Scrapbook
of the
Dead

Scrapbook of the Dead

Mollie Cox Bryan

KENSINGTON PUBLISHING CORP.

http://www.kensingtonbooks.com

KENSINGTON BOOKS are published by

Kensington Publishing Corp.
119 West 40th Street
New York, NY 10018

All Kensington Titles, Imprints and Distributed Lines are available at special quantity discounts for bulk purchases for sales promotions, premiums, fund-raising, and educational or institutional use. Special book excerpts or customized printings can also be created to fit specific needs. For details, write or phone the office of the Kensington special sales manager: Kensington Publishing Corp., 119 West 40th Street, New York, NY 10018, attn: Special Sales Department, Phone: 1-800-221-2647.

Kensington and the K logo Reg. U.S. Pat & TM Off.

ISBN-13: 978-0-7582-9358-9
ISBN-10: 0-7582-9358-5
First Kensington Mass Market Edition: October 2015

eISBN-13: 978-0-7582-9539-2
eISBN-10: 0-7582-9539-1
First Kensington Electronic Edition: October 2015

10 9 8 7 6 5 4 3 2 1

Printed in the United States of America

Dedicated to my mom Sandy Cox,
who inspired my love of words, reading, and writing,
with much love.

Acknowledgments

Five books in to the Cumberland Creek series, and two e-novellas, I'm still thrilled to be here and still grateful to readers for taking time to read my books, leave me reviews, and write me e-mails. It's an honor to be a part of your lives. Thank you.

As ever, I lucked out in the crazy world of publishing with a fabulous publisher and editor—Martin Biro, a writer's dream editor. Thank you for your steadfast support for me and this series. Thank you for being the best kind of editor—smart and kind.

Special thanks to my beta readers Anne Carley, Jennifer Feller, and Amber Benson. Beta readers are a special kind of people, giving their free time to read and offer comments, suggestions, or help spot those tricky typos before I send the books off to the publisher. I remain in debt to you all.

Also, thanks so much to the folks at the Writer's Police Academy. Much inspiration for me there, which just happened to come out in this book. I e-mailed and asked questions to several of the officers after the academy and they were always very professional and informative. Thanks guys! (You know who you are. Out of respect for your privacy and safety, I'm not using names.)

I want to give a shout out to some of the scrapbooking folks and businesses who have been very supportive: Lain Ehmann, Angela's Happy Stamper in Herndon, VA; the Michigan Scrapbooker; the Scrapbook Super Station in Butler, PA; and Scrapbook Expo, which is a traveling scrapbook show.

Thanks so much to Sharon Bowers, my agent of many years, who never gives up on me. Here's to many more years of an inspiring partnership!

In addition to all of the folks already mentioned, I want to acknowledge my family. I've taken advantage of many long road trips to work out plot points (captive audience), corralled my daughters into selling books at events (paid well in pizza), and left my husband to take them to dance and voice lessons and do homework, make sure they are fed, and so on (which he always does with much aplomb), while I run off to book signings and conferences. Thanks so much Eric, Emma, and Tess.

In gratitude,
Mollie

Chapter 1

She hadn't shown up for work a few days in a row. Had she been in the sub-zero room that whole time, slowly freezing to death?

"With these immigrants, you just never know," Pamela said. "They are hard workers, but sometimes things go wrong." She wrung her hands, which were white with tension.

"What do you mean by that?" The sheriff placed his hands on his hips, as camera flashes went off. Crime scene technicians buzzed around the room.

Annie stood with her arm wrapped around Randy, who was trembling—but her recorder pointed toward the sheriff and Pamela, owner of Pamela's Pie Palace, where the body of a young woman had just been found.

"I mean sometimes they just take off, disappear. Who knows where they go or why? Just last week, one of them disappeared, never showed up for work, and I couldn't reach her," Pamela said, her voice quivering.

Randy had discovered the frozen body early this

morning. He'd called the police, then Pamela, then Annie. After that, he began to fall apart. When Annie first walked in, she had barely recognized him because he was so pale.

"Maybe they go back home? Maybe they find another job?" Pamela flung her arms out.

Annie wished she could make an educated guess— but she didn't know many of the local foreign population. Foreign to Cumberland Creek, anyway. In fact, she was surprised to hear there even *was* an immigrant population in the small town.

"She was legal, right?" the sheriff asked, leaning in toward Pamela, but Annie heard every word. A big man, Sheriff Ted Bixby sported a twisty mustache that looked like it belonged on a Spanish conquistador, not a sheriff from a small county in Virginia.

"Absolutely," Pamela replied, her jaw stiff.

Nobody should look this good at five AM, not even Pamela, Queen of Pie, wife of the wealthy Evan Kraft. She always looked like she'd stepped right out of the pages of a 1950s pinup calendar. Curvy did not begin to describe her figure. And she was not afraid to show it off.

"I need to see the victim's papers," Sheriff Bixby said more to his deputy than to Pamela. "In fact, I need to see all of them. All the papers for every damn one of them."

Annie didn't like his tone when he said the word "them." But she'd gotten used to the "white men of a certain age" attitude about some things— like foreigners. In this part of Virginia, they seemed to be ignored, treated with suspicion, or made fun of. She had bitten her tongue so many times she counted herself lucky that it didn't have a huge gash.

The sheriff faced Annie and Randy, who'd already answered a barrage of questions. "Get some rest, son." Bixby looked at him with warmth and sympathy. He was a man who knew that discovering the frozen body of a coworker in a freezer was a jolt to the system. A man with deep family roots in that part of Virginia, he had seemingly been sheriff forever.

Annie knew that Detective Adam Bryant of Cumberland Creek's police force did not care for the man. She remembered a conversation she and Bryant had had about Sheriff Bixby during one of the other cases she had covered as a freelance reporter. But this most recent crime had taken place outside of Bryant's jurisdiction, so he hadn't been called in. She thanked the universe for that. On this, her last story, she didn't want to deal with his attitude.

"Coming through," yelled someone from inside the freezer.

The body of the small, dark-haired woman came through the doorway on a gurney. One thin line of red marred her neck where her throat had been neatly slit, and a big gash glistened over the artery where she had probably bled out. A craft knife was still lodged there. Pink and white polka-dotted tape covered her mouth, left in place for the autopsy.

So neatly done. Where was all the blood?

She had taken a good look at the scene earlier, but the light shone brighter outside the metallic, dimly lit walk-in freezer and she could see the young woman in detail. "How old did you say she was?" Annie asked Pamela.

"Her papers say she's twenty-three," Pamela replied with a tone leading Annie to believe that Pamela didn't believe it. The young Mexican woman looked liked she was sixteen, at most.

Why would Pamela hire her if she were suspicious about her age? Annie felt the ping of intuition pulling at her. Something about this was off. Way off. She needed to talk with Randy after he calmed down, then Pamela and the rest of the restaurant staff. It might be an even bigger story than a murder at the local, much beloved, Pamela's Pie Palace.

An older, dark haired woman sobbed and a young, wet-eyed man slipped his arms around her.

Friends? Annie made a mental note to speak with them.

"Shhh, Irina," the man said.

Irina, what a beautiful name, Annie thought amidst the chaos.

One of the technicians held a baggie with some colored paper and a photo inside.

"What's that?" Annie asked.

The young woman smiled politely. "Evidence." She held it up higher.

"Really? A scrapbook page?" Randy flung his hands up in the air. "I'm going back to the B and B. I need a drink and bed." Never mind that it was only five AM.

Since moving back to Cumberland Creek, he had taken a room at the new bed and breakfast in town until he found a house to purchase.

A loud commotion erupted from around the corner.

"Randy!"

Paige and Earl, Randy's parents, rushed in.

"Oh thank God you're okay. Your daddy heard about an incident on the scanner. We were so worried."

"What happened?" Earl asked.

Randy opened his mouth, but no words came out. His face grew even paler.

"Listen, Paige, why don't you take Randy home? I don't think he should be driving," Annie said.

"That's right," the sheriff chimed in. "At least someone around here has a good head on their shoulders." He gave Annie an approving glance.

"Sheriff." Earl nodded, the appropriate manly greeting in the region. Not "hello." Not "hi there." Just a name and a nod. "My boy in trouble?"

"Oh no, no," Sheriff Bixby said. "I'll let him do the explaining on the way home." He started to walk away.

"Now, Sheriff," Pamela called to him. "I can't let you leave without a couple pies. You said we'll have to close today and I have all this pie that needs to go. Please grab one or two."

The sheriff looked liked he knew his way around pie. "Why, thank you."

Pamela had several pies already boxed up. A young man with dark skin and sullen, almost black eyes stood next to her, helping tie the boxes shut. He was the same man Annie had spotted a few moments ago holding the older woman, Irina.

Where is Irina, now? Annie eyes searched the room to no avail. The woman was gone.

"That coconut cream?" Sheriff Bixby asked, mulling over the boxes.

"It's actually pumpkin cream, a fall special," Pamela said.

Annie surveyed the scene. The sheriff and a few others gathered around the counter where Pamela doled out her treats.

"I'd just have to throw it away," she said. "You all may as well take some."

Annie turned and looked out the window at the dead body of the young woman being slid into the back of the ambulance. She glanced back at Pamela handing out boxes of pie and the sad-looking young man next to her. It had to be the oddest crime scene she'd ever witnessed.

"Annie?" Pamela said. "Do you want some pie? I have the cherry that you like so much. I also have some of my special mincemeat."

Annie knew the special mincemeat was only available for two weeks during the fall. It was one of her favorites—a delicious mix of hard-to-find local seasonal ingredients, the kind that was barely legal.

Pamela always remembered everyone's favorites.

Annie's stomach tightened. "Thanks but not today. I just couldn't."

"Well now, young lady, are you a little queasy?" the sheriff said with a patronizing tone.

Why, yes, I think I am. I just saw a frozen person with her throat slit being carried out of here on a gurney. But, on second thought, she took a deep breath. "Never mind," she said, ignoring the sheriff and speaking just to Pamela. "I'll take whatever you've got there."

The sheriff turned with his boxes of pie and started to walk out of the Pie Palace.

"Sheriff," Annie called out as she followed him. "Might I have a word?"

He turned to look at her just as he started to open

the front door of the restaurant. His tan uniform stood out against the black and white tile floor and red booths.

She found the place kitschy and cute, but for some reason, this morning all the cuteness looked menacing. Murder amid the kitschiness. She didn't like it.

"What can I help you with, Ms. Chamovitz?" he asked, smiling.

Oh, this is different. Very different, indeed. A smiling law official. No Adam Bryant with his sideways, smirking grins. "What do you think happened here?"

"I don't speculate," the sheriff said. "Call my office later today. We might know something then. But it being Saturday, you never know."

"A walk-in freezer is an odd place for murder," Annie said, watching him tense.

"Well, now, who said anything about murder? It could have been an accident or suicide. As I say, Ms. Chamovitz, I don't speculate. I deal with facts."

An accidental throat slashing? Let him think I'm that gullible. "I'll call you later, then," she said, noticing the medical examiner getting ready to leave. She wanted to catch her before she left. Annie extended her hand to the sheriff. "Later, Sheriff Bixby."

He could not take her hand—his arms were full of pie boxes—but he nodded back at her, turned, and left the building.

"Ms. Jones?" Annie said as she walked over to the ME.

Ruth Jones looked up at her. She was an older, studious woman who had run into Annie frequently around town. "Yes?" Ruth dug her car keys out of a jacket pocket.

"What can you tell me about the body? About the death?"

"Not much at this point," Ruth said. "It looks like she bled to death. But I need to run some tests, of course, to be certain."

"How would someone get trapped in a freezer long enough to bleed or freeze to death?" Annie asked.

Ruth walked out of the Pie Palace carrying a big bulky bag and a pie box. Annie followed her outside into the fall morning. The sun was just beginning to rise, giving the sky a slate blue tinge. The waning moon was still visible.

"Why didn't she just open the door?" Annie wondered. "If she was in there struggling with someone who slit her throat?"

"No, she wasn't inside with someone. I don't think so, anyway. Not like what you're suggesting. There were about five hundred pounds of sugar blocking the door. She couldn't have possibly moved it. I'm sure she's less than a hundred pounds."

"But that means someone else placed the sugar in front of the door while she was in there."

"She was probably already dead when they did. But restaurants get deliveries all times of the day and night. Check with Pamela on that," Ruth said, opening her car door. "Call me later. I may have some answers for you then."

"Okay," Annie said and stepped back from the car. She had enough to file her first story on the case. But she'd need more for the complete story. A lot more.

She mentally sorted through the evidence and possibilities. She didn't know which was worse—the fact the young woman could have met her death in the freezer, crawling inside to get away from someone or that someone had killed her and then stored her dead body inside.

Chapter 2

Beatrice and Jon were having breakfast at Elsie's B and B. Elsie had invited them several times and they had finally run out of excuses. Jon didn't mind Elsie, but Beatrice would rather not spend any more time with her than necessary. In fact, there weren't many people with whom Beatrice liked to spend time.

"This is delicious," Jon said.

The stuffed French toast was a bit rich for Bea's taste, but she had to agree that it was delicious—perfectly spiced with cinnamon, sugar, and nutmeg.

"What kind of cheese is inside?" His slight French accent was even slighter since he had moved to the States to be with Beatrice.

"Ricotta." Elsie beamed. "I'm so glad you like it, Jon." The woman sparkled every time Beatrice's new husband was around her.

Bea was not a jealous woman, but it was beginning to annoy her. She harrumphed and Jon's eyes met hers. He knew what she was thinking. He grinned and sipped his coffee.

Beatrice turned toward the commotion she heard at the front door. In walked Randy, Paige, and Earl.

What on earth are they doing here at six AM?

"Do you have any bourbon?" Paige asked, frantic.

"What? Why? Of course, I do," Elsie said.

Beatrice's estimation of her went up. Just a tad. "What on earth is wrong? Whiskey so early in the morning?"

Paige led Randy to an overstuffed chair.

"Randy discovered a dead body this morning at the Pie Palace," Earl said after a moment. "Just a little drink will calm his nerves. It's always worked before."

"A dead body?" Jon exclaimed.

Beatrice's heart jumped and Elsie gasped.

Randy nodded. "In the freezer. I went in early to help move the sugar. It had been sitting there . . . I don't know . . . a few days. I opened the door, turned the light on, and saw this heap. Turned out it was Marina."

Elsie handed him a glass filled with a few shots of whiskey poured over ice. Randy took a sip and closed his eyes.

"Good Lord," Beatrice said. "How did that happen?"

Randy shrugged and stared off into space.

"They don't know if was an accident, suicide, or foul play," Paige said.

"Foul play?" Elsie said, her eyes widening and face whitening.

Beatrice knew Elsie was thinking of the incident that had occurred right in her beloved B and B. She and Jon had been shot in the very room and were lucky to have survived. Maybe that's why Beatrice put up with her busybody ways and her flirting with Jon.

Paige shrugged. "Nobody knows anything at this point." She sighed. "Of course."

"I've got to get to work," Earl said. "Take it easy, Randy."

"I'll try," Randy said, looking up at his father. "Thanks for everything, Dad."

"Sure, thing. You're going to be fine," Earl said, as if trying to convince himself as much as Randy. Earl shuffled his feet awkwardly and walked out to his car.

Beatrice was glad to see Earl and Randy once again in the same room and speaking with one another after their years of estrangement. But Randy did not look well at all. He had never struck Beatrice as a fragile sort, but then again, walking in on a dead body was no way to start the day.

"Can I get you something to eat?" Elsie asked Randy.

He waved his hand and shook his head. "No, thanks. I'm fine with the whiskey. Almost lost the breakfast I already had. Don't want to rock the boat."

The place went silent as Beatrice and Jon sipped their coffee and finished their French toast.

"Who is Marina?" Beatrice finally asked. "Is she from Cumberland Creek?"

Randy swallowed his next sip of whiskey and shook his head. "No. She's from Mexico."

"Good heavens," Elsie said. "She was so far from home. What was she doing here?"

"Working and sending money home, from what I understand," Randy said, his eyes watering. "She was just so sweet." He took another drink as his color gradually returned. "She made the most magnificent mango pie," he muttered.

The front door of the house opened and Bea turned to see the new arrival. It was Annie, thank goodness. Maybe she could shed some light on the situation.

"Hey Bea, Jon, Elsie. Where can I find—"

Beatrice nodded in Randy's direction before Annie could finish her question.

"Annie!" Randy sat up straighter in his chair. "What did you find out? Anything?"

"Unfortunately, no. I talked to the sheriff, talked with the ME. It's all speculation at this point. But how are you?"

Randy shrugged. "I've never seen anything like that. . . . You must think I'm such a coward."

"Not at all," Annie said, pulling a dining room chair over to him. "I've seen a lot of murder victims and while you sort of get used to it, it never gets any easier. It bothers me every single time."

"Of course it does," Beatrice said. "You're human. It would bother anybody."

"Now I understand a bit about how Sheila felt on the cruise," he mumbled. "Tripping over a dead body. Thank God I didn't trip over Marina."

"How long had that sugar been sitting in front of the freezer?" Annie asked.

"I don't know. I think a couple days. Too long," he said. "We've been having staffing problems and the person who usually takes care of stock was out sick. I finally got tired of it sitting there and I needed to get into the damn freezer. I've really never seen such lackadaisical handling of stock. It would never go over in New York."

Annie nodded.

"I'm not surprised to hear it," Beatrice said.

Transitioning from New York City to Cumberland Creek was no easy task—even for a young man who grew up and had family there. Being openly gay was just an additional part of Randy's challenge as he tried to settle back down in his hometown.

"All the time I spent in the big city . . . well, let's just say I never once ran into a dead body," Randy said.

Beatrice grimaced. She knew Paige and Earl were ecstatic to have their only child back in the area—but she wondered how long Randy was going to be happy in Cumberland Creek.

Chapter 3

"Murder? Not again!" DeeAnn exclaimed. "Good God, what is happening to this community?"

True, the Pie Palace was not in Cumberland Creek, quite, but still, it was close enough.

It was Saturday night so the croppers were all gathered in Sheila's basement scrapping room for their weekly crop. It was DeeAnn's favorite day of the week. After a hard day of work, a nice and relaxing dinner with her husband, spending the night with her girlfriends was exactly what she needed.

Annie placed her beer bottle down on the table. "According to the ME, Marina was dead before she was placed in the freezer. She bled to death before she was dragged inside the freezer. Yet there was no blood in the freezer."

Annie opened a pie box, reached in, and grabbed the pie.

DeeAnn moved the box away. "Why would a killer place a dead body in a freezer? I mean, it's so blatant. Don't you think you'd want to hide the body?" She paused. "I've always admired that freezer. I'd love to have one as big as that." DeeAnn owned a thriving bakery in town.

Annie grunted. "Well, the killer certainly wasn't concerned with hiding the body, were they? That says something, but I'm not sure what." She held the pie up and took it in. It smelled like a cakey, chocolate-covered cherry—Annie's idea of culinary heaven. "Pretty," she said as she admired the craftsmanship.

It was Pamela's Cherry Chocolate Delight, a cherry pie with chocolate drizzled over the lattice crust and a fine layer of chocolate on the bottom crust.

Sheila, hunched over her laptop, looked up. "If there's one thing I've learned over the past few years, it's that criminals are not the brightest."

"What are you doing?" Vera asked, setting down her scrapbook and reaching for a paper plate as Annie sliced the pie and began doling it out.

"I'm working on a Halloween-themed scrap journal," Sheila responded. "It's for work. I've got a deadline next week."

DeeAnn surveyed her friends around the table. Sheila was a designer with a huge craft company in New York City. She journeyed between the city and Cumberland Creek so often it was becoming commonplace, but DeeAnn knew her well enough to see it was wearing on her. She always looked tired. And she wasn't her cheerful self anymore. Annie had said Sheila was still getting over the incident that had happened on the cruise ship last Christmas. One thing was for sure, Sheila was changing.

"Did you try those pumpkin-ginger cookies?" DeeAnn asked her. "I think you'd like them." In her experience, cookies made everything better—at least for the time being. For that matter, so did pie.

Sheila reached for a cookie over her computer. "I'll take a slice of pie, too. I don't really care for cherry, but the chocolate adds something to it."

"Those cookies are good," Vera said, holding up a page. She was working on a scrapbook about Eric, the man with whom she lived. She had gathered all of his old photos and sorted through them, then decided it was time to make a scrapbook for him. "Eric's mom wasn't into scrapbooking," she explained, noting DeeAnn looking at her page.

"What a cute photo," DeeAnn said. "Eric was adorable." It was a photo of him dressed as a cowboy for Halloween, placed on a cowboy-themed page, complete with a horse and a rope that outlined the page.

Vera beamed. It was so clear how much she loved the man, yet she would not marry him.

Maybe it was smart, mused DeeAnn, *given how her last marriage had turned out.* The scrapbook of that wedding had been destroyed—Vera had torn up the pages and thrown them in the Cumberland Creek. DeeAnn smiled to herself, even as a wave of weariness overtook her. She sighed.

"Busy day?" Vera asked.

"Since the Pie Palace was closed, everybody and their brother came to my place," DeeAnn said. "We were packed all day."

"I saw that," Sheila said. "I was out running errands and saw the line. I wonder if you might consider expanding soon."

Paige had mentioned the same thing to her last

week. DeeAnn glanced over at Paige and Randy's empty chairs. After the day's events, they had decided a quiet night at home was in order. It certainly was emptier in Sheila's basement scrapbooking room without them. Paige was DeeAnn's dearest friend and she loved Randy as if he were her own.

"I'm considering some changes," DeeAnn said. What she didn't tell them was one of those changes she was considering was retirement. She'd gotten into the business because she loved to bake, but it was an extremely physical job. She was more tired than she should be and her bones ached. Her back was a constant problem. Even with all her good help, it was a bit too much.

"Change is a good thing. Take it from me," Vera said, grinning.

"Things are working out well with Eric, then," Annie said, as she placed a rub-on embellishment on her page and started to rub it with a craft stick. She pulled the plastic backing off gently, leaving a pumpkin on the page.

Vera nodded and smiled.

"You know, I love these rub-ons. So much fun and they look so delicate on the paper." Annie was working on a Halloween card. She'd taken an online class on how to make cards and was zooming along with it.

"Are those David's Designs?" Sheila asked, cutting a piece of her slice of pie with her fork. "We have a gorgeous line of them."

"Hmm. I don't think so." Annie turned the paper over. "No, not David's."

"I'll see if I can pick up some next time I'm in the city," Sheila said, bringing a bit of pie to her mouth.

"Oh, that would be great," Annie replied. "Voilà, this is done. I now have a lovely homemade card for my brother." She held it up—a soft-tan card with pumpkin rub-ons. The center to the card had a torn darker brown strip. The words "Happy Halloween" were stamped on the bottom of the folded card-stock.

"Does he like Halloween?" Sheila said.

Annie nodded. "I'd say. If he could get away with it, he'd still go trick or treating."

"So, are you going to cover the weirdness at the Pie Palace?" DeeAnn asked Annie.

She nodded. "I filed my first story in the series. I'm hoping this will also be my last story. I'll see this one through, but I'm earning enough from my books now so I don't have to freelance. We're waiting for my next royalty check to be sure." She sat back in her chair. "You know, it feels good to finally be done with reporting. It's been a long, painful good-bye, but I'm really done. Or I will be, after this."

DeeAnn wasn't so certain. Annie seemed so driven. Could she really give up journalism and be happy?

"What will you do with yourself, Annie?" Vera asked.

Annie laughed. "You might be surprised. That's all I'm saying."

"You are an evil woman," DeeAnn said. "Teasing us like that."

Annie just smiled and fingered through her stack

of cardstock. "You know, I almost forgot about the scrapbook page."

"What?" DeeAnn said.

"Marina was holding a scrapbook page when they found her," Annie said.

The room silenced.

"Disturbing," DeeAnn finally said.

Chapter 4

The Cumberland Creek scrapbooking club quieted as the soft jazz music played and the sound of Sheila's clicks on the computer dotted the soundscape, along with appreciative murmurs about the pie.

"Why would a young woman from Mexico have a scrapbooking page in her clutches when she was killed?" DeeAnn finally said after taking her last sip of wine. "I mean, that's bizarre!"

"Not only is it bizarre, it could also be a clue," volunteered Annie.

"What do you mean?" Vera said, her blue eyes wide with speculation. "How could it be a clue?"

"Maybe it didn't belong to her. Maybe it belonged to the killer," Annie said. "Or maybe she was just scrapbooking when she was attacked. I don't know, but it could definitely be a clue."

"Or maybe the page had poison on it," Sheila said. "Maybe that's what killed her—poison."

"How did I know you were going to say that?" Vera laughed. "You just better get it off your mind. The next thing you know, we'll have Bryant and FBI agents and everybody and their brother hanging out here."

"Maybe it will tell them more about her. Maybe she wasn't who people thought she was," DeeAnn chimed in. "Like with Maggie Rae. Remember? We found out a lot about her by scrapbooking about her. We also found out a lot about Cookie by looking at her Scrapbook of Shadows. Any word from her?"

Annie glanced at Cookie's empty chair. Their old friend, Cookie, had been back in Cumberland Creek for a few months and sometimes joined the group, but since she was struck by lightning she had not been the same. She was under a doctor's care for her memory loss. Annie nodded, twisting her mouth. She was annoyed by the situation—but she was certain she wasn't as frustrated as Cookie herself, who described the way she felt as "lost."

Annie had given up trying to make sense of Cookie's "escape" from jail. She had been arrested under the suspicion of murder and one day just disappeared from her jail cell. Her claim was she hadn't left on her own accord and had been struck by lightning sometime while she was away, leaving her dealing with profound memory loss. She was back, living off a steadily dwindling savings account in her little house at the end of a cul-de-sac.

"But this is just one scrapbook page," Annie pointed out, keeping them on track. "And I have yet to see it. It could be any one of those things." *But it could also be nothing at all—which was probably the case.*

Sheila closed her laptop, stood, and stretched. "There's been some very strange things going on in this town. I'm just hoping it will calm down soon. I've got enough going on in my life without murder of a mysterious foreign woman on my horizon. I'm hoping the scrapbook page wasn't a clue. I don't want to have any more murder in my life."

It was true; Sheila did have a lot on her plate. Her daughter Donna had been diagnosed recently with epilepsy and had decided to take time off from her design studies at Carnegie Mellon University. Sheila was tending her, plus running her household, scrapbooking business, and working for David's Designs.

Annie knew how she felt. She wanted to be done with murder, as well. Just one more story. She meant it. She'd been itching to try other kinds of writing, rather than her journalism, like fiction, or maybe get back to writing poetry.

"Have you tried this chocolate?" Vera said to Annie, scooting a plate full of homemade chocolate toward her.

Annie bit into a truffle and her taste buds sat up at attention. The flavor was deep and rich, with a smoky hint of tea. "Oh my God. That is orgasmic!"

"What? Oh Annie, the things you say!" Sheila said over the laughter.

"Well, hell, if it's orgasmic, I need a couple of 'em," a red-faced DeeAnn said as she reached for some.

They all indulged and swooned over the chocolate. Vera's new hobby was making chocolate—much to the group's good fortune. Randy was helping her; he was a highly trained pastry chef, with a specialty in chocolate.

The thought brought Annie square back to him, wondering how he was doing after happening upon the dead body of his colleague.

"You know, Vera," DeeAnn said, "why don't you try to sell some of your chocolate at my shop?"

Vera waved her off. "I don't think I'm ready to go pro. It's just for fun."

"Are you sure? You could make a little extra money," DeeAnn said.

"Hmm, well, I'll think about it. I certainly could use the money." Vera's dance studio had bounced back a bit from the bad economy, but it had never completely recovered.

"You won't need to worry about money if you marry Eric. I mean, he is a doctor, " Sheila said.

"Oh for God's sake!" Vera snapped. "I'm not marrying Eric for his money. In fact, I'm not marrying him at all. If you're so hell-bent on marriage and Eric, just marry him your damn self!"

They all looked up from their chocolate, pie, and scrapbooks. Sheila looked as if she had been smacked.

"That's a bit of an overreaction, don't you think?" DeeAnn finally said.

"Honestly, I don't know," Vera said. "She's been on my case about this since he asked me to marry him. I said no. And I meant it."

"On your case? I just want you to be happy." Sheila flung her arms out.

"We all want you to be happy," Annie said.

"Hell, we all want all of us to be happy," DeeAnn said and lifted her glass. "To happiness."

"Happiness, indeed!" Vera said and lifted her glass in return.

Chapter 5

When Beatrice woke up, Junie Bee was sitting on her chest staring at her. Elizabeth's cat made herself right at home, no matter where she was. Of course, Bea's house had been the cat's home before her daughter Vera had moved in with Eric . . . and taken her daughter Elizabeth with her.

Junie Bee was purring and Beatrice had to admit she loved the sound and the feel of Junie Bee on her chest. Well, she'd admit it—but only to herself. "What do you want?" she asked the cat.

"Hmmm?" A startled Jon awakened.

"Not you. I'm talking to Junie Bee," she said and elbowed him. "Good morning, Jon."

He pulled the covers up around him and muttered a good morning.

Beatrice ran her hand down the length of the cat and Junie Bee seemed to smile at her. She couldn't remember why she'd never let Vera have a cat when she was a kid. They were wonderful.

Beatrice sat up and the cat hopped out of the bed. Bea untangled herself from the quilts and slid her feet into her slippers. Her bones were aching a bit—but she knew movement was the best thing for them. *Got to keep moving.*

She walked down the hallway and peeked in on Elizabeth, still sleeping. *Precious girl.* Bea loved her Saturday nights and Sunday mornings with Elizabeth. But every other weekend was not enough, even with the cat tagging along. It sure was hard to get used to modern family life, with everybody divorced two or three times over and schlepping the children from pillar to post. Still, Elizabeth knew she was loved. Her dad Bill had finally settled down alone in a house between Cumberland Creek and Charlottesville. He had a part-time law practice along with working as a law professor at the University of Virginia. He said he didn't have time to date. Thank the universe for that. He'd made a bloody fool of himself over the past few years. *Mid-life crisis, my ass.*

Bea padded down the steps—and clutched her chest when she saw Cookie Crandall lying on the floor. "Cookie?"

Junie Bee sniffed Cookie and walked past her. The cat had only food on her mind.

Beatrice crouched over Cookie. "Are you okay?"

Cookie stirred and lifted her eyes. "Beatrice?"

"Well now, don't Beatrice me. What are you doing lying in the middle of my floor? Get up from there."

The young woman was one of the strangest people Beatrice had ever met—and that was even before she'd been struck by lightning. Since she'd found her way back to Cumberland Creek and was trying to make sense of the world, she'd gotten even stranger.

Beatrice yanked gently on her arm and helped Cookie rise from the floor.

"Sorry Bea. I forgot to tell you she stopped by last night," Jon said as he came down the stairs.

Beatrice's eyebrows lifted as she shot daggers with her eyes at her new husband. "Why yes, Jon, I reckon you did."

Cookie was standing up. "Sorry Beatrice. Last night, I just had this feeling that I wanted to be near you."

Land's sakes. Sometimes, Cookie comes up with the strangest things.

For some reason her words reached in and grabbed Beatrice by the heart. *Damn her.*

"Whatever for?" Beatrice said. "Am I going to die soon? Did you have a freaky premonition? Is that what this is about?"

Cookie's eyes widened. "How would I know something like that, Beatrice? I just missed you. I'm so hungry. Let me make everybody breakfast."

Just a minute ago, she had been lying on the floor and now she wanted to make breakfast. Just like that.

Jon moved past them both, muttering something about coffee.

Beatrice was trying to regain her bearings as Elizabeth came bounding down the stairs. "Granny! Cookie? Cookie!" She ran into the odd woman's arms.

Beatrice stood back and watched. The two of them got on very well.

"I'll make breakfast," Beatrice said. "Chocolate chip pancakes?"

"Yay!" Cookie and Elizabeth cheered.

When Beatrice entered her kitchen, the scent of

brewing coffee greeted her, along with fishy cat food. The refrigerator door was open and Jon was pulling out the eggs, butter, and milk.

"Sorry Bea," he said quietly. "I did not want to wake you. I made up a bed for her on the couch. I don't know why she was on the floor."

Cookie was popping up in the strangest places. Beatrice thought she was trying to get rid of the doctor who was always tailing her. Must be nerve-racking.

"Well, I just about had a heart attack," Beatrice said, reaching into the cupboard to get the chocolate chips.

Jon reached over and kissed her. "I am so glad you did not have a heart attack, *ma chere*." He reached into the bottom cabinet for the mixing bowl.

Cookie and Elizabeth giggled in the next room.

"Let's be sure to make enough for Vera and Eric," Beatrice said.

"Will they be joining us?" Jon asked with a knowing look.

"It's not official, but they always seem to pop over about this time," Beatrice said and smiled. "Now, let me at the coffee."

By the time Beatrice was downing her second cup of coffee and the world was becoming a little less murky, Vera and Eric had joined Cookie and Elizabeth in the living room.

After breakfast, Eric took Elizabeth to the park and Vera, who was feeling a little under the weather, stayed behind with Cookie to help Bea clean up the kitchen.

"How's Randy?" Beatrice asked as she handed Vera a rinsed off plate to put in the dishwasher.

"I have no idea," Vera said. "He didn't show up last night. Neither did Paige."

"That's a first," Beatrice said.

"I think she's missed once or twice before—when Randy was little and sick," Vera said. "But you're right, she rarely misses a Saturday night crop. I mean Randy comes and goes. Not Paige."

"I hope she's okay," Cookie said as she wiped off the table.

"I'm sure she'll be fine," Vera said. "It's Randy I'm worried about. Imagine opening the freezer door and finding a frozen dead body inside. Troubling."

Beatrice leaned back on the counter. "It is, but I'd think he'd need to keep busy. At least, that's the way I think I'd handle it. If you sit around too long, that's all you think about. It could be bad. And to happen to Randy, of all people, who just came back home from New York."

"Annie saw the body, too," Cookie said, looking up from her task.

"Yes, but she wasn't surprised. She knew it was there. I think the shock is . . . you know . . . opening the door and finding something like that." Vera folded a towel and patted it flat.

"I have to wonder about her family," Cookie said. "Imagine being in Mexico and receiving word about your daughter." She smoothed over a placemat and set the sugar bowl in the center of the table.

Beatrice had already thought about that. Each time she did, a feeling of dread overcame her. Losing your child to murder in a distant land would be a living nightmare—more horrible than she could imagine.

Chapter 6

DeeAnn rarely left the house on Sundays as it was her day to relax. Sometimes her daughter Karen would come over for Sunday dinner. She was living in Charlottesville. It wasn't Cumberland Creek, but it was better than Texas.

Instead of relaxing, DeeAnn baked a coffee cake for Randy, thinking he'd appreciate it, poor guy.

As she stood on the front doorstep of Elsie's B and B, the door opened.

"Why, DeeAnn, how lovely to see you," Elsie said.

"Thanks, nice to see you, too. Is Randy here?"

Elsie shook her head. "I'm afraid not. He's at his folks' place."

"Oh, okay. I'll catch you later," DeeAnn said and turned to leave.

One good thing about Cumberland Creek was most of it was so close together a person could walk almost anywhere. The town proper was only six blocks long. DeeAnn's bakery was right in the center, along with all of the other businesses. The neighborhoods were built around it, with the park traveling the length of town along the river.

DeeAnn stood a moment and looked over at the mountains. The fall colors were even deeper and richer than usual. Seeing the crimson, golds, and fiery oranges against the blue sky made her stop, take a deep breath, and take it all in. She wasn't originally from Cumberland Creek; she was from Minnesota. When she'd met Jacob and they married, she'd moved to Cumberland Creek with him and never looked back, much to her family's chagrin.

She spotted Paige's home with the brick chimney spouting smoke. DeeAnn was cheered at the thought of a roaring fire as she walked up the sidewalk and knocked at the front door. The coffee cake was getting heavy in her arms.

"Why, hello there," Paige said as she opened the door. "Come on in."

DeeAnn never liked Paige's country-themed décor, but she kept her mouth shut about it. It was not her place. This morning, it nearly smacked her over the head with its tackiness. Teddy bears and hearts and pictures of barns and quilts were everywhere. Not to mention the funky-colored afghans over all the chairs and the sofa.

"I'm not staying," DeeAnn said, "but I stopped by the B and B to give Randy this and Elsie said he was here." She handed the coffee cake to Paige.

"He stayed here last night. Fell asleep in front of the TV, just like old times." Paige's eyes were bright. Her boy was home—and DeeAnn knew it was all Paige could do to keep from shouting it from the rooftops. "I know you said you've got to go, but can you stay for just one cup of coffee? Randy just made some really good stuff."

Suddenly, DeeAnn wondered if Randy, the gourmet, would appreciate her silly coffee cake. "Well, okay," she said after a moment and followed Paige into the kitchen where Earl and Randy were sitting at the table drinking coffee, which smelled downright heavenly.

"Oh hey, DeeAnn. What do you have there?" Randy asked.

"Just a coffee cake," she said. "I thought you could use a little something from the oven this morning."

"How sweet!" He rose from the table, took the cake from her, and gave her a hug. "Mama, get a knife. Have a seat, DeeAnn."

DeeAnn sat down and marveled at him. He seemed fine. She wasn't so certain she'd be. But he seemed to have bounced right back.

Paige set a cup of coffee in front of DeeAnn and Randy set a slice of her own cake in front of her.

"How do you like staying at Elsie's?" she asked.

"It's fine. I just can't wait for my own place, though. I'm going to see some houses this afternoon."

"So you're staying?"

"I'm not going anywhere," he said. "I don't scare off that easily."

"You're feeling better?" DeeAnn took a sip of the best coffee she'd ever had in her life.

"I'm getting there. I'm sure it's just a matter of time. I need to keep busy to keep my mind off it, you know?"

"Good way of looking at it," DeeAnn said.

Randy took a bite of her coffee cake and rolled

his eyes with pleasure. "Ahh. DeeAnn, my culinary professors have nothing on you, woman. I've always said you're the best baker I know."

DeeAnn beamed. Maybe she wouldn't retire. Not quite yet. "Why, thank you. That's very kind of you."

"Not at all."

Just then, the doorbell rang, and Paige wandered off to see who it was.

"Detective Bryant?" DeeAnn heard Paige say. "Please come in. We're all in the kitchen."

As the detective entered the room, DeeAnn caught her breath. He was such a handsome man, so confident. He walked with an interesting little swagger. And he was built like a brick house. A moving, hard-flesh one.

"Hello," he said as he entered the room.

"Well, what are you doing here?" Earl said and started to get up from the table.

Bryant made a gesture for him to sit. "Unfortunately, I'm here on business," he said, looking at Randy.

Randy's brows knitted. "Are you here about Marina?"

"In a roundabout way."

"Please sit down," Paige said. "Can I get you some coffee?"

"Normally, I'd say no, but it smells so good, I can't resist," Bryant said.

Who is he kidding? The man never could resist a treat. DeeAnn grinned.

"It's great having Randy around. He insists on grinding his own coffee and using a French press. It makes such a difference," Paige said, as she poured the detective a cup of the brew.

"So Randy, are you squared away with the sheriff?" Bryant asked.

"Yes, I told him everything I know. Exactly what happened."

"Pamela closed the place yesterday?"

Randy nodded.

Why is Bryant here? The Pie Palace isn't his jurisdiction at all. DeeAnn started to get a bad feeling. When Bryant was on the scene, it meant bad news. True, he was eye-candy, but still bad news.

"So what did you do with your day afterward?" Bryant asked.

"I spent it with my mom and dad," Randy said. "I know, for you it might not be a big deal to see something like that. But for me . . . I just—"

"Oh, I completely understand," the detective interrupted. "But here's the thing. Last night, another dead body was found. Marina's sister."

The room silenced.

"I didn't even know she had a sister," Randy said after a minute. "How awful." He said it as if his lack of knowledge was a sin.

"She cleaned houses for a living. Name was Esmeralda," Bryant said.

Randy paled and sucked in air. "I did know her! She worked for Elsie. They were sisters?"

The detective nodded. "They were sisters and they both knew you. So, you see why I'm here."

"Now just hold on here," Earl said, then cleared his throat and started to rise again from the kitchen table.

Bryant held up his hand. "Randy is not a suspect. I'm just hoping he can answer a few questions and shed some light on these young women."

"I didn't know them that well," Randy said. "I'm sorry. I don't know how I can help."

"Mmm. This is the best coffee I've ever had," Bryant said, abruptly changing subjects.

"Thanks," Randy said.

"You put cinnamon or something in it?" Bryant asked.

Randy nodded. "Along with some other spices. Do you want a slice of coffee cake? DeeAnn made it."

Bryant looked over at DeeAnn. "How could I resist a slice of cake from the town's best baker?"

He was being such a charmer—which was thoroughly unlike him.

"If you're on this case, it means Esmeralda was found somewhere in Cumberland Creek," Paige said, setting a piece of coffee cake on a plate in front of him.

Bryant nodded. "Down by the river."

DeeAnn shivered. Another murder in Cumberland Creek.

Chapter 7

Annie got to the second crime scene a bit late. Bryant had already been there and gone, but she was in time to see the body before they had disturbed it. The victim's face had a ribbon tied around it and a bow over her mouth. The ribbon was bright orange with black pumpkins printed across it.

It chilled Annie. *How strange. Why would someone decorate a body like that?*

It was so deranged.

"Esmeralda Martelino," the cop told her.

"Martelino? Same last name as Marina?"

The cop nodded. "Sisters." He looked over at the mountains. "Foreign."

"She's not a drowning vic," Annie said almost to herself. "How did she die?"

"Don't know yet," Ruth the ME said as she walked over.

"You again," Annie said.

Ruth nodded.

"Have you gotten any more medical results back for Marina?" Annie asked, but she already knew the answer. It was Sunday. Hardly anybody in Cumberland Creek worked on Sunday and even the rest of the state moved at a slower pace.

"No, I'm sorry," Ruth said. "Call me tomorrow afternoon. Might have something on the first one by then."

"What do you make of it?" Annie asked.

"I'm just the medical examiner. I don't know anything about these young women besides the stories their bodies will tell me."

It was an interesting way of putting it.

Ruth shrugged, then nodded toward Esmeralda. "I can tell you her sister was a healthy specimen. She was thin, but not malnourished, had good teeth and so on."

"No guess on cause of death for this one?" Annie asked.

"None. I think it's fair to say she didn't drown. But other than that, I have no way of knowing at this point."

Annie nodded.

Ruth walked off, carrying her medical bag with her.

Annie zipped up her coat and pulled her scarf in closer around her neck. It was getting cold. The sky was so blue it was almost painful to look at and the fall leaves looked like colorful, fluffy blankets spread over the mountains. She turned to look at a police officer as he was filling out some papers. "Who found her?"

He pointed. "The guy over there. Sitting on the bench. He was out for an early morning walk and there she was, lying on the ground near the water. Great way to start the day, huh?"

"Can I talk to him?" Annie asked.

"He's in shock. I'd wait awhile," the officer said. "He's not making much sense. We've been trying to take him to the hospital, but he won't go."

"No insurance?"

"Look at him. What do you think?"

Annie took a good look at him. Maybe he was Mexican, as well. He was dark, and he had hooded, almost black eyes. But maybe not. Only one way to find out.

A female officer was sitting next to him, writing in her tablet.

"Excuse me," Annie said as she wandered up to the bench. "I'm Annie Chamovitz, a reporter for the *Washington Herald.*"

The man looked up at her, but his eyes were vacant.

Annie looked at the cop, who shook her head. "I'd leave him alone for now," she said.

"Can I have his name?" Annie asked.

"Juan Mendez," the officer said. "Let me write down his contact information for you."

"Thanks."

A medic brought the man a blanket and wrapped it around his shoulders.

"He seemed fine at first," the officer said. "But then . . ."

"We all react differently," Annie said, thinking of Randy, so pale and shivering head to toe, just yesterday. "It's perfectly normal to be spooked."

The officer nodded and handed Annie a slip of paper with the man's phone number and address on it.

"Thanks so much."

The scene was grim. Amidst the beauty and splendor of the mountains surrounding them, sat a man who had happened upon a body. A man who would never really be the same. Oh, he'd be okay, eventually. But something like this might haunt him for years. He could tuck it away and function, but it would visit him at odd times.

Annie knew that.

For her, haunting came in dreams. Not when she was working a case, usually, but after. Sometimes she'd dream about murder victims from years ago. She'd never forget any of them. The odd thing was, she thought she'd left it all behind when she moved from DC. Cumberland Creek had turned out to not be the safe haven she and her husband Mike had predicted.

She walked up the path next to the river, which snaked alongside the town. She decided to stop by Paige and Earl's to check up on Randy. If she knew him at all, that's where he'd be.

She turned the corner onto Paige's street and saw Detective Bryant's car. Her immediate reaction was, *This can wait. I'd rather not see him.* But her hackles were raised. If he was there, that meant he was questioning Randy. She'd be damned if she would allow his presence to stop her from going inside and doing her job—even though a big part of her wanted to turn around. She walked up to the front door and rang the doorbell.

"Why, hello Annie," DeeAnn said when she opened the door. "C'mon in. I brought Randy some coffee cake this morning," she explained as they walked into the kitchen. "And then look who showed up."

"Annie," Detective Bryant said.

"Adam," she responded. "What's going on here?"

"Just asking Randy a few questions," he said a little too nonchalantly.

"And what's that?" Annie pointed to a sheet of paper encased in a plastic bag the group was mulling over.

The detective cleared his throat. "It's a scrapbook page. Evidence. I was wondering if anybody here knew anything about it."

"How did you get it?" Annie asked.

"I was at the crime scene first thing this morning, of course. How do you think I got it?" Bryant replied.

Annie chilled. "Do you mean you found this on the body—on Esmeralda's body?"

He nodded. "In her hand, actually."

Annie smirked. She knew something he didn't. Should she tell him?

"What gives, Annie?" he said and took a sip from his mug. He read her too well.

"Well, there was a scrapbook page at yesterday's murder, too," she responded.

The detective almost choked on his gourmet coffee.

Chapter 8

Beatrice sat in her chair and looked out over her clan—Jon, Vera, Eric, Elizabeth . . . and Cookie. Cookie and Elizabeth were on the floor playing cards and Jon, Vera, and Eric were watching a football game. Cookie troubled Beatrice. Hell, she troubled everybody. Nobody knew when she'd show up and her short-term memory loss came and went, much like her long-term memory loss. She was not quite the same woman they had gotten to know and love a few years back.

"Go fish!" Cookie said to Elizabeth, who reached down for another card. Cookie had always been very good with Elizabeth, even when she was a baby. They had a connection.

Cookie's long, black hair had been cut short—Beatrice preferred her short hair because her long hair had engulfed her tiny face. And Cookie was gaining weight—not that she would ever be fat or even plump, but finally the young woman was getting some meat on her bones. She looked healthy—most of the time. The doctor who was her caretaker made sure that she ate. Sometimes, she'd sort of slump over and get a faraway look in her eyes, but her spark was back as she focused on the game in front of her.

Bea could only take so much of the noise of the football game. She went to the dining room and switched on the computer.

"Go, Steelers!" Jon yelled, "Touchdown, yes!"

It was irritating, the way her sophisticated French husband was turning into a couch potato football fan. She bit her tongue—for the time being. Okay, the football culture was new to him; maybe it was just a stage.

She read over the local news headlines. HALLOWEEN PARTY TO BE HELD AT FIRE HALL. *Hmm. That's new.* A News Flash streamed across the screen. She clicked on it and began to read.

> The body of a young woman was found today along Cumberland Creek. It has been identified as the remains of Esmeralda Martelino, sister of Marina Martelino, whose body was found yesterday at Pamela's Pie Palace. The bakery will remain closed until further notice.

"I'll be," Beatrice said. "Sisters? Their killings most assuredly had something to do with one another."

"What's going on, Mama?" Vera had gotten up to put the tea kettle on and was behind her mom. Beatrice filled her in.

"Whoa!" Vera gasped. "Another murder in Cumberland Creek." She sat down at the table, her mouth agape.

"It's nobody we know, thank goodness, but still a tragedy," Beatrice said, her heart thumping. Her home. Cumberland Creek. What was becoming of it? What to do about it? There was a killer on the loose!

"Sisters." Vera said as she pulled up the chair and looked over Bea's shoulder.

"Odd, isn't it? I never realized there were any Mexicans living around here," Beatrice said.

"They sort of keep to themselves," Vera said. "Several families live over at those Riverside Apartments on Druid Lane."

"I had no idea." Bea was ashamed that she didn't know who was living in her community anymore. Though the apartment and mobile home dwellers were not quite in her neighborhood, she still considered them a part of her community.

"A couple of their daughters have started ballet lessons," Vera said. "They pay on time and the children are so well behaved."

"Well, that says a lot, doesn't it?" Beatrice said and crossed her arms. "I don't know half the people in Cumberland Creek anymore. I used to know just about everybody."

"I know, Mama," Vera said. "It's changing. Some of it's good. I'm really glad Elizabeth will be getting to know some kids from other cultures."

"Some of it's bad, though," Beatrice said. "I mean look. Two women murdered. We went for years without any murders in our community. Now all of a sudden, it's one after the other."

Vera thought a moment, her mouth curled. "Yes, but most of the murders had nothing to do with the new people in town. Look, many of the murders were committed by locals or people with local ties."

Beatrice nodded. "True enough."

"At the same time, it kind of scares me. It doesn't quite feel safe anymore. If I let myself, I'll get paranoid about Elizabeth and won't let her out of my sight," Vera said, her brows arching higher over her eyes.

"But you're lucky. The child has so many people who look out for her," Beatrice pointed out. "No need for paranoia."

Vera was already a bit overprotective of Elizabeth— a baby she thought she'd never have. Unfortunately, Vera's relationship with Bill, the father of the baby, had run its course when she had found out she was expecting.

"Look Mama," Vera pointed to the screen. "There's a little article about Marina.

"The body of Marina Martelino, age twenty-three, was found at Pamela's Pie Palace, Saturday at four-thirty AM. Marina, a recent immigrant to the United States, had been working at Pamela's for eighteen months. According to Pamela Kraft, owner of the Pie Palace, Marina was from Mexico City and lived with her sister at Riverside Apartments in Cumberland Creek. According to Sheriff Ted Bixby, an investigation is pending," Vera read. She looked at her mother. "Well, now is that all they are going to say?"

"Evidently," Beatrice said.

The whistling tea kettle invaded their conversation.

"Tea, Mama?"

"Sure."

"You'd think they'd let people know what's going to happen with her body or if she has any relatives around," Vera grumbled.

"Well, we know about her sister."

"Yes, but what about the people at home? Will we ever know? I feel like we should reach out to her family in some way."

Beatrice beamed. Her Vera. A heart as wide as the sky. Trouble was, it got trampled on a lot. Beatrice used to worry more about her—but that had changed. She had a great feeling about Eric. He loved Vera and was showing an incredible amount of patience.

"We can ask the police or Pamela for some information on how to reach her family," Beatrice said as Vera brought her a steaming cup of tea.

"What's going on in here, ladies?" Eric asked, entering the dining room.

"What is it, halftime?" Vera rolled her eyes.

He grinned. "How did you know?"

Chapter 9

DeeAnn slid the chicken back into the oven and went to work mashing the potatoes. It was time for Sunday dinner, one of her favorite times of the week. Karen was coming. Visits from her were rarer than what DeeAnn would have liked. Karen was a nurse at the University of Virginia Medical Center and, because she was so new, she had very little control over her schedule. Her first year was turning into nothing but work and sleep.

DeeAnn had wondered recently if her daughter was dating someone. She had received a phone call from someone canceling an outing and had been obviously disappointed.

DeeAnn tried not to pry in Karen's personal life. She was a grown woman—at least that's what DeeAnn kept telling herself.

"You and your strawberry kitchen," Karen said as she walked in the door.

DeeAnn looked up from her mashed potatoes before she plopped more butter in. "I like strawberries. They make me smile."

Karen laughed. It was the same sweet rippling laugh it always was, just a bit deeper. "What can I do to help?"

"Set the table. Everything else is in hand."

"Chicken smells great," Karen said as she reached into the cupboard for plates and headed into the dining room. She was tall and thin like her dad and it was her habit to reach the tallest shelves for DeeAnn, who was a bit shorter but a lot rounder.

"Yes, it does." DeeAnn's husband, Jacob, came into the room.

"It needs a few more minutes," DeeAnn said as if trying to hold him back with her voice. He was so impatient sometimes.

"Just heard about the woman they found this morning," Jacob said, reaching into the silverware drawer.

"What woman?" Karen called from the dining room.

"Esmeralda Martelino," DeeAnn said, sprinkling more salt into the potatoes.

"How did you know?" asked Jacob.

DeeAnn reached down in her cupboard to get a serving bowl for the potatoes and a sharp pain ripped through her back. It flattened her, stomach-first onto the hard linoleum floor. *What's happening? Where is my breath?*

"DeeAnn?" She heard Jacob say through her haze of pain.

"Mom? What is it?" Karen crouched down beside her.

"My back," DeeAnn managed to say. "I'll be fine. Just give me a minute." *Just breathe,* she told herself. But she wasn't sure she could. It felt like her lower back was on fire and if she moved an inch it would erupt.

"Hold on," Karen said. "Don't move. Dad, can you get the heating pad warmed up?"

"Heating pad? Do we have a heating pad?" he said with panic in his voice.

"Yes, Dad. It's in the closet next to the bathroom, third shelf down. What does it feel like, Mom—a dull thud? A sharp pain?"

"It was sharp," DeeAnn said. "It's easing off into dull. Feels like something is out of place."

"How long have you been having problems? Can you twist around onto your back?" Karen asked.

"I think so."

"Here it is," Jacob said, coming into the kitchen and proudly holding up the heating pad.

DeeAnn and Karen exchanged looks.

"Can you plug it in next to the couch? Also get more pillows. We're going to need to prop Mom up." Karen was taking charge of the situation.

Had DeeAnn not been in such pain, she'd have told her how proud she was of her daughter, the nurse. A grown woman.

The scent of the chicken reminded DeeAnn that the bird needed to be pulled out of the oven. "The chicken."

"Don't worry," Karen said. "I'll take care of the chicken. We need to get you to the couch first."

Karen. What a kind, knowledgeable, sensible young woman she's become. DeeAnn looked up into her daughter's face and saw a woman she could not be more proud of and started to cry.

"Oh now," Jacob said, as he helped her up from

the floor, his arm around her shoulder. "DeeAnn, don't cry, sweetheart."

"Are you in that much pain?" Karen asked.

"I am," DeeAnn said, sniffling. *But that's not why I'm crying,* she wanted to say. They would never understand the way she just had seen time stand still, move back and forward, in just a flash. Her daughter, a grown, capable woman . . . with the same face, the same eyes, hell, the same freckles she'd always had. The same freckles DeeAnn's mother had had. Lord, the woman was a lot like DeeAnn's own mother. She had a moment of existential dread and panic. *Stop,* she wanted to say. *Stop growing up. I want to hold you here forever.*

Her back jabbed at her and brought her back to the present. She carefully sat on the couch, with Karen lifting her feet and Jacob propping pillows up behind her.

"That okay?" His blue eyes were full of concern.

Dee Ann nodded. Yes, it was okay. It would be okay. Time marches on, the way it's meant to. It felt like just yesterday she was a new bride, a new mom, and now, here she was—an old, fat woman with a bad back.

Her husband handed her a tissue. "Get yourself together, woman," he said and grinned.

"I better see to the chicken," Karen said and left the room.

"I love you, Jacob Fields, even if you don't know where the heating pad is kept. Jesus Lord, man, where do you live?"

Jacob laughed. "I never had to use it, I guess. Is it getting hot?"

DeeAnn nodded.

* * *

When they were gathered around the TV after eating dinner and watching the Steelers game, DeeAnn filled them in on what she knew about Esmeralda.

"How about that? My mom is in on the scoop," Karen said.

DeeAnn beamed. "Of course, they figure the killings are linked. They're sisters. Both killed within a day of one another."

"Nobody knows how yet?" Jacob asked.

"Nope," DeeAnn said. "But you know what is the oddest thing?"

Jacob and Karen looked in her direction.

"Both of them were found with scrapbooking pages in their hands," DeeAnn watched as her daughter almost spilled her after-dinner coffee.

Chapter 10

"Rat poisoning?" Annie said into the phone.

"Yes, it's very easy to get a hold of and very easy to kill someone with it. Both sisters had it in their systems. Marina was probably almost already dead when she was attacked with the craft knife. Esmeralda was probably dead when the ribbon was tied around her mouth and nose," Ruth replied.

"Could the poisoning have been accidental?" Annie wondered more to herself than the medical examiner.

"It's possible," Ruth said. "I hate to say it, but maybe the apartments where they lived had a rat problem and they were trying to get rid of them. Maybe."

"Where did they live?" Annie asked.

"Um, let's see." Papers were shuffled in the background. "They lived on Druid Lane. Riverside Apartments. Know where it is?"

"No, but I guess I can find it," Annie said. *Druid Lane? In Cumberland Creek?* It was an odd name, that was for sure. The town was so small. How had she never run across it?

"But what about the scrapbook pages?" Annie asked. "Why would they have had a scrapbook page?"

"I have no idea. I haven't seen the evidence. Have you?"

"Yes, I saw one of the pages, but not closely," she said, thinking back to yesterday at Paige's kitchen table. Her eyes wandered over to the cupcakes she had cooling on the kitchen counter. She glanced at her watch. "Thanks for talking with me. You might hear from me again."

"You know where to find me," Ruth said and hung up.

Annie reached for her box and placed the cupcakes inside. Today was the library bake sale at her sons' school. She'd pledged to donate chocolate cupcakes with orange frosting—very Halloweenish. She was getting to be a better baker. She hadn't burned anything in a long time. After she dropped the cupcakes off, she would stop at the grocery store and pick up a few things for dinner. She'd make dinner and leave it on the stove for when Mike got home. Meanwhile, she'd be at their son Ben's soccer game.

Things sure were getting complicated with their schedules. Sometimes she was tempted to just swing into a drive-thru. Most of the time she resisted, but every once in a while, it was the only way. This wasn't why she became a stay-at-home mom. But then again, she was always in-between a freelancer and stay-at-home mom. Very few people could relate.

She grabbed her purse and her box of cupcakes.

When she opened the door, Cookie was standing there with Dr. Stevens.

"Ms. Chamovitz, do you have a minute?" Dr. Stevens asked.

"No, I'm sorry. I'm off to the school." Annie loved Cookie with all her heart and they were good friends, having bonded over being outsiders in a place where most people traced their heritage back several generations. But Annie'd gotten bad vibes from Dr. Stevens. She couldn't quite put her finger on what she didn't like about him.

"Let me take that for you," Cookie said and reached for the box. "Can I come with you?"

"Sure," Annie said.

"I will catch up with you later," Cookie said to her doctor, who looked a bit miffed.

"Cookie, we are right in the middle of something—"

"It will have to wait. Annie is busy. I told you we'd have to schedule a time to meet with her," Cookie said, following Annie to her car. "You can't just pop in on people and expect they can drop everything."

Annie caught a strange look between them before she slid into her car.

Cookie opened the passenger door and sat in the seat with the box of Halloween cupcakes on her lap. "I am just getting so sick of him," she said as they pulled away. "I don't know what he wants from me."

"He's trying to help you, remember."

Cookie grimaced. "Is he?"

"What's that supposed to mean?"

"I mean we've been at this therapy for months now. Nothing is helping. Maybe there's a reason I don't remember much of the past. Maybe deep down I don't want to," Cookie said with a flatness Annie found hard to bear.

Did Cookie not care about the people she may have left behind while she was missing? Did she not know how Annie herself had grieved for a year until Bryant told her that they found Cookie and she was okay?

"Well, I'm sure we all have parts of our past we'd like to forget," Annie said after a minute. "I know I do. But don't you think you'd like to know more? I mean we were very good friends."

"Aren't we still?" Cookie said, looking a bit hurt.

"Yes, of course. But I'm just pointing out there may be others in your life like me. Others missing you," Annie said as she clicked on her turn signal to pull into the school.

Cookie hung her head a bit and quieted. She sat in the car to wait for Annie to deliver the cupcakes.

When Annie returned, Cookie was gone. It startled her—but then she remembered. *This is who Cookie is now. She just comes and goes willy-nilly.* Annie looked around for her friend, but she was nowhere to be seen. She refused to carry a cell phone, so Annie couldn't even call her.

Annie sighed deeply. What she wouldn't give for Cookie to be healed completely. She opened her car door, slid in, and her phone buzzed. It was Sheila.

"Hey, Annie. We're starting a food train for DeeAnn. She's thrown her back out and won't be able to work for at least a week."

"Wow, that sucks. She okay?"

"No. She's miserable. But I wanted to let you know to check your e-mail. You can sign up for the food train online. It's very efficient that way. I'm taking them dinner tonight and then leaving for the city tomorrow. We'll see you on Saturday."

Annie pulled out of the school parking lot and headed for the park to situate herself. She wanted to look up Druid Lane on her phone. When she turned into the park parking lot, she spotted Cookie.

She was sitting on a bench, looking out over the river, legs crossed, one open hand on each knee. Was she meditating or just trying to remember?

Either way, Annie felt like an intrusion, so she turned the car around and left the park.

Chapter 11

Beatrice knocked on DeeAnn's door and Jacob answered. He looked haggard. It had only been a few days of DeeAnn being out of commission and the man looked like he was going to keel over.

"Hey, Bea," he said.

"How do?"

"Come on in. Let me help you with that." He took the fried chicken from her.

"I know how much DeeAnn likes my fried chicken," Bea said.

"She's on the couch." Jacob tilted his head in the right direction.

When Beatrice walked into the room, the sound of the TV blasted her. DeeAnn was watching the news.

"Hey Bea," she said. "Thanks for coming by."

"Brought you some chicken."

"Thank you. You know I love that chicken. You gave me the recipe, but mine never turns out as good as yours."

"What do the docs say about your back?" Beatrice asked, but DeeAnn had gone back to watching TV.

"What?"

"Turn the friggin' TV off," Beatrice said in as nice a tone as she could muster. After all, DeeAnn was hurt.

DeeAnn clicked her remote. "I was watching the news. Sorry."

"The doctors?"

"I just have to rest until it's better. I have a slipped disk. They recommended surgery, but I haven't made up my mind about it yet. It would mean time off from work . . . and to think I was thinking about retiring. Then this happened."

"What? Why would you retire? You're still young," Beatrice said.

DeeAnn's lips pursed. "That's precisely why. I want to enjoy life a little. Baking is hard work, Bea. My back has been bothering me awhile. And my feet."

"Pshaw. Let the younger people do the hard work."

"Yes, but I got into baking because I love it. It's hard to not do it. I'm not sure what the answer is."

Beatrice thought it over. DeeAnn was not quite fifty. She had a lot of good years left in her.

"In any case, you've got to take care of yourself now," Bea said.

"Can I get you something to drink?" Jacob asked as he entered the room.

"No thank you. I can't stay long. Just wanted to bring the chicken by and see how Ms. DeeAnn is doing," Beatrice said.

"The medicine makes her a bit loopy"—he smiled—"but at least she's not in any pain."

"Can I bring you some books? Puzzles? Ya can't sit there all day watching TV. Good Lord," Beatrice said.

"I'm not much of a reader," DeeAnn said. "I've never sat still enough to get interested in a book. But maybe now is the time."

"What do you think you'd like to read? I've been reading some mysteries. Would you like that?"

"I can try it out."

"I'll stop by with some books tomorrow. In the meantime, try not to watch too much trashy TV. It will rot your brain."

"I was watching the news about the recent murders," DeeAnn said with an edge to her voice.

"Is it what they are saying? Murder?" Beatrice's heart skipped around in her old chest.

"Yes. They were scrapbooking sisters, evidently," Jacob offered.

"Scrapbookers? What does that have to do with anything?" Beatrice asked.

"Who knows? DeeAnn said, her eyes widening. "Maybe nothing. But maybe everything."

"Uh-oh," Beatrice said. "Something tells me it's a good thing you're laid up right now."

Jacob agreed. "Let's leave the sleuthing to the professionals this time."

DeeAnn shrugged. "We never meant to get involved with any of the other investigations."

"Humph," Beatrice said. "Tell that to the man you knocked down over on Jenkins Mountain."

"Well," DeeAnn said, grinning and crossing her arms. "It was him or me, Ms. Matthews."

Chapter 12

Later that same day, DeeAnn threw knitting needles across the carpeted floor and yarn went flying.

"It sure was nice of Elsie to try to teach you to knit," Jacob said and laughed.

"I can't do it. I'm a scrapbooker, but I can't quite sit up enough to actually scrapbook. It upsets me. I'm so bored. I hate knitting."

Jacob pursed his lips off to the side. He stood with his hands in his pockets and rocked up on his toes and back. "But you said you wanted to try. That knitters look so peaceful, that—"

"Oh be quiet, Jacob," DeeAnn interrupted.

"You need anything? I'll be out in the garage."

She crossed her arms. "I'm fine." *I just need a new, younger back.*

He handed her another pain pill and a glass of water. She swallowed both and watched him pick up the needles and yarn. He started to hand it back to her.

"Don't bother," she said and waved him off. She watched him walk off.

He had taken a few days off work to help her out a bit. And bless him, he was trying. But she was not handling it well. DeeAnn was a doer, not a thinker. She didn't like to be left alone with her thoughts. She wasn't much of a reader, like Paige—the teacher—with her nose always stuck in some historical romance book, or Annie's nose in some memoir. She liked to be baking, cooking, cleaning, and moving. If she sat still too long, feelings of dread would overtake her. She'd start thinking about her mother's death or about her sister's diagnosis of breast cancer. All she could do was stew. There was nothing to be done about any of it.

When Jacob left the room, DeeAnn picked up the TV remote, hoping she could find something decent to watch. *Dr. Phil? Lord, no.* She couldn't stand to watch people airing their dirty laundry on TV. *MTV? Good God,* what had happened to MTV? It used to show music videos—now it was all reality TV stuff. And there was nothing real about it. Who did these people think they were kidding? *Click, click, click.*

Local news? Okay. Maybe.

"And now we turn to the double murder of two sisters. Marina and Esmeralda Martelino," the anchorwoman said. "Both bodies were found within twenty-four hours of one another. Marina had been working at the local favorite Pamela's Pie Palace."

Local favorite, humph.

A shot of Pamela with her place behind her came into view. She spoke to the TV camera. "Marina was a talented baker and a wonderful, sweet, young woman." She looked sincere and gorgeous—as usual.

Did the woman ever have a bad-hair day? Or break a nail? Or get a zit? Anything?

Pamela continued. "I don't know who would have wanted to kill her. It's just such a tragedy."

A photo of Esmeralda flashed onto the screen behind the news anchor, who spoke again. "Marina's sister Esmeralda worked as an independent contractor cleaning homes in the area. Elsie Mayhue was one of her employers."

The camera flashed on to Elsie. "She was quiet, friendly, and a very good worker. Can't think of anything bad to say about the woman. Of course, we didn't talk to each other much. It wasn't like we were friends," Elsie added with emphasis.

No, of course not, DeeAnn thought.

"Cumberland Creek detectives and the county sheriff's office are combining efforts to solve this double murder," the anchorwoman said. "If you have any information on either of these young women or anything having to do with their murders, please call this toll-free line."

The telephone number came over the screen.

DeeAnn dialed Annie.

"How are you, DeeAnn?" Annie asked after they exchanged hellos.

"I was just watching the news."

"Uh-oh," Annie said.

DeeAnn pictured her smiling. Annie had a lovely smile; she should do it more often. She was just way too serious sometimes.

"I saw the bit about the sisters being killed," DeeAnn told her. "Isn't it odd? I know we talked about all this earlier at Paige's, but have you heard anything about the way they were killed? The news didn't say."

"They were exposed to rat poisoning. Marina probably bled to death, though, and Esmeralda was suffocated. That's all they know at this point."

"What? It's awful! What an awful thing to happen to someone, especially in a foreign country. Have you found out anything about them?" DeeAnn asked.

"I have their address. They lived in the Riverside Apartments on Druid Lane. Know where that is? I haven't even mapped it out yet," Annie said.

DeeAnn heard shuffling in the background. *What's Annie doing?* "I've never been there, but Jacob has mentioned it to me before, as in not to ever go there alone."

"Why?" Annie asked.

"He said it's rough over there. Gangs and such."

"Gangs? In Cumberland Creek? Really?"

"I know it's hard to believe. But you remember the young woman who was attacked and raped a few months ago? It was gang-related. Very hush-hush," DeeAnn said.

"I don't know what to say. Where have I been?"

"I have no idea, dear. Jacob heard about all this through the grapevine, of course. I checked it out. It's all true. So if the women lived on Druid Lane, maybe this is gang related."

"Women gang members who scrapbook?" Annie asked facetiously.

DeeAnn shrugged. "It's no weirder than some of the other stuff we've seen around here."

Annie paused. "Isn't that the truth?"

Chapter 13

Well, no wonder Annie didn't know about Druid Lane. It was a brand new road. That much was obvious.

How new is this place? She pulled into the parking lot of the first apartment complex. It was almost empty of cars. Of course, it was the middle of the day. Everybody was at work or school. Almost everybody. A group of men were standing at the end of the parking lot huddled around a motorcycle, checking it out. She exited the car and looked around for the leasing office.

The apartment complex looked like a million others she had seen, except this one was newer. It was nondescript, architecturally speaking, painted in tones of gray and brown, with the window frames and doors painted white. She spotted the office and headed over.

Inside, she was assaulted by an odor.

Mildew? She walked over to the counter, her nose itching. "Hello?"

A woman came from behind a wall. She was short

and round. "Yes, may I help you?" She had an accent, but Annie couldn't identify it immediately. She was well-coiffed. Hair, makeup, and a cheap, but clean suit.

"Yes," Annie smiled. "I'm a reporter. I'm here about the Martelino sisters."

The woman's smile vanished.

Annie noticed the creases around her eyes. "I'm working on a story about their deaths."

The woman knitted her brow. Was she going to cry or cuss Annie out? Emotion played over her face—but what emotion was it?

"Did you know them?" Annie persisted.

She nodded. "Yes," she said in a hushed tone and her eyes went to the floor.

"They lived here, right?" Annie said.

The woman nodded. "I can't let you into their place. The police won't let anybody in right now."

"Oh, I completely understand," Annie said. "It seems like you knew them well. I am so sorry for your loss. Such a tragedy."

The expression on the woman's face grew more pained. Yes, she would cry at any moment. Then the woman's eyes traveled to the door and in walked a man.

Was he one of the men who was checking out the bike?

He was tall, wore glasses, and his black hair was cropped close to his head. He wore khakis and a blazer.

"Mr. Mendez," the woman said, "This is—"

"I know who you are," the man said to Annie. "What do you want? To come in here and write a story about us? About the Martelino sisters? What tragic lives they led?" His tone was sarcastic, almost vicious. "We don't need your stories. They are gone. Gone. What does it matter now?"

Annie drew a breath. "I'm sorry, Mr. Mendez. I didn't mean to offend you or anybody. I'd just like to give people a complete story of what happened to them. And maybe it would help find the killer. Maybe it would help save someone else."

His face was suddenly closer to Annie's. She smelled cheap aftershave, with a hint of a breath mint—or was it mouthwash?

Her heart started to race and pings of intuition raced through her. She needed to get out of there fast.

He sneered. "*Bruja.*"

Annie stood straighter, looked him in the face, and said, "*Perdón, me permite, ¿cómo?*"(*Sorry, but how do I allow this?*)

Surprised, he drew back.

Nobody calls me bitch and gets away with it.

"Look, if you don't want to talk to me, fine. I'll find other people who will. Or hey, maybe I'll make some stuff up," Annie said, starting to walk toward the door. "Or maybe all I need to do is tell the truth about you and I'll have the feds here in about five minutes, breathing down your back. Threatening a reporter? Not bright."

She trembled as she reached for the door, opened it, and walked out. *Stop shaking. Don't let him see you shake.* The cool air hit her with relief. The guys at the end of the lot looked at her, then turned their faces. One of the young men looked vaguely familiar. She didn't want to stare, but where had she seen him before? Something wasn't right about this place. Mendez was hiding something.

All the more reason to leave. She couldn't get in her car quickly enough.

She checked out the dashboard clock. She had about an hour before Sam and Ben came home from school so she decided to swing by the police station to see Detective Bryant. She had been so busy with her boys, her books, and life in general, that maybe she'd somehow lost track of what was happening in her own community.

Annie pulled into the parking lot of the police station. Detective Bryant's car was there so she girded her loins. There was nobody else who had their fingers on the pulse of Cumberland Creek like he did.

She walked into the station and the woman behind the desk, looked up at her. "Can I help you?"

"Is Bryant available?"

"Just one moment," the receptionist said, picking up the phone. She spoke quietly for a moment, then offered, "Annie Chamovitz." After a pause, she hung up the phone and said, "Go right in."

When Annie walked into Bryant's office, she was surprised to find another man there.

"Hi, Annie," Adam Bryant said. "This is Detective Mendez."

Annie frowned. "Mendez?"

"Yes?"

"I just met a Mendez at the apartments on Druid. Any relation?"

The man started to say something, but Bryant interrupted. "What were you doing down there?"

"I'm working on the Martelino story," she replied.

"I'd advise you to not go there alone," Bryant said.

Annie crossed her arms. "What the hell is going on in this town?"

The detectives looked at one another but didn't say a word.

Chapter 14

As Beatrice was gathering up some books to take to DeeAnn, her doorbell rang.

"I'll get it," Jon said. He was so helpful.

Bea placed a few books in a bag, then removed a couple. She didn't want to overwhelm DeeAnn. She'd just tell her there were more, if she was interested. Bea placed the bag on her kitchen table next to the lasagna she had made for DeeAnn and Jacob. It should last them a few days.

"Hey, Bea," Annie said, walking into the kitchen.

"Well, hello there. Have a seat. I'm just getting some things ready to take to DeeAnn."

"The lasagna looks good," Annie said, picking up a few books and looking at them. "I love these. They are a lot of fun, yet they aren't stupid, you know?"

"I've got so many of them and DeeAnn is bored out of her mind," Bea said.

"I've been taking my books down to Blue Moon Bookstore," Annie said. "They sell secondhand books along with new ones."

Beatrice sat down. "You know, I haven't been there in a while. I forget about that place. Nice bookstore."

"I've been spending a lot of time there. They have book groups, writer's groups," Annie said, sitting down.

"Hmmm, interesting," Bea said. "Can I get you something to drink?"

"No, I'm not staying. The boys will be home in about ten minutes. I've just come from the police station and I don't like what I heard. I wanted to run a few things by you since you've lived here your whole life."

Beatrice looked up from her stack of books.

"I went over to Druid Lane where those new apartments are. It's where the Martelino sisters lived. I just wanted to have a look around and maybe talk to some people."

"And?"

"Well, I started to speak to a woman behind the counter at the office. She seemed nice, but then this man came up behind me and he was rude and threatening."

"Oh dear," Beatrice said.

"So I hightailed it over to the police department. Come to find out, it's a hotbed of gang activity."

Beatrice's mouth dropped open.

Jon walked by on his way to the sink. "What? Gangs in Cumberland Creek?" He said, stopping at the table. "Did I hear that right?"

"Evidently it's been a problem for quite some time," Annie said. "For the most part, it's not been in the news, but a few months ago when the young woman was raped and attacked . . . well, that was gang-related. I learned about it from DeeAnn. It checks out."

"Do you think that's the case with the Martelino sisters?" Beatrice asked.

"I have no idea. It certainly seems personal— sisters killed within twenty-four hours of one another." Annie paused a moment before continuing. "But Beatrice, I wanted to ask you what you make of this gang business and what you know about Druid Lane and the neighborhood."

Beatrice thought about it for a moment, sifting through images and memories. "Where exactly is it? Don't think I've ever been there. And I thought I knew this town pretty well."

"It's over near the park across the river," Annie told her. "It looks pretty new. Newly paved road, new apartments."

"Hmm. I don't know a thing about it." Beatrice shrugged. "I know Cumberland Creek is growing and there's been a lot of new construction, but I don't know about that area."

"Is that where the gangs are?" Jon asked.

"I don't know," Annie replied. "That's what the cops say, but I covered gangs in DC and many times where you think they are is just a cover for where they really are."

Jon's mouth twisted. "Sounds sophisticated."

"Wait a minute," Beatrice said. "Did that property used to be a farm? I think it did."

"Interesting," Annie said. "I'll look into who owned it."

"I know who owned it. That was the old Drummond homestead, I believe," Bea said. "When did they sell it to become apartments? Where have I been? How did I miss it?" A wash of nostalgia overcame her. She had such fond memories of the Drummonds, their house, and their orchard—one of the oldest in the state.

"You have a full life, Beatrice," Annie said after a moment. "You've been busy with your new husband."

"*Oui,*" Jon said and grinned. "Plus, so many other things."

"But I read the paper every day and I talk to people every day. I mean, I consider myself well-informed." Beatrice was indignant. It didn't make sense. How could something be happening and she not know anything about it?

"As far as the gangs go," Annie said, "the police are watching very closely. I guess they are trying to keep things quiet so as not to set off panic."

Beatrice thought a moment. "I never thought I'd see the day I'd agree with the police. But a lot of the old-timers around here would welcome a reason to fight off a group of foreigners. Pains me to say it. Just the other day, someone was complaining about the Mexicans and other foreigners taking their jobs."

"Really?" Annie said. "Was that at the senior center?"

Beatrice nodded. "Over bingo." She reached for Jon's hand. "They completely ignored the fact that a foreigner was sitting right next to me."

Chapter 15

DeeAnn held the laptop on a pillow on her knees. She never thought she would like one of these things, but it turned out Karen had been right. She did like it.

"I've got a couple digital scrapbooking programs on there for you to play with and I uploaded some of your photos," Karen said.

"So thoughtful of you, sweetie." *Upload? Digital?* Those words didn't make a whole lot of sense to DeeAnn. Oh, she knew what they meant, but she didn't know how to use those words in the context of everyday life. But she didn't want to let her daughter know that.

"I'll be back tomorrow to take you to your appointment," Karen said, getting up from the couch. "I'll get you some more apps. You can even watch movies on it."

"Movies?" DeeAnn said. "I might like that."

Karen leaned down and kissed her forehead. "Anything you need before I go?"

DeeAnn looked at the little couch-side table

holding a glass of water, tissues, medication, and the books Beatrice had brought over. "I'm fine. Besides, your dad will be home soon."

After Karen left, DeeAnn called Sheila.

"How's it going?" Sheila asked. "How are you feeling?"

"I need to get up off this couch before I kill someone," DeeAnn said. And that was the absolute truth.

"Wouldn't that hurt?" Sheila laughed.

"You're damn straight it would hurt." DeeAnn thought about the pain, muted because of the medication she was taking, but it was still there. Maybe she should take another pill? "But listen, Karen brought me a laptop."

"Wow," Sheila said. "Nice."

"She loaded some scrapbooking programs on it," DeeAnn said. "And I didn't want her to know how stupid her mother really is."

"Oh, DeeAnn!"

"Seriously? Upload? Download? What the heck?"

"Would you like for me to come over and explain some things? I'm happy to come over."

"Yes, I'd like that. And maybe you can show me how to get the Internet on this thing. I want to read the news. I'm so curious about the Martelino sisters. Know anything new?"

"Today, Annie went to where they lived," Sheila said. "Evidently, it was not a good situation."

"What do you mean?"

"A man threatened her. And Bryant told her to never go over there alone."

"Over where?" DeeAnn asked.

"Druid Lane."

"Humph. That's what Jacob said too."

"Evidently, there are gangs over there."

"That's what Jacob said. I don't know if I believe that. When I get my back straightened out, I'm going over to have a look for myself."

"Now, I don't think that would be a good idea," Sheila said. "Annie is not easily intimidated and she was so upset that she went to the police station right after."

"Humph. She needs a bodyguard." DeeAnn laughed.

Sheila laughed, too. "That would be you."

"Yep. So, see you in a bit?"

"Coming right over."

Gangs in Cumberland Creek? Surely not, DeeAnn thought as she looked at the clock. She felt a twinge of pain shoot through her spine. It was almost time for another pill, so she might as well take it now. She picked up the bottle and looked over the instructions and saw that yes, she could take two if the pain worsened. She shrugged and took two. She'd be very comfortable by the time Sheila came over for a visit.

DeeAnn next dialed Jill over at her bakery. "How's everything going?" she asked when Jill picked up.

"Well for the third time today, I'll answer that everything is running very smoothly," Jill said, sounding exhausted and stressed. "You've got a good crew here, DeeAnn. It's okay. You take care of yourself and don't worry."

"Have you thought about what to do for Halloween? I think we should do the Harry Potter theme again this year. I'm not sure I'll be back on my feet in time."

"We will take care of it, I promise."

"We should be getting some flour in tomorrow," DeeAnn said.

"Yes, it's on the schedule." Jill paused. "Anything else?"

"I'm sorry to be such a pain," DeeAnn said after a moment. "But it is my shop. At least for the time being."

"What's that supposed to mean?" an exasperated Jill said.

"Oh nothing. It's . . . my back. I'm not sure . . ." DeeAnn said, holding back tears. *Oh Lord, what is wrong with me? Am I going to cry over the phone to Jill?* "I better go." She clicked off her phone. Things were going well without her. Maybe it was a good time to step back from the business. If not sell it, then let Jill take over the day-to-day.

But what would DeeAnn do with herself? The boredom of lying on the couch all the time was driving her mad. What if she didn't have the bakery to go to everyday? What would she do with herself?

She reached over for a tissue and blew her nose.

DeeAnn was a person who needed to keep busy. She didn't like to sit around and think. It was no good. No good at all.

The doorbell rang.

"Come on in," she called.

"Well hello there," Sheila said, not looking at her yet, but reaching for the laptop. "That's a nice laptop! Wow, you can do some cool stuff with this."

"Well, that's good," DeeAnn managed to say.

Sheila took a look at her. "Have you been crying?" She sat down in the chair next to the couch. "Oh,

DeeAnn." She said it with so much pity in her voice that it made DeeAnn cringe.

"Listen," Sheila said after a few minutes. "We'll get you squared away with this digital scrapbooking and the next thing you know you are going to be completely caught up before you go back to work."

"Well, now," DeeAnn said, feeling a little better. "That would be a minor miracle."

Chapter 16

Annie looked over Sam's homework. "Looks like you've gotten it all right." Her eyes were burning. She had thought she'd get some research done this evening but she was tired. Or maybe it was stress.

After all, one of the reasons they had moved to Cumberland Creek was because it was safer.

"Bath and bed," Annie said to Sam.

He sniffed.

"Are you okay, sweetie?"

He nodded. "I hate math."

"I know. But remember what I said. It's one of those things you just have to get through."

He kissed her on the cheek and she beamed. Her Sam.

"Hey Annie, did you put the last load of clothes in the dryer?" Mike said, walking into the kitchen.

"Yep," Annie said, getting up from the kitchen table and heading to the sink to rinse a few dishes.

"What's wrong?" Mike asked after a few minutes of silence.

"I found out there are gangs in Cumberland

Creek. I was over at those new apartments on Druid today and was threatened. I was surprised by it and went to the police and found out about big problems over there."

Mike leaned up against the sink and crossed his arms. "Does this have anything to do with the Martelino sisters?"

Annie shrugged. "I bet it does. I'm hoping to get some research done tonight."

"How big a problem is it?" Mike asked.

"It can't get any bigger than murder," she said, reaching for a towel to dry her hands. "But what bothers me is that I didn't know anything about it, you know? They are keeping it hush-hush. I'm a reporter and I'm a mother. I need to pay more attention to my community."

Mike reached for her and wrapped his arms around her. "I think you're doing fine. You're the best mom I know."

She relaxed into her husband's arms and placed her head on his shoulder. "I was scared today. I didn't expect to be threatened. It was a shock. I mean, I'm sure I can handle the story. I just need to be more careful, like I used to be."

Mike brushed a long, curly strand of hair out of her face and kissed her lips. "Annie, you've been in some tight situations, but you are a mom, now." He sighed. "I'm glad this is the last story. I don't want to raise these boys alone."

A shiver traveled up Annie's spine and she pulled away from her husband. "Don't worry. You won't." She smiled. "At least not if I have anything to say about it."

A few years ago, the conversation might have

ended differently. But something had shifted in Annie. She didn't crave the danger anymore. She was still curious and still liked writing and finding some semblance of justice, but after being tied up and almost killed at the B and B and witnessing Jon and Elsie being shot, images of her children being without their mother taunted her. She had chosen to be a mom. They had worked at becoming parents. It was what she wanted. She wanted to be there for her kids. It was more important than anything.

Dreams shifted. Life changed.

And gangs were invading Cumberland Creek.

"Gangs?" Randy said, the next day at the scrap-booking crop. "Here?"

Annie nodded and sipped her beer.

They had decided to meet at DeeAnn's. She couldn't leave the house and Sheila thought it would cheer her up to have the croppers at her place. They had set up card tables and chairs around DeeAnn and her couch. DeeAnn was scrapbooking on her new laptop.

"Never thought I'd see the day," Vera said after a minute. "This is my hometown, and I've never been frightened for my safety until the last few years. It's just sad."

"Do they think that's who killed the Martelinos?" Paige asked.

"I don't know," Annie replied. "But I've been researching them. The sisters have been here about eighteen months. They came together. Marina has been working for Pamela ever since she came here."

"I wonder why the other sister didn't go to work for her," DeeAnn said.

"It's tough to get a job there," Randy said. "Unless it's as a dishwasher, you have to be qualified. I don't think people realize that Pamela's hired some highly qualified professionals."

"Well, we know that you are," Paige said. "But are there others like you?"

"Absolutely," he said. "Marina was very gifted. Knew her stuff. I don't know where she was trained. I never really have the time to talk to people when I'm working. It's a very fast pace and I'm really still figuring out the way things work."

"I'm curious," Annie said. "You've said that the place isn't managed well."

"No, the supplies don't seem to be," Randy said, placing a brown, jewel-embellished paper photo frame around a picture.

"Nice," Paige said, looking over his shoulder.

"I find that very surprising," Vera said. "I mean, for such a successful place, you'd think she'd be more careful."

Randy grunted, holding up his page. "I'm not sure what the problem with the supplies is. I'm looking into it." The page was gold with a Halloween photo of him and his dad sitting on a porch swing. He was dressed as Superman and only about three years old. The cranberry jewel embellishments he'd placed on the page added just a bit of flair. "I love those jewels. And they are so easy to work with. Now they have peel-off backs."

"Does Pamela employ a lot of Mexicans?" Annie

asked while searching in her bag for an envelope of photos she had stuck inside earlier.

"She employs mostly foreigners," Randy said. "I'm one of the few locals there."

"What?" Vera said, dropping her scissors.

"To be fair, most of them are doing menial jobs. Dishwashing, chopping, mixing," said Randy. "Pamela mentioned once that she couldn't find Americans to fill those positions."

The room quieted.

"That's hard to believe," DeeAnn said. "I've never had a problem. In fact, I maintain a file of people who'd be happy to work for me, even if it's just washing dishes."

"How much is she paying those people, Randy?" Annie said, unable to ignore the pings of reporter's intuition surging through her body.

"I imagine minimum wage," he said, sliding his finished page into a plastic page protector. "But I really have no idea."

"Has anybody gotten a good look at the scrapbooking pages they found with the sisters?" DeeAnn questioned.

"They've both been sent to the crime lab in Richmond," Annie said, sliding out her photos of their day of hiking at Sherando Lake. She had bought some paper with stylized blue mountains in the background and couldn't wait to preserve the memory of that day. It had been one of those moments when she wished she could stop time. The boys were so busy with soccer, music, and school that it was tough to get away as a family, even if it was just to a local lake.

"Cute pictures," Randy said.

Annie beamed. She played around with the placement of the photos. "How open would Pamela be to chatting with me?"

Randy twisted his mouth. "Who knows?"

Chapter 17

Beatrice and Jon looked forward to Saturday nights with their granddaughter when they babysat while Vera was at her weekly crop meeting. But they were also happy when Elizabeth finally went to bed. The child was exhausting. Bea was ready for bed way before Elizabeth. Jon, on the other hand, was still playing around on the computer.

Beatrice sat in her chair reading the newest Louise Penny mystery and Jon sat in front of the computer reading intently.

"What are you doing over there?" Bea asked.

"Reading about gangs in small towns. It's troubling. I don't think we have gangs like this in France." He looked at her with a sideways glance and a grin.

"The hell you don't," Beatrice said. "Maybe you should be reading about gangs in Paris or Mexico City."

"Mexico City?"

"That's in Mexico."

"Yes, of course it is, but we are in Cumberland Creek."

"Yes, but the murder victims were from Mexico, right? So maybe we can learn something about where they lived. Maybe it will give us a better understanding of why the women were here," Beatrice said.

"They were probably here because wherever they grew up was terrible. They were very poor and lived in terrible conditions. They thought America was, how do you say, the land of opportunity," Jon said.

Beatrice's stomach sank. What Jon said was probably true and that was what made it all the more tragic. What could she do? She felt obligated to do something. She couldn't not help out. It was the Southerner in her. It was frustrating because there was nobody to take a casserole to, nobody to offer a shoulder to. *What must the girls' parents feel like?*

"Jon, we need to find out where to send our condolences. Maybe we can help their family somehow."

Jon's face softened. "What a lovely thought. You, my love, have a big heart."

Beatrice grinned. "Let's keep that between us, shall we?"

He went back to the computer and she to her book.

That didn't last long. Bea looked up. "I don't know much about Mexico at all. Here I am, eighty-five years old and there's so many places in the world that I know nothing about. Ed, my first husband, and I traveled around the states a bit. And there was my big trip to Paris. But life gets so busy. It all goes by too quickly to visit every place you might like to."

"I know exactly what you mean," Jon said.

"Well, hand me the phone."

After Jon passed it over Bea dialed Vera's cell.

"Yes, Mama?" Vera said.

"I want to send condolences to the murder victims' family. Anybody have any address?"

"Well, how would I know?"

"Ask Annie, would you? I know she's there," Beatrice said.

"Hold on," said Vera.

A few seconds later, Annie's voice came over the phone. "Hey Bea, how are you?"

"Feeling bad about those girls who were killed. I want to send their folks something. Can you help me out?" Beatrice asked.

"I can try. Right now, there's not much to tell. As soon as I find out who to contact, I'll let you know," Annie said.

"Why is it such a big deal? Why doesn't someone have their mother's address?" Beatrice said, exasperated.

"Pamela might," Annie said after a minute. "But it's complicated. Privacy issues. Immigration issues."

"Are you saying they were here illegally?"

"No. Pamela said they were legal. But Marina was her employee and there are legal guidelines for that. I plan to talk to Pamela this week. Maybe we can get somewhere. I'd like to reach out to their family, too, even if it's just to send a card, you know?" Annie said.

"Land's sakes. Guidelines," Beatrice said. "Guidelines for everything. Why do they have to make things so complicated?"

"I can't answer that, Beatrice," Annie said and laughed.

"Well, please let me know when you know something. Now, go ahead and get back to your scrapbooking. Sorry to interrupt."

"You are never an interruption, Bea. Good night."

Jon was deep into reading something on the computer. When Bea got off the phone he piped up. "Fascinating report on gangs in rural America. They are trying to figure out how gangs start. But no matter how it starts, it's clear that young people are targeted. One key factor is many of the gangs in rural areas are close to a major highway."

"I've always hated Highway 81. They say there's a lot of drugs transported there." Beatrice yawned. She wasn't sure what she wanted more—sleep or that last piece of apple strudel.

Of course, the strudel won out.

Chapter 18

DeeAnn mulled over the whole *Pamela hiring only foreigners* thing. What was that about? "Randy, how does Pamela find her help?"

"Who? What?" Randy was obviously concentrating on his father-son scrapbooking project.

"Pamela!" DeeAnn said. "How does she find her foreign help? I mean, I wouldn't even know where to begin, say, if I wanted to specifically hire immigrants."

He shrugged. "I'm sorry, DeeAnn. The hiring is done by Pamela. I have no idea how she finds them."

"Maybe she runs want ads in their Mexican papers," Vera suggested.

"Online, more likely," Annie said.

"It's not only people from Mexico. Sal is from Brazil and some of the others are from the Philippines," Randy said.

It was perplexing. DeeAnn couldn't get over it. She didn't know about any of it, of course, and it troubled her. Even though Pamela's Pie Palace was on the outskirts of town, she was in the same business and wondered if she was missing an opportunity. But what was the advantage? Her employees were the best. She paid them a fair wage and they worked hard for her. She sucked in air as a twinge of pain ripped through her lower back.

Sheila noticed. "DeeAnn? Is this too much for you?"

"Nah, I probably need another couple pain pills." DeeAnn reached for her bottle as she looked at the clock. *When was the last time I took a pill? Oh never mind.*

It hurt, so she took a couple more.

Annie's head tilted as she looked up from her scrapbook. "Where do all these immigrants live? I mean, I never see them wandering around Cumberland Creek."

"I have no idea, Annie," Randy said. "We know where the Martelino sisters lived. Maybe the rest of them live there, too."

"But even then, where are they hanging out? Doing their grocery shopping? I never see them," she insisted.

"That is odd. I figured since I moved onto the mountain, I'm a bit out of touch with things. That's why I don't see them. There are several girls in dance class, though," Vera said and placed a button onto her page. It was a button that looked like a medal. She was working on Eric's triathlon page.

"I think they keep to themselves," Randy said after a minute. "I mean, imagine being in a foreign country surrounded by people you don't know. It's natural to want to hang out with other people from your own country. Right?"

DeeAnn searched through her brain to remember

if she'd ever seen any of the new people in the bakery. She couldn't remember. She closed the lid on her laptop to rest her eyes, which were burning.

"You okay?" Vera said.

"Yes, stop fussing over me. It's just that my eyes are burning from using the computer," DeeAnn said.

"Yes, that will happen. That and pain in your hands and such. It's a good idea to stop, rest your eyes, and stretch," Sheila said.

"Sheila, how is Donna?" Annie asked after taking a sip of beer.

"She's doing okay," Sheila said after a minute.

DeeAnn took a good look at Sheila. "But you look like hell."

"DeeAnn!" Paige said. "Those drugs are messing with your head!"

Sheila's mouth dropped open, then closed.

Vera reached over and took her hand. "She's right. You look very tired. Are you okay?"

DeeAnn watched as Sheila's lips started to curl downward. Her cheeks twitched and a low sob came from deep inside of her. "No! I'm not okay. I have deadlines, big deadlines, a very sick daughter who wants to go back to Carnegie Mellon, another child getting ready to go to school, and I have no energy. I simply don't know how to manage anymore." She snapped her laptop shut.

The room went completely silent.

Cookie spoke up first. She had been quiet for most of the night, which was her usual way these days. She'd come and eat and work on a page or two. Nobody knew what memories she was scrapbooking, since she really didn't remember much of her past.

"Sheila, maybe you need to pull back, give something up," Cookie said.

Sheila made a noise, something between a laugh and a sob. "But what? I have this dream job . . ."

"Sometimes what we think is a dream turns out to be a nightmare," Cookie said.

DeeAnn bit her tongue. *How would she know?* Half the time Cookie didn't remember a thing. How could she be dispensing advice?

Sheila took a deep breath. "You know, Cookie, for somebody who is still not quite well . . . I think you've hit the nail on the head. I love my work. But the deadlines, the travel . . . If Donna were okay, I think it would be different. But maybe I need to talk to my company about pulling back a bit. My first product line comes out next week. It's going to be crazy busy."

"Is this your scrap journaling project?" Annie asked.

"That's part of it. There's a Halloween digital scrap journal and a line of papers and embellishments and so on. All designed by me." Despite her stress, Sheila beamed with pride.

"That's fantastic," DeeAnn said.

"The company is having this huge event to roll it out next week. My whole family is going with me to the city to celebrate."

"Oh Sheila, that's wonderful!" Vera said.

Sheila nodded. "A dream come true. If only I felt better."

Chapter 19

"Hey, Pamela," Annie said as she walked in the door of Pamela's Pie Palace.

"Hey Annie," Pamela called out from behind the counter.

The place was packed. She was having a grand reopening celebration since the place had been closed for several days. Annie was often impressed by Pamela's business acumen.

"Let's go into my office," Pamela said, leading her through a door that led to some stairs. Annie followed her up the stairs to what looked like more of an apartment than an office.

"Sorry about the mess," Pamela said, walking over to the futon and plopping down on it. A poster of Marilyn Monroe hung on the wall behind the futon. "Lord, that's quite a crowd down there! Take a seat. What can I do for you?"

DeeAnn always went on about how beautiful Pamela was. *And it was true,* Annie mused. But she was uncertain how pretty Pamela would be without her makeup. Likely Annie would never find out;

she looked as though she'd stepped out of a poster herself.

"I'm here to ask a few questions about Marina," Annie said.

Pamela's mouth curled. "I figured."

"She'd been here two years?"

"Just about, well, closer to eighteen months, actually."

"I'm curious as to how you found her. How you find the other internationals that work for you," Annie said, trying to be as careful with her words as possible.

"I used to work with an agency," Pamela said, tucking a stray hair behind her ear. "But then word got around. I have families working here, cousins, nephews. They come over and send for others. I haven't had to use the agency in a while. For the most part, I never have problems. Most of them are very good workers."

"So you don't work with the agency at all anymore?"

"Not too much. Every once in a while they contact me," she said.

"Is that how you found Marina?"

Pamela tilted her head. "Actually, the agency came to me. Marina was known in Mexico City as a good baker. She had run into trouble of some kind . . . and she needed to get out."

Zaps of intuition and curiosity were zooming through Annie. "What kind of trouble?"

Pamela made a gesture that Annie had seen Vera make a thousand times. She called it the "Delta Burke-Suzanne Sugarbaker" dismissive wave. "I never ask about such things. I find it's better if I don't know about my employees' personal lives. I don't want to get too involved. They move on from here pretty quickly most of the time. Marina was different. I was surprised she stayed as long as she did."

"Why do they move on so quickly?"

Pamela sank back into a pillow. "They find better work, I suppose. It's typical in the restaurant business. I have some servers and bakers that have been with me for years. But for the most part, workers are here less than a year and move on."

A wafting of some delicious pie baking downstairs filled the room. Cinnamon and apple? Mince?

"But Marina had been here eighteen months. Did you think she'd stay longer?" Annie said, reminding herself that her visit was not about pie.

"I thought she was a talented baker. She was on a different pay scale, than say, a dishwasher. I was hoping she'd stay." An emotion played over Pamela's face. Sullen. Sad. "I don't understand why someone wanted to kill her. She was so sweet."

"And her sister . . ." Annie said. "You mentioned that there was trouble in Mexico. Any way you can find out what that was?"

"I can make some inquiries, I suppose. But why? You don't think their trouble followed them here, do you?"

Annie shrugged. "I don't know what to think. Two sisters killed within twenty-four hours of one another. And they both lived over on Druid Lane in apartments that I didn't even know existed. Come to find out those places are gang infested."

"Gang?"

"According to the cops," Annie said.

"I'm sure you're mistaken," Pamela said, her eyes widening.

"What makes you so certain?"

"First, we're talking about Cumberland Creek, right? Second, Marina would never be involved in such shenanigans, third—"

She was interrupted by a knock at the door.

"Come in," Pamela yelled.

"Sorry to interrupt." It was Randy. "I need your signature on a few things." He handed her a pen and a clipboard. She read it over.

"Hey Annie," he said, while Pamela was signing. "How are you?"

"Good. Yourself?"

"Fine," he said.

Pamela handed him back the clipboard.

Annie glanced at her watch. Pamela had pushed back their meeting several times, which meant it was close to the time her boys would be getting home from school. She'd have to wrap this up and try to get another meeting scheduled. She explained to Pamela that she'd have to go. "I'm sorry. I hope we can meet again soon."

"Hey, just call or e-mail me. It might be quicker," Pamela said, leading Annie out of the room to the stairs.

When Annie walked into the dining room, she was surprised to see Vera, Sheila, Beatrice, and Jon sitting in a booth. She walked over to them after saying good-bye to Pamela. "Well, hello there. What are you all doing here?"

"Pie," Beatrice said. "We're here for pie. Care to join us?"

"It's the grand reopening," Vera said. "She's got some great specials today."

"I've got to go. The boys will be home soon. Sorry," Annie said.

"What are you doing here?" Vera asked.

"I was chatting with Pamela about Marina," Annie replied in a quieter voice.

"Find out anything interesting?" Beatrice asked.

"Maybe. I'm not sure what to think," Annie said.

"Did you get an address for me?" Beatrice asked, looking hopeful.

"Shoot, no. I forgot," Annie said.

"I'll ask Pamela myself," Beatrice said. "No worries."

"If you want to get anything done, you've got to do it yourself" Annie heard Beatrice mutter as she walked away.

Chapter 20

Beatrice savored the last bite of her chocolate custard pie. Heaven on earth. Creamy. Rich. Just the right texture. "Sin on a Plate" Pamela called it. She had come up with cute names for all her pies.

She had that one right.

Vera took a sip of her coffee and placed the cup back in the saucer. "Delicious. Even her coffee is the best."

"How was your Key-Lime Kiss pie?" Beatrice asked.

"Extraordinary," Vera replied.

Beatrice sat back and watched the crowded scene before her. A small group of people were waiting at the cash register to pay their bills. Servers skirted in and out between people and aisles of tables. Not one of the servers appeared to be foreign. Hadn't Randy said they were mostly foreigners? Wait. He must have been talking about the kitchen staff.

Pamela was chitchatting with folks at a table in the corner. She moved from table to table asking how her customers were enjoying their pie. Good business move. She was more like a hostess than an owner who sat on high ordering people around. It made you feel good for paying $3.50 for a slice of pie. But not today—it was half-off today, it being a special grand-reopening.

Sheila was quieter than usual. She seemed tired. But it was more than that really; she seemed worn down. Like the reality of life was suddenly too much for her. She did have a lot on her plate.

"How was your pie?" Beatrice asked her.

"The Cherry Divine was divine," Sheila said and smiled. "Love that chocolate layer between the cherries and the crust. Genius."

"I agree that this place has extraordinary pie," Jon said.

"Good to hear that," Pamela said as she approached their table. "Coming from a Frenchman, that's a big compliment."

"Everything was very good, of course," Vera said.

"Can I ask you a question?" Beatrice began. "I'd like to send my condolences to Marina's family."

The smile vanished from Pamela's face.

"Would you happen to know how I can reach them?" Beatrice continued.

Pamela pasted on a fake smile.

It was as if I'd asked her to kill someone for me. I only want Marina's family's address, thought Beatrice.

"I'm sorry, Ms. Matthews. I don't have that kind of information. She came through an agency."

"What agency? Maybe they have her address?"

Another customer came by the group and congratulated Pamela on the best pumpkin pie he'd ever eaten.

Pamela turned back to Beatrice. "I'm sorry. What was your question?"

"What's the name of the agency Marina came through?" Beatrice was getting miffed. *A simple question demands a simple answer. Why can nobody give me this woman's family's address?*

"Hathaway Transatlantic Employment Agency," Pamela finally said. "Good luck. They are not quite easy to deal with."

"Thanks for the warning. I'll manage," Beatrice replied. *How odd.* She was getting the strangest vibes from Pamela. *What is the problem?*

As if sensing Bea's thoughts, Pamela leaned over the table. "Ms. Matthews, I hate talking about it. It's very upsetting to me. She was the sweetest person I'd ever met." She blinked.

Beatrice felt an immediate pang of embarrassment. Of course, that was it. Pamela was grieving. She apparently thought very highly of the young woman. Perhaps Marina was more than an employee.

"I'm sorry," Beatrice said. "I didn't realize you were so close."

Jon elbowed her gently.

"Well, I would not say close," Pamela said. "But there was something about her that made me feel sort of protective. And I'd feel awful if anybody I knew met the end that she did."

"Of course," Sheila said. "It's a human reaction. No matter who the person."

Pamela stood up straighter. "Right." There was a flash of emotion in Pamela's eyes—something beneath the carefully applied eyeliner, blue eye shadow, and mascara.

Beatrice couldn't say for sure what it was. Regret? Sadness? Fear?

As Pamela turned to leave, Beatrice turned to Jon. "What are you elbowing me for, you old coot?"

"Coot? What is this word?" he shot back at her.

She waved him off. "Look it up."

Chapter 21

DeeAnn was a bit miffed that everybody went to Pamela's grand reopening and she was stuck on the couch. The medicine didn't seem to improve her pain for very long anymore so she was taking the maximum dose. Tomorrow, she was off for X-rays and more tests.

She suddenly heard a bunch of noise at her door and then the doorbell rang.

"Who is it?" she called.

The door swung open. It was Beatrice, Vera, and Jon.

"Hello there," Beatrice said. "Brought you some pie."

"How nice of you! What kind did you get me?"

"Sin on a Plate," Vera said. "You look like you could use it. Lord, woman, have you even brushed your hair this morning?"

DeeAnn ran her fingers through her hair. She really couldn't remember. Had she? "What's the point? I'm not going anywhere. Stuck here on this couch."

"Oh my," Beatrice said. "Are we having a pity party?"

"Pity party?" Vera exclaimed. "I haven't heard that term in a long time. Well, not since I was a kid and you used to ask me the same thing."

Beatrice waved her off and spoke to DeeAnn. "I'm going to get you a real fork to eat that with. No point eating with a plastic fork."

"It's okay," DeeAnn said. "I don't mind."

"Suit yourself." Bea sat down.

"How are you feeling, dear?" Jon asked with concern in his voice.

Such a nice man. What did he see in Beatrice? thought DeeAnn. "I'm going to see the doc tomorrow. I feel about the same, actually."

"Are the pills helping?" Vera asked.

DeeAnn took a bite of her pie and nearly swooned, it was so good. She nodded, chewed, and swallowed her bite. "But not very long. I have to keep taking more. I think I'm taking the maximum dose now."

Vera picked up the pill bottle. "You're out."

"Jacob's on his way with more," DeeAnn replied. "How was the Pie Palace?"

"Big crowd," Jon said.

Beatrice shot him a look of rebuke and he shrugged in return.

"It was good," Vera said. "Annie was there chatting with Pamela upstairs for a bit . . . about Marina."

"Really? What did she find out?" DeeAnn asked.

"Well, we've gotten the name of the agency she came from," Beatrice said. "I hope they have an address for the girls' parents."

DeeAnn swallowed another bite of pie. Suddenly, she was weary, but she wanted to know more. "What's the name of the agency?"

"Hathaway Transatlantic Employment," Vera answered.

"I used to get brochures in the mail from them," DeeAnn said. "I know who they are."

"Really?" Beatrice asked. "What do you know about them? Pamela said they were difficult."

"I don't know anything," DeeAnn said. "I pitched their stuff in the trash. My files are stashed with American citizens who need work. I don't need the hassle."

"Now, DeeAnn—" Vera began and looked uncomfortably at Jon.

"I've got nothing against foreigners, of course," DeeAnn said. "I'd hire some if they came to me looking for a job and I needed someone. But to go through an expensive agency? It just always seemed strange to me."

The room was silent.

"You know it *is* very strange," Jon said. "You say there are plenty of people here looking for work. Why would Pamela hire only people from overseas?"

"Who knows why Pamela does what she does," DeeAnn said. "Money has never been an issue for her, right?"

"Oh no," Beatrice cackled. "Not at all. She went from her rich daddy to her rich husband."

"Very difficult for me to relate to," DeeAnn said. "I've had to struggle and work hard for everything I have, including the bakery. I can't do fancy events and mark my goods down to reel people in." Her heart began to race as she thought about the unfairness of all of it. *How can I compete with people like Pamela?*

"Now hold on," Vera said. "What you're saying is true. But she's always been good to you. She's never said a bad thing about you or the bakery. And she's so filthy rich I've often wondered why she bothers working. She could be sitting around all day or doing lunch with the ladies, or whatever rich women do. Instead, she works."

"Well," DeeAnn said after a moment. "I guess you told me."

Vera laughed.

"We've got to get going," Beatrice said. "Is there anything we can get for you? More books?"

"No, I haven't finished the ones you already gave me," DeeAnn said. "Jacob will be home soon. Don't worry about me." Her back was beginning to jab at her again. Damn, she wished he'd hurry home.

After everybody left, she opened her new laptop to the scrapbooking program that Karen had loaded for her and began to place graduation photos onto a virtual page with virtual paper she had selected.

Karen had graduated top of her class in nursing school. DeeAnn had just started to journal a little bit about it—Karen in her cap and gown. She loved thinking about her and her sister, a year behind in nursing school. She was thinking about studying midwifery in England. *England,* for God's sakes! Fear tore through DeeAnn's body. What if she went to England and something happened to her, like it did with Marina and Esmeralda? How would she know? Suddenly, Beatrice's busybody-ness—finding the girls' family—made sense. It wouldn't take away their pain and confusion, but it might provide some comfort.

DeeAnn sifted through the memories of Hathaway Transatlantic. Things were pretty fuzzy. It was the damn drugs. She could not think clearly; she was still in pain. Why did she have to choose between pain and more pills? Couldn't anybody help her?

Chapter 22

"Sit down, please," Sheriff Bixby said to Annie. "What can I help you with?"

The sheriff's office was nice, clean, and warm with plants in the room and pictures of flowers on the wall. Sheriffs were very different from police officers. They served at the will of the people. It was important that their constituency like them.

Is that why Sheriff Bixby is so polite? Annie wondered. "I'm writing about the Martelino sisters. I'm here because Marina was found in your jurisdiction and I have some questions."

"Fire away. Hasn't been a murder in the county since 2001 and that was a crime of passion, a domestic dispute. It's rare for us to have a homicide."

"Were you the sheriff back in 2001?"

"I've been the sheriff for twenty-six years. I'm proud to serve the people of Albamont County." Sheriff Bixby tapped his fingers on his desk, keeping time to some unknown tune in his head.

"Do you know Pamela Kraft and her husband well?"

"No, they run in different circles." He grinned and stopped tapping.

"But she is on the up and up?" Annie persisted.

"What do you mean? Permits and so forth?" Sheriff Bixby asked, leaning forward, reaching for a pencil.

Annie nodded.

"As far as I know, she's as legit as it gets," he said, tapping the pencil. The man just couldn't sit still.

"Isn't it odd that she has so many foreigners working for her?"

"I'll grant you, that is strange. But she's a good businesswoman. I reckon she knows what she's doing."

"What do you know about the rumor that there are gangs in Cumberland Creek?"

The sheriff stiffened. "Not my jurisdiction. You have to talk to the police about that."

"I find it hard to believe myself, but I was over at Druid where new apartments are and I was threatened. So I went to the cops and they told me not to go there alone."

"I'd take that advice if I were you," he said.

"But if the Martelino sisters were killed over some gang dispute—"

"Now, hold on. Nobody said anything about that." He had finally stopped tapping.

"I'm sorry. I'm just thinking out loud. Here's what we know. Two sisters were killed within twenty-four hours of one another. They lived in an apartment complex, which is evidently the hub of gang activity. Do you follow me?" Annie said, cocking an eyebrow.

The sheriff leaned back in his chair, placed his hand behind his head and then clicked his tongue against the roof of his mouth as if to say *shame on you*. Annie found it hard to look him in the eye—his mustache was distracting.

"First of all, it seems to make sense that the murders were related," Annie went on. "And second of all, if they were involved in these gangs—"

"They were not involved in gangs," he finally said. "They were two young women wanting to work and start a new life. That's all."

"Are you certain?" Annie asked.

"Look, you're making all sorts of assumptions here. Not everybody at those apartments are gang members. Just because they were poor immigrants doesn't mean they're criminals."

Annie's face reddened. "That's not what—"

"There's plenty of decent families living over there. A few bad apples—"

"I think if this was a gang-related incident, people should know. The people need to know what's going on in their community."

"Is that all?" Sheriff Bixby said, annoyed. "Is that all, as far as your questions go?" His pleasant demeanor had vanished.

"No," Annie said. "I promised some of the women in Cumberland Creek that I'd get the address of the Martelino family in Mexico so that they can send their condolences. Do you have any information?"

"We're working on it, but as far as I know they had no family," said Sheriff Bixby.

"I imagine the process is convoluted."

"At best." Sheriff Bixby's buzzing phone interrupted the conversation. "Just a minute. I have to take this." He picked up the phone and began talking.

Annie busied herself looking around his office. The man had a lot of photos of himself with other officials. *Interesting*. And very different from a police officer's office.

Sheriff Bixby cleared his throat. "Yes, sir. I'm on my way." His face was white as he hung up the phone. "Ms. Chamovitz, I'm sorry. I need to get going."

"What is it?" she asked.

"I'm sorry. I need to go," he repeated and stood. Reaching out his hand to Annie's, he shook it then quickly ushered her out the door.

Chapter 23

Beatrice punched the company name *Hathaway Transatlantic Employment* into the search engine. It had a nice Web site, very sophisticated. But what she wanted was a phone number. Aha—there it was. She grabbed her phone and dialed.

"What are you doing?" Jon said and Bea shushed him. He stood nearby with his hands on his hips.

"Transatlantic Employment, this is Linda Smoke. How can I help you?" the pleasant voice said on the other end of the phone.

"Yes, my name is Beatrice Matthews Chevalier and I live in Cumberland Creek, Virginia. One of your workers was recently killed here. Her name was Marina Martelino. There's a group of us in town that would like to send condolences to her family. Is that possible?" Beatrice asked.

"What are you asking? For an address?" Linda said.

"Yes, I'd like the address of her parents." *Parents that have lost two daughters here in Virginia, where they*

were sent to work to send home money to help out the family.
Beatrice's stomach tightened.

"One moment please," Linda said.

Jon gave up his stance and sat down on the couch next to Beatrice. Weird 1970s music played over the phone as the minutes ticked away.

"Mrs. Chevalier?" Linda Smoke interrupted the groovy music.

"Yes, I'm still here," Beatrice said.

"I'm sorry. I can't find any records for Ms. Martelino."

"What?"

"Maybe they have been misplaced. Or—are you certain you have the right agency?"

"Yes, yes, I'm certain." Beatrice was trying not to show her impatience.

"May I take your phone number and get back to you? I'll continue to search when I can," Linda said.

"Mighty nice of you," Beatrice said and then gave her phone number. "Now, are you in Mexico?"

"No, Ma'am. The agency is housed in China."

"Well, I do thank you for your help. Folks here just want to reach out to the family." Bea was tempted to add *and I can't believe how difficult this is.*

"Kind of you," Linda Smoke said.

After Beatrice hung up the phone, Jon said, "No address?"

"Marina's files have been misplaced," Beatrice said.

"I smell something—how you say?—fishy," Jon said. "Misplaced files? Everything is on the computer these days. I don't understand."

"Maybe not in China," Beatrice said.

"But an international employment agency, surely," Jon said.

Beatrice thought a moment. "You're right. Why would she not want to give me the information? I'll call back and find out."

Beatrice dialed the number. No answer. None. The phone rang and rang. She slammed the phone down. "All I wanted to do is send my condolences, but this is a bit much. You'd think I was asking for the moon."

"No answer?" he said. "Maybe it's nighttime there and the woman has gone home for the day. Let's try again tomorrow."

"Sounds good to me," Beatrice said.

Beatrice's phone rang. It was Mike Chamovitz.

"Sorry to bother you, Beatrice," Mike said, "but Annie is out on a story and I've gotten a call from a client who's in town and wants to meet for coffee. I can tell her no, but it would be a good thing if I could tell her yes. The boys are in bed. I'd really appreciate it if you could stay here until Annie or I can get back home."

"A client this time of the evening?" Beatrice asked. Mike was a pharmaceutical sales rep.

"Very unusual," he agreed.

"Well, of course I'll be there. But where's Annie?"

"She had a meeting with the sheriff and something came up," Mike replied.

"The Martelino case?"

"I'm not sure."

"But duty calls," Mike said. "See you in a few?"

"Of course," Beatrice replied.

"What is it?" Jon asked, leaning in toward her.

"I'm going over to watch Annie's boys," Beatrice said, getting up from the couch. She found her purse and keys. Jon was on her heels.

She frowned. "What are you doing? You almost knocked right into me."

"Sorry, but I'm coming with you, of course."

She reached over and touched his cheek. "Thank you, Jon."

On the walk over to Annie's house, they were quiet. They walked past the Jensens' yard decorated with dancing but ghoulish ghosts, backlit, providing an eerie ambience. Their new neighbors had decorated with huge mock spiderwebs in their tree and big furry spiders strategically placed. Another neighbor had made a fresh-looking grave and headstones with bloody hands reaching out from the ground. Beatrice had thought she was in the Halloween spirit by carving a few jack-o-lanterns to sit on her front porch.

As Beatrice and Jon walked along, there was not much to say as the chilly autumn night circled them. Half a moon hung in the sky and stars twinkled at them. Beatrice's old heart hung heavy. She couldn't shake the feeling of trepidation and fear, even as she reached for her husband's hand.

Chapter 24

DeeAnn's day began the same as any other day since she'd hurt her back—except that she left the house. She visited the doctor, who said she needed to start physical therapy.

She was able to get around with a walker and sit up. The doctor gave her different pain medication that worked with a lower dosage. She didn't feel as high from them.

The week dragged on with visits from Karen, Bea, and Sheila. Paige was exhausted from all of the testing going on at the school, but she texted DeeAnn every day.

Saturday night, the crop had once again been moved to DeeAnn's place and she sat propped up on the recliner in a much better frame of mind—except for the one thing everybody was worried about, that everybody had been talking about. The murder of the sisters.

"Something odd going on there," DeeAnn said.

"Why are all these women who worked at the Pie Palace getting killed?"

"Marina's sister didn't work there," Annie pointed out.

"I agree with DeeAnn," Vera said as she turned the page on her scrapbook and looked over a fresh, blank spread of paper. "I love Pamela's pie, but I've always found her a bit off-putting and now all this. I wonder what's going on."

"Why do you find her off-putting?" Cookie asked.

"The way she dresses for one thing," Vera said. "Like she's a showgirl instead of a restaurateur."

"She has her own style, that's for sure," Randy said.

"But you know there's something else. Mama has been trying to reach the Martelinos' parents to send her condolences. She has yet to be able to do that. I think she's just about given up. But I don't understand what the big deal is," Vera said.

"What do you mean?" DeeAnn asked.

"She's talked with Pamela. She's called the employment agency. No luck," Vera said. "It's like these women have no ties. I find that hard to believe."

"Maybe that's the way they wanted it. Maybe they never wanted to go back." Cookie said it quietly, but the words had weight, coming from her. She was still working on remembering. Still in therapy.

DeeAnn had considered on more than one occasion that maybe Cookie didn't *want* to remember.

"Why?" Sheila spoke up. "I'm sure they have family."

"Maybe not," Cookie persisted. "Life in some of

those countries is difficult. Their parents might not be alive. There may not be anybody."

"That's true," Annie said after a few minutes of silence, save for the sounds of paper being shuffled and scissors snipping. "I have a few calls in to Immigration. It may be awhile for them to get back to me. But I haven't really found Pamela helpful, either. She claims she doesn't know much about them."

"That's probably true," Randy said. "I like Pamela. She's a pro, very polite, very friendly. But she's not one you can easily warm up to if you know what I mean. Now, what do I do with this?" He held up a piece of blue netting.

Sheila rose from her place at the card table and went over to where he was. "Pull it, then place the sticky-side down on the page."

"Very cool," said Randy as he attached the netting.

"Now you can place paper or a photo on top of that. What a great picture," she said.

DeeAnn saw that it was a photo of him and his dad at Halloween. *How about that?* It inspired her to see Randy at the scrapbooking table and to know that he and his father were getting closer. That surprised her. She knew that Paige was thrilled with the way things were working out.

"Have you found a house yet?" DeeAnn asked him.

"Not yet. I'm not in a hurry. I want it to be the perfect situation. I love living at the B and B. Elsie is such a character."

"Elsie!" Annie said. "You know, I hadn't remembered until right now that she employed Marina's sister. I should talk with her."

"Good idea," DeeAnn said, feeling a slight pinching

in her back. Should she take another pill? It was almost time—so she'd go ahead and take one.

"Let's see how you're doing," Sheila said to Vera and Annie, who were seated next to one another because they were working on the same project—Halloween scrapbooks. The holiday was in a few weeks and Annie, Sheila, and Vera were the only three who had kids that still celebrated. They were working on mini-scrapbooks in preparation for their celebrations. Blank spaces for pictures and journaling, already embellished and so on. It was a clever and efficient way to scrapbook that worked out most of the time.

"I love working this way," Vera said.

"I'm not sure how I feel about it," Annie said. "I just don't know how it's going to work. I guess I normally take all of my design clues from photos, so I'm a little unsettled."

"It will work out. You'll see," Sheila said.

"What is that?" DeeAnn said, noticing a colorful paper sticking out from under Sheila's laptop.

"What? Oh, that's a paper dress," Sheila said, holding it up.

"I can see that," DeeAnn said. "Like for a paper doll?"

Sheila nodded and sat down, then dug around in her bag and pulled out an envelope. "Donna and I have been making paper dolls."

DeeAnn's heart nearly burst. Paper dolls! She was transported to her childhood when she had spent hours playing with paper dolls. In fact, she still had some of them. Her hand went to her ample bosom and tears stung her eyes.

"DeeAnn?" Paige said. "What is it?"

"The dolls are so charming." DeeAnn watched Sheila spread them out on the table. "I remember my mom and I cutting them out. The stories we would tell with them. . . ." She started to cry—not sweet little nostalgic tears, but huge, ugly sobs. *Oh time, what have you done to me?*

"DeeAnn?" Randy said, handing her some tissue. "Are you all right?"

She pointed to the dolls and tried to gather herself.

"Good Lord, I didn't mean to make you cry," Sheila said and began to gather up the dolls and their paper clothes.

"Leave them!" DeeAnn said. "I want to see them."

"I agree," Paige said, her face flushed with excitement. "They're delightful."

"Not just delightful . . . but remarkable," Randy said in a hushed tone.

A silence came over the group as they pored over the homemade paper dolls. Tiny paper girls and women of all shapes and sizes with long, red hair, short, black hair, and many shades of brown. Paper dresses and shirts, skirts, and pants—blue, orange, red, all colors. But what made them extraordinary, DeeAnn thought as she ran her fingers over the smooth paper, were the details so meticulously drawn on. The lace collars, the colorful buttons, the floral prints.

"My goodness," Sheila said. "They are just simple paper dolls. It's something Donna and I have made together since she was a girl. It's become a habit. And now that she's home . . . well . . . we've started doing it again. This time, with a little more flair, I suppose."

"You should show these to your boss," Randy said.

"What? Whatever for?" Sheila said.

Randy shrugged. "Who knows? Maybe they could start an upscale paper dolls line."

"Nobody plays with paper dolls anymore," Paige said. "It's all about electronics these days."

DeeAnn drew in a breath and hoped she was wrong. Oh the hours she spent with her paper dolls as a girl. She and her sister Diane wiled away the hours with them.

The doorbell sounded. They all wondered who it could be. Everybody, except Beatrice was already assembled.

Randy answered the door. "Detective Bryant. Please come in."

Chapter 25

Detective Adam Bryant and Sheriff Ted Bixby walked into DeeAnn's living room. The scrapbookers all looked up from the paper dolls and sat back in their chairs, watching the two men.

"Good evening, ladies," Bryant said. "Change your locale?"

"Well, DeeAnn's back has been out so we thought we'd have the crop here," Sheila said.

"Yes, we talked to your husband," the sheriff said. "Good evening, ladies. We won't bother you too much. Just have a few questions for you."

Annie sat back and crossed her arms. This was odd. The county sheriff and Detective Bryant working together. She knew they didn't like one another.

"Never thought I'd see the day you two would be walking into my house together." Leave it to DeeAnn to say what they were all thinking. "Has hell frozen over?"

Both men smiled, but did not look at one another and shifted their weight around in discomfort.

"We're pooling resources on the Martelino cases,"

Bryant said, holding up a plastic bag with a scrapbook page in it.

The sheriff held his own plastic bag up. "Same paper. The labs could tell us nothing. Meaning, there are no fingerprints. Nothing distinguishing about the paper or the photos."

The two of them set their papers down on the card table.

It was fairly typical scrapbook paper—green with a floral pattern. Each page had one photo. One of them featured a black-framed picture of a group of people at a picnic. Along with the picture, someone had started journaling in Spanish. Annie couldn't decipher it. The handwriting was difficult to read.

"The writing there is about Marina's new home. How lovely it is. How she loved the mountains," Bryant said.

Annie's heart sank. Once again, a woman killed in her prime.

The other scrapbook page had orange-framed photos. The picture was of a group of women—including one of the sisters, Esmeralda.

"Check out that picture," Sheila said. "Look at the background . . . on the picnic table. There are scrapbooks and paper and I think . . . some embellishments."

The detective nodded. "Yep, these women scrapbooked together regularly."

"Holy shit," DeeAnn said.

"Turns out you're not the only scrapbookers in town," Sheriff Bixby said.

"Well, of course, we aren't. I run a scrapbooking business and at least half the women in this town have bought materials from me," Sheila said. "But I don't think these in the pictures have ever come to my basement to buy supplies."

"What can you tell us about this paper? These women?" Detective Bryant asked.

"The women look vaguely familiar, but I don't know that paper," Sheila said. "It's not in my line of products."

Annie recognized one of the women. She was the same woman who had been behind the counter at the apartment complex. Annie kept that bit of information to herself.

"Are you certain?" Bryant asked Sheila again.

Sheila thought a moment. "If we carry it, it's very old. It's possible that I don't remember it."

"It looks familiar to me," Cookie piped up.

"You've seen one floral design, you've seen them all," Paige said and waved her off.

"No," Cookie persisted. "This is different. The green isn't typical. It's very dark."

"True," Paige said. "But for a while, that was all the rage."

"Two years ago," Sheila said, "all of our floral paper had that antique look to it."

Cookie stood up. "I think I have this paper."

"What?" Bryant said, lurching back.

"Let me see." She walked over to her bag where she stored her paper supply and rifled through it. "Yes. Here it is."

"Where did you get it?" Sheriff Bixby asked her.

"I don't remember," she said automatically. "I'm sorry. But I never buy my supplies from anybody but Sheila."

"Well," Sheila laughed nervously. "I guess that answers that question."

"Oh, look at the other side," Paige said.

Cookie turned the page over and set it in the middle of the table. The back of the page was black and the corners looked ragged, with bits of green coming through. The top of an orange moon peeked up from the bottom of the page.

"Ah," Sheila said. "Yes, now I remember this paper. It was a part of the Summer Dream pack from two years ago, I think. I can look that up for you." She opened her laptop.

Paige went back to her project in front of her, as did Randy. Annie watched as DeeAnn watched Sheila with her laptop, her fingers moving quickly over the keyboard.

"Yes," Sheila said finally. "It was two years ago and it was part of a pack. I gave out several of these at a public Fourth of July crop last year. Let's see, I gave out . . . twenty-six."

"Did you keep the names?" Sheriff Bixby asked.

"I have the names of everybody who attended the crop, but not who received which pack as prizes," Sheila said. "If they bought the pack, I have those records."

"Sounds like a good start," Annie said.

"Indeed." Sheriff Bixby looked at her, once again, with an approving glance.

Bryant picked up on it and shot daggers with his eyes toward her.

What the hell? she thought.

"I can print the list of Fourth of July croppers for

you," Sheila said. "And a list of people who bought the paper."

"No need. Just e-mail it to us." Bryant handed her his card. "We can print it."

After the sheriff gave Sheila his card, too, he looked over the table with the food. "What do you ladies have there?"

"There's plenty here," DeeAnn said. "Pumpkin bread, muffins. Chocolate. You should try the chocolate. Vera's really getting good. I'd like to sell her stuff at my shop."

"Oh, DeeAnn!" Vera blushed. "Thanks so much. Maybe I will take you up on that offer. I love making it."

"You're a fabulous student," Randy said. "You pick things up quickly."

"How are you doing?" Sheriff Bixby asked Randy as he patted him on the back.

"I'm doing okay," Randy said. "I'm fine. Every day I feel a little better."

People had stopped asking Annie if she was okay. They had assumed, of course, that she was because, well, she had seen so many dead bodies, so many murder victims. But it truly never got much easier for her. She was so looking forward to the next stage of her life . . . when she wouldn't have to will away the bad dreams at night.

"We were trying to reach the Martelino family," Annie said.

"For what?" Bryant asked, his mouth half full of chocolate.

"We wanted to express our condolences," she said.

"Well, that's mighty kind of you," Sheriff Bixby said.

"Mama tried to find them through their employment agency. So far, nothing." Vera said.

The detective and the sheriff exchanged uncomfortable glances.

"Pamela doesn't seem to know much either," Annie said.

"Pamela is a shrewd businesswoman. She knows she has to be careful what information she gives out," Sheriff Bixby said, pausing. "I know it's the tendency of good-hearted women like yourselves to reach out at times like these, but I think in this case, it's better left alone."

"I agree," Bryant said.

Annie's pings of intuition started up again. Anytime a cop said to "leave it alone" it meant there was more to the story than what they wanted to tell.

"It's a complicated mess," Sheriff Bixby said. "And as far as we can tell, the girls' family is long gone."

"Did they have any other family here?" DeeAnn asked.

"No," Bryant said a little too quickly.

"They lived together over on Druid?" Annie asked.

He nodded. Once again, uncomfortable looks were exchanged between the two officers.

"Well, I guess we better go. Thanks, ladies, for the goodies." Bryant loved his sweets. He was a man who knew good food.

"Before you go," Vera said, "can I ask you about these gang rumors?"

"It's more than rumors, I'm afraid," Bryant said.

"In Cumberland Creek? Absurd!" Vera set her scissors down with a thud.

"Everywhere," Bryant said. "Cumberland Creek is not immune to the vagaries of modern life, ladies. I thought you'd know that by now."

"Is it just over there on Druid?" DeeAnn asked with a note of hope in her voice.

"Much of it, but not all," Bryant said and paused. "As I told Annie, it's best to stay away from there. Don't go alone, in any case."

"Hmmm," DeeAnn said.

"Don't get any crazy ideas, DeeAnn, not with your back out," Sheila said.

"I'm getting better every day," DeeAnn said indignantly.

Detective Bryant looked at the sheriff and rolled his eyes.

Chapter 26

Beatrice grabbed Jon's hand. "Let's go."

They had parked their car at the far end of the park and were walking up one of its ancient, twisty trails. Leaves were crunching beneath their feet and the sky was bright blue, with the sun warm enough that the brisk air didn't matter.

Beatrice led Jon off the trail.

"Where are we going?" he asked.

"I'm curious about something. Bear with me. I remember that I used to walk over here and stop by and see Emma Drummond. They were an old Cumberland Creek family. Farmers, most of them."

"What happened to them?"

"Most of them died off. I think Emma's still over at that assisted living place. I can never remember the name of it. Maybe it's Mountain View?"

They stepped over a small mound and Beatrice stopped. "Yes, the house is still there."

"It's barely standing, from what I can see."

"And look over there," Beatrice pointed to the apartments on Druid. They could see only a part of them from where they stood. "That was the Drummond apple orchard."

"I don't see any apple trees," Jon said, squinting.

"Gone," Beatrice said in a hushed tone. Swirls of sadness moved through her, mixed with a longing for simpler days. But were they really simpler? Or just slower? Or was it another one of those tricks of time?

"'You must have been warned against letting the golden hours slip by; but some of them are golden only because we let them slip by,'" Beatrice said, quoting J.M. Barrie.

Jon clicked his tongue on the roof of his mouth.

Beatrice started moving again, searching for the clearing in a small forested spot on the Drummond property where she and Emma used to sit with their babies and chat about life. How had they lost touch? Beatrice had loved her.

"Too bad about those apples," Bea said. "The flavor of those apples has never been matched. The family had been farming this land for two hundred years. They'd been given a land grant by Washington himself. The apples were what they call heirloom today. They were tasty, not like the crap you get at the grocery store."

"Shiny and beautiful but no flavor," Jon said, moving away some brush for Beatrice to continue walking.

"There it is." She pointed to a rock large enough for both of them to have a seat. They sat down, with a little groaning from both of them.

"Nice spot," Jon said after a few minutes.

"The Drummonds thought it was important to leave a little of the land wild. Emma and I found this little clearing and the girls would play here and we'd chat," Bea said. Her memories of that place and time had been buried long ago.

"What happened? Why have you never talked about her before?" Jon asked.

Beatrice mulled over her time with Emma. "You know me. I can't stand most people." She tried to laugh it off, but memories pricked at her brain. "I think it had something to do with her husband . . . I couldn't stand the man. The way he treated her. And I couldn't keep my mouth shut."

"Of course," Jon said.

After they had been sitting quietly together for a few minutes, Jon spoke again. "Let's find her and visit her."

"Good idea," Bea said. The thought of it excited her and filled her with shame. She had let her good friend down. She looked toward the apartment buildings and saw the apple orchard in her mind's eye. *Old fool. I am an old fool,* she thought, willing away the tears.

Jon's arms went around her and pulled her toward him. "The past is gone. And we are here, now. Let's make the most of it, shall we?"

Sweet Jon. So in tune with her emotions. He was a good husband, a good man.

When they got up to leave, a tiny sparkling something caught Beatrice's eye and she moved in the direction of it, toward the old farm house. "What is that?" she said and blinked.

An old rose bush had been hung with trinkets on its branches. They moved closer to it and saw that the trinkets were something from the dollar store, cheap metallic charms and beads. A cross. Dollar symbols. Peace symbols. Hearts.

"Lawd," Beatrice said. "I haven't seen one of these in years."

"What is it?" Jon said.

"It's what we used to call a fairy tree," Beatrice said. "Emma used to make them—much prettier than this one. This is like a cheap rendition of the real thing. It's like a prayer and a warning all in one."

"That this place belongs to someone else?" Jon asked after a moment.

Beatrice nodded as tears streamed down her face.

"What is this? Why the tears?" Jon asked quietly.

"I think it also means that the Drummonds haven't given up completely. They were an old Scotch Irish clan and clung to some old ways. This tree gives me great comfort. The family is still here," Beatrice said. "We just have to find them."

Chapter 27

DeeAnn still could not take the stairs up to her bedroom. Thank God she could walk around a bit downstairs and tinker in her own kitchen, still stocked with casseroles and goodies from half of Cumberland Creek's population. Jacob and Karen had tried to maintain some semblance of order, but it wasn't the same. She liked things a certain way. After rearranging the casseroles in the fridge, a sudden wave of weariness overtook her.

She sat down at the table, opened her laptop, and clicked on the local newspaper's icon to read the news. Scrolling through the mundane stuff—school news, accident news, and so on, she tried to find the latest updates on the Martelino cases. There was nothing new.

"What are you doing?" Jacob said as he walked into the kitchen.

"I was trying to get some news of the murders."

"Anything?" he said, reaching into the cupboard for a glass.

"Nothing new. Now, Jacob, tell me what you know about the Druid Lane apartments."

He filled his glass with water. "That's where the woman who was attacked a few months ago lived."

"That could happen almost anywhere," DeeAnn said, wishing the conversation wasn't necessary, that she would wake up from a dream, and that there were no gangs close by.

"Yeah, well, I know some guys who were over there and their tires were slashed. Other stuff, too."

"What were they doing there?"

"One of my mechanics was dating someone who lived there. Evidently, someone didn't like it," he responded.

"Is he still seeing her?"

"I don't know, DeeAnn. I don't follow his personal life. I just know about the tires because he bought some from the shop."

"What else do you know?" It confounded her how he could work with someone and not know about who they were dating.

"I've also heard that if you want drugs, that's the place to go," he said and sat down at the table with his glass of water.

"What kind of drugs?"

"Hell, how do I know?"

"Probably meth, pot, cocaine," she said, feeling her heart race.

"Calm down. You look like you're getting ready to explode." He smiled. "I doubt there's anybody dealing cocaine over there."

"Lord, Cumberland Creek's turning into a cesspool of murder, drugs, gangs." She reached for her husband's hand. "I'm so glad our girls aren't going to school here anymore."

"I think you're exaggerating a bit. But I'd be troubled, too, if our girls were still in school. What's Paige have to say about all of it?"

"Not much," DeeAnn said. "She's so ready to retire, but they keep sucking her back in. And I think she's so happy now that Randy's back home, nothing else matters."

Jacob smiled. "I get that. It's good when they come back home. Karen's been a godsend."

Indeed, their oldest daughter had been wonderful. It was a shock to many people to see her change into such a fine upstanding young woman. She'd had a rough few years in high school—had gotten in with the wrong crowd and involved with alcohol and started having sex way too early. Now, she was a nurse and had tended to her mother as much as she could while still working at the hospital. Her sister would be graduating soon, as well.

"So do you think the Martelino sisters were murdered because of some gang thing?" DeeAnn asked.

"You're sitting around imagining all sorts of things, aren't you? You need to get back to work."

"I wish. It's so clear to me the murders are connected, plus the Martelinos lived over there where all the gang activity is."

"They need to look into Pamela." Jacob had never liked her, and it wasn't just about the business competition. "I think if I were investigating a murder, I'd start there."

"Oh Jacob," DeeAnn smiled. "Pamela's a bit strange, but she's no killer."

He looked at her with one eyebrow cocked. "How do you know? There's something off about her."

"I've always thought so, too. The way she dresses like she's living in the 1950s. I thought it was all about the Pie Palace, you know, and being in character. But anytime you see her, that's how she's dressed. She doesn't ever seem to go out unless she's in the complete getup. I don't know what that's all about, but I do know that any woman who bakes pies like she does could not kill people."

"DeeAnn! That doesn't make any sense at all."

"Don't you know that pie is about love?" She smiled but then a twinge of pain shot up through her center. "Jacob, can you get my pills?"

"Pie is not about love," he said, going into the next room to fetch her pills and then bringing them back and setting them on the table. "Pie is about dough, and fruit, and sugar."

"Men. You don't understand." She reached for the pill bottle and it fell, scattering her pills across the table.

"Good Lord, DeeAnn, how many of those pills have you taken? I just got them for you yesterday. Not many left."

"I've lost track. I just take one when it hurts."

Jacob's brow knit. "I don't think that's the way it's supposed to work."

"Of course it is," she said and swallowed a pill. "That's what they're for—pain."

Jacob picked up the bottle and read the directions. "Did you ever read this?" He held up the bottle. "You're not supposed to take more than two a day."

"Doctors! What do they know?" She shrugged.

Chapter 28

"What are you suggesting, Annie?" Pamela said over the phone.

"I'm not suggesting anything. Please calm down. I'm only saying there might be a link. A woman who worked for you has been killed. Plus you have had all those employees go missing over the years."

"Don't you think I know that? Couldn't it be a coincidence? I mean Marina's sister had nothing to do with me," Pamela said with a bite in her tone.

Annie thought it over. "Well, you're right, of course. It could be a coincidence. But if I were you, I'd look into their backgrounds and see if there's anything there."

"I've told you this before, Annie—so many immigrants come here to escape their backgrounds. They are running away from their countries. They want to start fresh. Most of the time, I don't know anything about them. The agency sorts through all that." Pamela's voice was getting shrill. She took a deep breath. "If I can think of anything, I'll let you know."

After they said their good-byes, Annie turned

back to her computer. Nothing. There was nothing on any of either sister in her databases. Pamela was right. It was as if they had appeared out of nowhere.

She had put in at least ten calls to Immigration but it was leading her nowhere. She had to take another tack. But what? Where did the recent immigrants gather? At a bar? A restaurant? Some sort of meeting place, other than where they lived?

Annie's alarm went off; she often set alarms throughout the day when she was working. Seemed the day slipped away and the next thing she knew her boys were home and she hadn't gotten dinner under way or anything else accomplished. The alarms kept her on track.

She grabbed her purse and her keys and headed to the store before they got home.

In the parking lot of the one grocery store in Cumberland Creek, she noticed Elsie loading groceries into her car. She stopped and helped her.

"Well, thank you, Annie," Elsie said.

"Can I ask you a few questions about Esmeralda Martelino?" Annie asked, glad that she might be able to question Elsie without having to go to the B and B. After having been almost killed there, she preferred to not ever go back again.

"Who?" Elsie said with befuddlement.

"Randy said she cleaned for you. Esmeralda Martelino?"

"Ah, yes, the little Mexican gal. She was so pretty. I talked to the news and the police about her. I don't have much to add. She was a good girl and a hard worker."

"Did she ever talk about her sister?" Annie asked.

"No. I don't generally talk with employees about their personal lives, and she barely spoke English."

"How did you find her?"

"I found her through my cousin who knew about this employment agency. Hathaway," Elsie replied.

Of course, Annie thought, *she used the same agency as her sister.*

"Thanks, Elsie. You know, if you can think of anything else, please give me a call." She turned and walked away.

Elsie waved as Annie hurried off. "See you, Annie," she called.

Annie glanced at her watch. There was no time to waste.

Rushing through the store, throwing items into her basket, the oddest feeling crept over her. She stopped and looked around. She didn't see anything out of place. Nobody unusual. She turned the corner and there she was. The woman from the apartment complex, pale, smiling nervously, with a basket over her arm.

"Hello," Annie said.

The woman nodded and looked off in another direction.

A zip of electricity running up her spine brought Annie's attentive powers to a point. The young woman was nervous. Annie wondered if Mendez was around. "Are you okay?" she asked in a hushed voice.

The woman's eyes met hers and shot a look of fear at her. Then she blinked. "Of course."

Annie slipped her hand into her bag and pulled out her card. "Keep this close. If you think of anything to tell me about the Martelinos, I'd appreciate it."

The woman's face fell, but she took the card. "My friends," she said almost involuntarily. She shoved the card into her bag.

"I'm truly so sorry," Annie said. "We wanted to send condolences to her family. Do you know how to reach them?"

Suddenly the man who had confronted Annie at the leasing office came from around the corner, a loaf of bread in his hand. He sized her up and shot her a look of disgust.

Annie smiled at both of them. "I'm very sorry for your losses."

He mumbled something under his breath in Spanish. Annie wasn't certain, but she thought he'd called her a bitch again. What was with this guy?

The woman said in Spanish that he should watch his filthy mouth; that Annie seemed to have good intentions.

But her voice shook with fear, and she walked off.

In the checkout line, Annie turned to see if she could spot them, but they were gone, either deep in the store or they had left.

After she loaded the groceries into her car and went to get in, she noticed that one of her tires was flat. Not a simple flat, but slashed, completely destroyed. A flash of fear moved through her. Someone had just slashed her tire. In broad daylight. Coincidence?

She called Bryant first, then her husband. Someone had to get home to the boys while she waited.

Before she knew it, Detective Bryant was in the parking lot. "That is one slashed tire," he said as he examined her car.

"I just saw that Mendez guy in the store and I think he called me a bitch," Annie said.

Bryant cocked his head. "Huh. Well, he couldn't have done this if he was inside the store."

"I think he had plenty of time while I was talking to the woman who works over at the apartments. Evidently, they were here together."

"It doesn't take long to slash a tire, but it does take a big blade and some strength," Bryant said. "I'm going to level with you. This is a warning. You need to back off."

"Back off of what?"

"Have you been back to the apartments?"

"No, I've only just seen the two of them now, here, in the grocery store. I spoke with the woman briefly and gave her my card."

"Annie, I don't want to scare you, and I don't want to see an article in the papers about this, but this gang stuff is very serious."

"You can't get more serious than murder," she said with a low voice.

"Nobody said anything about murder. Typical. You go from a slashed tire to murder."

"I think the Martelino sisters must have had something to do with this gang," she said.

"What do you base that on? That they lived on Druid?" He shook his head. "Annie, there's a lot going on over there. I'm not saying that we should mark it off the list of possibilities. I'm saying not to jump to conclusions."

"Where can I get more information about the gang?"

Adam turned away from her and answered his cell

phone. When he turned back around, he told her that he'd have to go.

The AAA truck pulled up at the same time.

Annie caught Bryant's arm, feeling one of his muscles. The man did love his workouts. "Please. Can't you tell me what's going on?"

"I'm sorry, Annie, I just can't." He looked at her with a hint of compassion. "Just be careful, okay?"

Something in Adam Bryant's eyes terrified her. She nodded. She would be careful, yes, indeed.

Chapter 29

Beatrice clicked through the pop-up ads on the computer screen. What a pain. When she finally got to the Google search screen, she keyed in *Emma Drummond*, which brought up a whole slew of Emma Drummonds, none of whom was the one she was interested in. She knew that Emma lived over at Mountain View Assisted Living, but she wondered if there was any clue on the computer what her physical or mental state was. Bea didn't want to go in for the visit unprepared. It would help to know what Emma's condition was.

But she was going to have to wing it. Elsie had enlisted Jon in helping pick out a new paint color for the dining room at the B and B (thank the Lord for small favors). Bea had been asked to go but told them she'd rather not.

So she was off to Mountain View, which was about six blocks away. She walked through her town toward the mountains—the ones that her daughter had always prayed to, the ones that she looked at every day of her life. They were a comfort to her.

She walked past where she used to get her hair done, now closed because Flo couldn't compete with the new Hair Cuttery. She walked past the fountain and nodded to several of the old people who were congregating there. A group of people walked out of DeeAnn's Bakery, which appeared to be hopping even though DeeAnn wasn't there to oversee. It was so lovely with its pink and brown color scheme. Then she walked by Vera's dance studio and across the street where Emily McGlashen's studio was—and where her body had been found when she was killed. *Such a shame.*

Beatrice walked down another block, wondering what the world was coming to. She crossed the bridge and hummed a tune that she made up right then and there. She paused after she crossed the bridge, caught her breath a bit, and turned to look at her town. She saw graffiti on the bridge. It was a weird squiggle painted in red. She'd seen that squiggle somewhere before. She reached into her pocketbook and took a photo with her cell phone. That was the only thing the damn thing was good for. That, and letting Vera know she was still alive— and apparently at her beck and call.

From where she was standing, she had a partial view of the park built along the river. She remembered the day it was dedicated as if it were yesterday. But yesterday she wasn't too sure about. She smiled to herself and kept moving.

Mountain View Assisted Living looks like a nice place, she mused as she came up over the hill. It sat tucked in a bit of a valley, but she was certain the place did have a mountain view, as the name promised.

Several old men sat outside smoking cigarettes and chatting among themselves. They completely ignored her, as she did them. At this point in life, one didn't like to mess around with trivial conversation.

She walked up to the counter and hit the desk bell, which stood next to a wooden black cat with its back arched. A sign hung around its neck that said HAVE A BOO-TIFUL DAY. Beatrice tried not to roll her eyes.

"Yes? Can I help you?" The woman behind the desk was small and bird-like.

"I'd like to see Emma Drummond. That okay?" Beatrice said.

"Is she expecting you?" The woman pushed her glasses higher on her nose. Her hair was completely white—but Beatrice didn't think she was a day over fifty.

Beatrice shook her head. "No. I wanted to surprise her. I'm an old friend,"

"Name?"

"Beatrice Matthews."

"Just a minute. Please have a seat, Ms. Matthews," the receptionist said and left the area.

The place looked clean and was furnished simply. It was run by the Mennonites so there were no fancy chandeliers or plush carpets like in some other places she'd been to visit. A group of women came around the corner. One held a cane, another was in a wheelchair and had an oxygen tank. The other two appeared to be fine.

"Are you the bus driver?" one of them said to Bea.

"No, I'm just here to see someone," she replied.

An attendant came into the lobby and said for Bea to follow her to Emma's room.

Beatrice followed her down a plain but cheerful and well-lit hallway. Rails ran along either side of them. Floral prints were set off by ornate frames and lined the walls.

"Right in there," the attendant said and pointed.

Beatrice's heart raced. How strange was this going to be? She probably hadn't seen Emma in thirty-five or forty years.

Emma poked her head around the corner. "Well, don't just stand there, Beatrice Matthews. Come on in."

Before Beatrice knew it, Emma had her by the hand and pulled her in for one of the longest hugs she'd ever had. "Beatrice," she said when she finally pulled away as if to get a good look at her. Then came another hug.

"Please sit down," Emma said. "I've got some iced tea. Can I get you some?"

"Surely. And thanks." Beatrice was gobsmacked at how wonderful Emma appeared to be doing. She looked good—same bright blue eyes, lively smile, and she still moved around like a bird flitting from pillar to post.

Emma set the glass of iced tea down on the table next to Bea and then sat down. "I'm so happy to see you, Bea." She beamed.

"It's been a long time," answered Bea. "I'm sorry about that."

"Oh, you know"—Emma waved her off—"life gets in the way sometimes. What brings you here?"

Beatrice paused a beat. "Memories. Good ones."

"Hear, hear," Emma said and tilted her glass.

"I was over by your place the other day," Beatrice went on. "Had my new husband over there."

"Married? Again?"

"Yes, I'll bring him by sometime. But we were over there and went to the clearing where you and I used to take the girls. Remember?"

Emma nodded.

"And you'll never believe what I saw."

"What?"

"A fairy tree," Beatrice said. "It reminded me of your fairy trees. How lovely they were. But I thought it odd since nobody's living at the house."

"You're wrong about that. My daughter lives there."

"What? Didn't look like anybody lived there."

"Well, I haven't been there in a while. I don't leave this room." Emma said it with a strange tone in her voice. "I never do. But I know that my daughter lives there. I imagine the place is run down. She doesn't have much help in tending to it. Just one woman who's a housekeeper and nurse."

Beatrice sorted through her memory of the place. *Could someone actually be living there?* She didn't think so. Emma must be mistaken.

Bea wondered if Emma knew about the apartments. Had anybody told her?

"Well, you know there's apartments over there," Beatrice said carefully.

Emma nodded. "We sold part of the land and they'd like to buy the rest of it. Ain't happening," she said with finality.

That answered a few questions. But Beatrice

still couldn't fathom someone living in that old dilapidated house. It didn't look safe.

Beatrice took a look around Emma's room, filled with lace tablecloths, antique glassware, and photos of her family. Everything seemed normal. Yet Emma said she didn't leave her room.

Maybe she was mistaken about the house.

"You know, after your husband died, I thought about coming over and seeing you. I don't know why I didn't," Emma suddenly said. "Your Ed was a good man." She paused. "I suppose sometimes it was hard for me to see you two together."

An uncomfortable silence ensued before Bea spoke.

"Well, he wasn't perfect," Bea said. "But we were very happy. Come to think of it, I don't remember reading anything about Paul's death. What happened?"

Emma sighed, then smiled, resembling the twenty-two-year-old woman that Beatrice knew so well. "I killed him."

"Come again," Beatrice said and leaned in closer.

"You heard that right. I'd never admit that to anyone but you. After his first massive heart attack, they gave him dietary restrictions. None of which I adhered to. One morning, he had another heart attack. It was as simple as that."

Beatrice's mouth dropped open.

"In fact, he asked me to get help," Emma said and looked off into her own distance. "And I told him to go to hell." She sat back in her chair and placed her hands demurely on her lap. "And then I watched him die."

Beatrice's hand clutched her chest. He had been terrible to Emma, had beaten her and berated her in public, but to kill the man? "Surely not."

"Well, I had to make sure he was good and dead," Emma said, lifting up her iced tea and taking a long drink.

Chapter 30

DeeAnn felt better than she had in a long time. If it kept up, she might be able to get back to work sooner that they had thought. *Maybe the physical therapy is helping,* she mused. God knows she hated it.

She dialed her bakery.

"Yes, DeeAnn, everything is fine here," said Jill when she answered the phone.

"Good," DeeAnn said.

"Did you go through that stack of mail?"

"Not yet. I'll do that today."

They talked a few more minutes before DeeAnn was satisfied all was well and then hung up.

One of the aspects of owning her own business that DeeAnn did not like was going through the mail and paying bills. But she guessed she better get to it. Then she hoped to get some scrapbooking in.

It was typical junk mail. She filled the wastebasket with it. Bill, bill, bill. She stacked those together. More junk mail. Then something caught her eye. Hathaway Transatlantic Employment Agency. *Hmmm.*

The same one Pamela had used. It couldn't hurt to call, could it?

DeeAnn dialed the number.

"Hathaway Transatlantic," the voice on the other end of the phone said.

"Yes, my name is DeeAnn Fields. I'm calling regarding the ad you sent to me."

"One moment please, I will transfer you," the voice said.

Music played while DeeAnn waited.

"This is Harold Angelo. Can I help you?"

"Yes," DeeAnn said and once again explained that she was responding to a brochure that had come in the mail.

"I'm very glad to hear from you," Mr. Angelo said. "It looks like we have several other bakeries and restaurants in your area that use our service and are quite happy with us. We'd love to help you."

"Why would I want to use your services rather than hire a local?" DeeAnn asked.

"Good question. Part of your payment goes to their relocation so you end up paying them less than minimum wage."

"You mean their employment package counts against their salary?" she asked. It was unfathomable.

"Exactly. They sign contracts to stay with you until they've worked off the complete amount."

"It doesn't seem legal." *Or ethical.* But she kept that thought to herself—for the time being.

"It's very above board. I assure you," Mr. Angelo said and then paused. "Many of these people are coming from very bad circumstances and you would be helping to give them a new life."

"By paying them less than minimum wage?"

"Only for a short time."

"How would they live on that?"

"Well, Ms. Fields, I'm so glad you brought that up. We have sponsors, you see. Sometimes it's families. Sometimes it's companies. But they help to house our workers."

It sounded almost altruistic. *What's the hitch?* wondered DeeAnn.

"I can send one of our representatives to speak with you. It's sometimes hard to communicate over the phone."

DeeAnn thought about it a moment. "Please do. I think I'd like that."

After scheduling the appointment, she felt quite pleased with herself—devious, she was devious. You could not keep her down. She might not be able to work at her shop, but she could conduct business from home. Even if it was a ruse. Of course, there was no way in hell she'd hire anybody from that agency. But she wanted information and so did her friends.

Next, she dialed Annie. "You will never believe what I did."

"What a great idea," Annie said after DeeAnn explained.

"I hope you'll come."

"I wouldn't miss it. And you won't be able to keep Beatrice away," Annie said and laughed.

Chapter 31

Annie's eyes scanned down the list of Sheila's customers who had purchased the Summer Dream scrapbooking paper from her. She didn't recognize most of the names—except for two. One was a woman whose kids went to school with hers. The other woman she didn't know—but her name was Mendez. Irina Mendez, who, according to the order form lived with and worked for the Drummond family. Annie would call to make an appointment with her and make sure it was the correct address. It was the third Mendez she'd heard of within a week. There was a Mendez at the police station with Bryant and it was the name of the man at the apartments. Her gut told her to start with the Mendez woman—and thank goodness she did not live at the Druid Lane apartments.

As she was getting ready to leave the house, her cell phone buzzed. It was the sheriff.

"Yes," Annie said into the phone.

"Sheriff Ted Bixby here."

"How can I help you?"

"I wanted to run something by you, if you don't mind?"

"Yes," Annie said.

"Is it strange for me to think these murders have something to do with scrapbooking? I don't quite know what to make of all the scrapbooking stuff, but it seems significant that the killer left scrapbooking stuff on site."

Stone cold fear crept into her stomach.

"Someone didn't like these women scrapbooking," Annie said, more to herself than to the sheriff.

"I thought the same thing. But why? Seems harmless enough" said Sheriff Bixby.

"Scrapbooking is harmless, but sometimes women getting together is not," Annie said. There was strength in communication and numbers—and some men didn't like it.

There was silence from the other end of the phone.

Annie continued. "What I mean is, in certain cultures, the men prefer their wives to be at home, without the friendship of other women." She felt a ball of fury form in her gut.

"I see."

"Especially if something is going on in the community that, I don't know, isn't right. And the women get together and discuss it," Annie said.

"Sounds a bit far-fetched."

"I agree," Annie said. "But these cases are very strange."

"True enough. These women lived in the US. Neither of them were married; they seemed to be alone. No boyfriends hanging around, either."

"No men?" Annie said. "Odd. Maybe we need to dig a little deeper to find them. I'm sure there must have been some men in their lives."

She was thinking she'd ask the woman who lived at the Drummond place, Irina, about boyfriends and so on—if she knew the sisters, that is. But Annie certainly was not going to tell the sheriff what she was up to. He was a lot more personable than Bryant, but he was still a cop. She knew what he'd say. *Leave the detective work to us.* But sometimes people would talk to her when they wouldn't open up to the police, especially if those people were from a foreign land in which police power was abused on a daily basis.

The sheriff chuckled. "Yes, you're right. They were young and healthy women. Why didn't they have men around? No boyfriends?"

Annie gathered her belongings, found her keys, and drove to the address Irina had given her when she called to make the appointment, on the other side of town—the Drummond place. As she pulled up into the driveway, she checked the address again. It, indeed, was the address on the scrapbook supply order form and the address Irina had given her. Funny, it didn't even look like anybody was living there. It was an old farm house on the edge of town. Annie noted that the Riverside Apartments buildings were visible from there, as was a sliver of the park.

She walked up the sidewalk to the front porch and door. To say the house needed a paint job was an understatement. The sidewalk was a bit crooked and the porch stairs were warped and creaky.

She rang the doorbell, almost certain it was not the right place. Getting ready to turn around, she was surprised when the door opened to a small, older, dark-skinned woman who smiled nervously at her.

"Hello," Annie said. "Are you Irina?"

She nodded. "Yes, you must be Annie. I've been expecting you," she said, plastering a cool, professional-looking smile on her face, even though that's not quite how she felt.

When Annie walked in, she was shocked to see how lovely and clean the inside of the house was. Beautiful Victorian furniture, well-appointed rooms, gorgeous, gleaming woodwork throughout—and yet the outside of the place had gone to hell. She tried not to show her surprise. "Is this your house?"

"I live here. But this is where I work. I work for the Drummond family," Irina said. "Please have a seat. Can I get you something? Tea? Water?"

"No thanks," Annie said, a little off-balance by the remarkable difference between the inside of the house and the outside. "This is such a lovely home."

"Thank you," Irina said. "I like to make things look pretty. What brings you here?" she asked with a pleasant expression on her face, smoothing over her dark skirt.

Where have I seen her before? Annie wondered. "As I said on the phone, I'm a reporter and I'm working on the story about the Martelino sisters." She reached into her bag for her recorder and clicked on the button. The woman appeared to be okay with it and Annie had mostly stopped asking permission anyway. If people didn't want to be recorded, they'd tell her.

"Yes," Irina said, looking down. "They were both

my friends. God rest their souls." She crossed herself.

Finally! Someone who knew them that will talk to me, thought Annie.

"Lovely young women," Irina said. "Horrible way to die." Her bottom lip quivered.

"I'm so sorry for your loss," Annie said, taking a closer look at her and wondering where she had seen her before? "I'm sure you'll agree that we need to find justice for them. Find out who killed them and bring them to justice."

The woman cracked a smile.

Odd.

But her cheeks quivered, escaping from the forced smile.

"Did the women have any other friends besides you?" Annie asked, after a moment and then she finally realized where she had seen Irina before. She was the woman who had been hugging the sad-eyed young man at Pamela's Pie Palace the day of the first murder. It made sense now. She was a friend of Marina's.

"Yes," Irina said. "We have a large community of people here."

"But did the women have any close friends?"

"A few," Irina said, after appearing to mull it over.

"Any men?" Annie asked hopefully.

Irina stiffened. "Not really. They were beautiful, loving young women and wanted to marry, eventually. But"—she shrugged and gestured with her hands—"it didn't work out yet. They were young." Her voice cracked.

"Hard to believe there were no men sniffing around," Annie said.

The other woman shrugged.

"I was over at their apartments and a man was there. Not very friendly. He has the same last name as you," Annie said.

The woman chuckled. "Half the Hispanic population has the same last name as me. It's like your Smith or Jones. We're not related."

"Oh I see. So you don't know him?"

"Oh, I know him," Irina said with an edge to her voice. "Not a very nice man. Thinks he's king of the hill because he manages apartments."

"You don't live over there. Why?"

"Why would I? This is a nice place. I like Ms. Drummond. There's plenty of room for me here."

Annie wondered if it was as simple as that. Why wouldn't she want her own place? And why wasn't the outside of this place as meticulously cared for as the inside? How could she even begin to frame such a question?

"Ms. Drummond even allows my friends to come here to scrapbook," Irina said. "She's very nice. None of the others have enough room in their homes."

"This is where you meet to scrapbook?" Annie looked around.

"Yes, in the dining room. There's a huge table in there. We're having a crop Friday night. The first night since . . . they passed away. Would you like to come?"

Annie could not believe her luck. Was it luck, karma, or kismet? She had to stop herself from jumping up from her chair and screaming, *"Yes!"*

She met Irina's smile with her own. "I'll have to check my calendar. But I'd love to come."

Chapter 32

Beatrice walked up the sidewalk to the Drummond house. Halloween was in a few weeks and it occurred to her that the place looked like something straight out of a clichéd horror movie. The sidewalk was cracked and lopsided. The house needed a good painting and the porch was sagging.

If Emma was dead, she'd be turning over in her grave—but instead she was at an assisted living place, afraid to leave her room and thinking that she'd killed her husband. A shiver traveled up Bea's spine. *Emma must be mistaken. Nobody is living here.*

But when she stepped up onto the porch, she glimpsed a movement in the window. And there were curtains! Bea rang the doorbell.

A short, dark-haired woman opened the door. "Can I help you?"

"I'm a good friend of Emma Drummond—"

"She doesn't live here anymore," the woman interrupted curtly and started to close the door.

Beatrice's arm prevented it. "I know that. I'd like to see her daughter, Michelle. She lives here, right?"

"Yes, come in." The woman sighed and reluctantly opened the door.

When Bea walked through the door, she was taken straight back to the last day she had been in the house. The day she'd witnessed Emma being smacked across the face by her husband. Beatrice had intervened, not thinking, and the man almost struck her as well.

The woodwork was polished and shining. The carpets and curtains were beautiful, clean, and well-appointed. *What's the deal with the outside?* thought Bea.

The woman gestured to the couch. "Please have a seat."

Well, Michelle must not be that bad off if she has a housekeeper. Just what's going on here?

"Hello." A small, childlike voice came from around the corner. Beatrice twisted around to see. The approaching woman was a wisp of a thing. A little younger than Vera, maybe, and pretty as she could be.

"Michelle? I'm Beatrice, a friend of your mom's," Bea said, standing and offering her a hand. The last time she had seen Michelle she had still been in diapers. Beatrice was certain she wouldn't remember her.

Michelle took her hand and shook it, only meeting Bea's eyes once.

"I was just visiting Emma," Bea said. "And she mentioned that you lived here."

Michelle sat down. "Irina," she called. "Can we get you some iced tea? Water?"

"Nothing for me, thanks," Beatrice said.

"Yes, for the time being, I live here," Michelle

said, returning to Bea's earlier question. "I love this old place. It's the only home I've ever known."

"I used to visit here back when Emma and Paul lived here. It is lovely. The other day I was walking over by the park and saw the place, which prompted me to look up your mom."

Michelle simply said, "Ah." She wore no makeup. She had pretty, big brown eyes, framed in long, dark lashes, a button nose, and an unfortunate, pointy chin. "How is she?" asked Michelle.

"Fine. She doesn't leave her room?" Beatrice asked. She liked that Michelle wasn't all made up.

"No," Michelle said, meeting Beatrice's eyes with her own. "Unfortunately, it runs in the family."

"You don't leave the house?"

She shook her head. "Oh I have, but not recently. That's why I have Irina. She gets me what I need. Between her and the Internet, I have no need to go out, really."

So that's why the place had gone to pot outside. Michelle never saw it.

What to say to something like that? Beatrice knew there were shut-ins everywhere. But this young woman appeared healthy. It must be a form of ago-raphobia.

"When I was walking the other day and saw the place it made me kind of sad. I didn't know anybody lived here. From the outside . . . well, I thought it was abandoned," Beatrice said carefully. That was as polite as she could put it. She was pleased with her-self.

"It's intentional," Michelle said, jutting that pointy chin of hers out farther. "I want people to stay away, especially the Kraft Corporation."

"What? Why?"

"We had to sell part of our land to help keep Mom in the nursing home. So we sold it to them. Then they built those stinking apartments, brought in bad sorts of people. I figure if folks think the place is abandoned, they won't be robbing me or bother with me at all."

"What makes you think they'd rob you?" Beatrice asked, thinking that Michelle sounded a bit paranoid.

"I've had a few incidents already. And the Kraft Corporation wants the whole shebang. I'll never leave here!" Michelle was getting hoarse. Her voice was draining.

"Ms. Drummond." Irina suddenly appeared. "Shall I get you some of your medicine?"

Michelle nodded. She sat very straight in her chair. Her body belied the look on her face, which was borderline panic.

"I'm sorry. I get a bit upset sometimes. They really have upset me. The men that come here and try to get me to sell this place. It's the last link I have to my family. I'm the last one. Well, aside from my mother and my cousin. And they want to take it all from me," she said.

Irina appeared again, seemingly out of nowhere, and handed Michelle a glass of water and a pill.

That was the thing about hired help, they were always around. It was something Beatrice could never have abided. "What men?" she asked.

"The Kraft Corporation. The ones who built the apartments."

Beatrice sank back into the cushions on the couch.

"They want this place and the rest of the land. They can have it over my dead body," Michelle said.

"Good for you," Beatrice said. *Kraft*, she thought. That was Pamela's last name. Was the Kraft Corporation hers? Or was it a relative? Kraft was a popular name in these parts. It could have no bearing at all. But it might be a little too coincidental—the women who were killed had links to the Pie Palace and also lived in apartments possibly owned by a member of Pamela's family. Just what was going on?

Chapter 33

DeeAnn and Sheila sat at her kitchen table with DeeAnn's laptop in front of them.

"So, after you place the photo on the page, you can change the color or texture or anything," Sheila said.

"But that's not *really* a page," DeeAnn said.

"Well, you know what I mean," Sheila said, exasperated.

"It's pretty cool," DeeAnn said. "But after I finish all this, then what do I do?"

"What do you mean?"

"I mean how do I get the pages off my computer and into my hands? Can I print them?"

"Well, sure. Depending on your page size. If you have a regular scrapbook page, there are places that you can send your pages to and they will print them. Or you can keep them on CDs, jump drives, whatever."

"Why would I want to do that?"

"Some people don't feel the need for paper and clutter. They lead digital lives." Sheila grinned.

"Sounds fancy," DeeAnn said, sliding her computer over and her sandwich toward her. Sheila had brought lunch. She made the most wonderful sandwiches—this one was avocado and cream cheese with lettuce and tomatoes. DeeAnn would never have imagined putting all of those ingredients together. But it was good.

"When are you going back to work?" Sheila asked.

DeeAnn shrugged. "I guess when the doc tells me I can."

"How are you feeling?"

"As long as I have the pain medicine, I'm fine. But when it starts to wear off, I'm not happy. And Jacob won't let me have more. I say if it hurts I need one. He says only two a day. Prick." She laughed.

"Guess the bastard likes you or something," Sheila said and then took a bite of her sandwich.

The two sat quietly for a few minutes as they each ate their sandwiches.

"I've been thinking about those paper dolls of yours," DeeAnn said. "I love them. Have you shown them to your boss yet?"

Sheila shook her head. "I'll be seeing him next week. I don't have much hope that they'll be interested in carrying a line of paper dolls, though. I don't think they are a popular toy these days."

"That makes me sad," DeeAnn said and then paused. "How is Donna?"

The color in Sheila's faced drained. DeeAnn was sorry she asked.

"I don't think she's going back to school anytime soon. They said they'd hold her scholarship for two years. She seems to be fine for days, and then . . ." Sheila gestured. "I don't know. She weakens. I don't like leaving her. In fact, I think I might quit my job."

"What?" DeeAnn dropped her sandwich. "Your dream job?"

"It is a dream job in a way. But it's not exactly how I thought it would be—and it came at such a bad time for the family. I feel . . . pulled so much of the time. I'm not sure it's worth it."

DeeAnn was surprised to hear it. She thought Sheila was so thrilled with her work. "Hey, you've got to do what you've got to do. Things happen. Priorities shift."

Sheila smiled. "Isn't that the truth?"

The telephone blared. It was a woman from Hathaway Transatlantic Employment. "Just confirming tomorrow's appointment," she said.

"I'll be here," DeeAnn said. And she wasn't the only one. Annie would be there and so would Beatrice. Sheila couldn't make it, as she was going to New York City.

DeeAnn finished the call, hung up the phone, and explained who had called.

"I wish I could be there," Sheila said. "It should be interesting."

"I'll say," DeeAnn said. "There's definitely something fishy about these folks."

"Maybe not." Sheila pushed her glasses back up on her nose. "Maybe they are exactly what they say they are. Nothing more, nothing less."

"I wish I could believe that. I don't understand why Pamela uses them when there are locals who need the work. Maybe it's because she can get away with paying them less than minimum wage."

"She does?"

"Good Lord, the woman has more money than God," DeeAnn said.

"Maybe that's why—she's very frugal with it."

"Baloney! She was born into money and married into it. She's a selfish bitch." DeeAnn couldn't believe she actually said that. But she did—and it felt good to acknowledge that it was exactly how she felt. It wasn't sour grapes because the Pie Palace was so successful. It was as if that feeling about Pamela had been swirling around inside her for a long time and she just now recognized it.

Sheila lurched back, her hand to her chest.

"I mean it, Sheila, no pussyfooting around about it. When you own a business, you need to treat the people who work for you as good as you can," DeeAnn said.

"True. Speaking of that, I brought dessert, too, from my favorite bakery." Sheila reached down next to her feet and lifted a "DeeAnn's Bakery" bag. Inside was a box of cupcakes.

When she lifted the lid, DeeAnn sighed. Four gorgeous cupcakes were decorated to look like witch hats.

"Chocolate raspberry," Sheila said. "So beautiful. I don't know how she does it."

A lovely, handwritten card was tucked inside the box from her crew.

DeeAnn held back a tear she felt stinging her eyes, then she took a deep breath and shrugged. Well, if she couldn't be at her shop, it was a good thing Jill was. Figuring she may as well enjoy the treats, DeeAnn reached into the box for a gorgeous cupcake and when she took a bite of it, it tasted like sweet heaven.

Chapter 34

Annie set the cereal bowls down in front of her boys. "Eat up. The bus will be here in fifteen minutes."

Mike came out of the bedroom and sauntered into the kitchen. He was dressed to the hilt in a gray suit.

"Well, good morning, handsome," Annie said and smiled.

He reached out for her and gave her a quick kiss. "Important meeting today. I can't wait to get this over with."

"I'm sure you will get the promotion, Mike. You've done so well since we've been here," Annie said.

They both had. They were able to save a little bit of money and were getting close to being able to buy another house. Their place was so small. Each year, as the boys grew, it became smaller. The incredible shrinking house.

"Stop it, Ben!" Sam slammed his hand on the table.

Ben laughed and continued to slurp his milk out of the bowl.

"Mom! Dad! Tell him to stop!"

"Ben, please stop annoying your brother." Mike turned and reached into the cupboard for a bowl and a cup.

"I'll get your oatmeal. Sit down, Mike," Annie said and poured him a cup of steaming coffee.

"Sam," Mike said. "Stop glaring at your brother like that. How did your math test go yesterday?"

"I did okay." Sam shrugged. "I'll find out today."

"Good," Mike said. "And what are you up to, Ben?"

"Soccer game this weekend. Can't wait."

Mike nodded. "That's right. And next weekend is Halloween."

"Halloween is for babies," Sam said.

"Well," Annie said. "You don't have to get dressed up. You can stay here and hand out candy with your father."

Sam smiled. "Sounds good to me."

After everybody had left and Annie finished cleaning the kitchen, she dressed and gathered her things for the meeting at DeeAnn's house. It should be an interesting morning. But maybe not as interesting as the evening she had planned at the Drummond house, meeting with another group of scrapbookers. Imagine that! Another group of women in town got together to scrapbook every week or so. Annie found it amusing. She couldn't wait to meet the women and find out more about the immigrant population in Cumberland Creek—especially Marina and her sister Esmeralda.

Pamela was not being much help—she and Annie

kept playing phone tag. At this point, it was pretty clear that it was a purposeful avoidance tactic on Pamela's part, which only led Annie to suspect her of knowing more or covering something up.

But what?

Annie slipped on her sneakers. Every time she put them on, she longingly remembered the days when she used to wear great shoes. Maybe soon, she'd trade in her sneakers for her designer heels again. Truth was, she didn't know where she was heading with her life. She simply knew she was done with reporting.

She grabbed her bag, locked the front door, and started the walk to DeeAnn's house.

When she reached DeeAnn's house, she saw that the man from the agency was already there. "Guess he couldn't wait," she muttered to herself. "But I thought I was early."

Annie rang the doorbell and Beatrice greeted her. She looked like that cat who swallowed the canary. Knowing Beatrice, it was one bloody canary.

"Come on in," Bea said. "He's just gotten here." She looked at the bag in Annie's hand. "Those muffins? I brought some coffee cake. We sure are going to sweeten him up."

Annie followed her into the kitchen where plates of food were being filled with cake, muffins, donuts, bagels, and other morning goodies.

DeeAnn was in the living room with the man while Bea was preening over the food. "Let's go ahead and take these in."

Annie grabbed a plate.

When they walked into the living room, Christo-

pher Hathaway looked up and his eyes widened.
"Now ladies, you all have gone to too much trouble.
It's not necessary."

"We want to make you feel welcome. Everybody
needs breakfast," DeeAnn said.

The women set the plates of food on the coffee
table and then proceeded to sit down.

Mr. Hathaway had coco-colored skin and dark
hair, graying at the temples. He had big, bright eyes
that hinted at intelligence.

"Please help yourself," DeeAnn said.

Mr. Hathaway selected a blueberry muffin and
took a huge bite. "Oh my God. This is so good."

"They're from my bakery," DeeAnn said proudly.
"So—we'd like to hear more about your company."

"Well, as you know, we provide a means for immigrants to come to this country. We help get their
visas and passports and whatnot, and help to find
them work." He took another bite of the blueberry
muffin and rolled his eyes in obvious delight.

Sounded good, but Annie had her doubts.

"So, the money I'd pay you would cover all that?"
DeeAnn asked.

"That and more," he said, looking around curi-
ously.

He was probably wondering what the hell all those
women were doing there.

"It would cover expenses in getting them here
and their first year of employment."

"So, they don't get paid the first year?" Beatrice
spoke up.

"I'm sorry. How are you connected with the
bakery?" he asked politely.

"I'm not," Beatrice said. "I'm a friend of DeeAnn's."

"But Bea's question is a good one," DeeAnn said quickly.

Mr. Hathaway continued, turning his attention to DeeAnn. "I know it seems harsh, but we've found that while they are adjusting to a new job, new country, and new culture, it's best that the first year they receive payment only from us. You pay us up front in a lump sum and we pay them. It helps us to keep track of them."

"Why do you need to keep track of them?" Annie said.

"Another friend?" he asked DeeAnn, who nodded.

"I'm unaccustomed to answering business questions from friends," Mr. Hathaway said. "I don't understand what these women are doing here."

"They're just curious," DeeAnn replied. "Because of the recent murders, you see. Everybody is curious about the Martelino sisters."

Mr. Hathaway's face reddened. "A very unfortunate incident. But they had been here for almost two years so I really have nothing to say about them."

"Meaning their first year was over so you didn't keep track of them any longer?" Annie asked after swallowing a bite of cranberry scone.

"Yes," Mr. Hathaway said. "During the first year their sponsors check in on them several times to make sure they are adjusting and so on."

"Sponsors?" DeeAnn asked.

"Usually, it's their employer. Maybe a social worker . . . sometimes it's landlords."

Landlords. Hmmm. An image of Mr. Mendez, the

landlord at the new apartments, came into Annie's mind. Could he be a sponsor?

Annie shivered. If he was, God knows what kind of lives the Martelino sisters had been leading. And no wonder they'd ended up dead.

Chapter 35

Beatrice was unimpressed by Mr. Hathaway's explanations. "They bring these young people here and track them for a year, then don't follow up?"

"Let me be clear," Mr. Hathaway said. "Many agencies like ours do nothing that first year. My father started the agency because he fell in love with a woman from India. Her family also needed to get out of the country because of a political situation in which their lives were threatened."

"So that's how this all began?" DeeAnn asked.

"It has evolved into a huge business," Mr. Hathaway went on. "My father's inclination was to help foreigners get out of bad situations, bring them here to work, and start new lives."

"Sounds very altruistic," Beatrice sad. "Except I'm not sure how I feel about them not getting a real salary that first year. Sounds like indentured servitude."

"I understand completely," Hathaway said, wiping the corner of his mouth with his napkin. "I know that's what it sounds like. But that's not what it is."

"So what do you know about the Martelinos?" Beatrice asked.

The man looked aghast. "I know they were killed," he finally said.

"No, that's not what I mean," Beatrice said. "We wanted to send their family our condolences, but we've been unable to find out anything about them."

Mr. Hathaway's face reddened. "I am sorry about that, but there's probably something you should know about them . . . well, they had no family. As far as I know, they grew up in an orphanage in Mexico City and were never adopted as children."

Beatrice's stomach sank. *Lawd, it keeps getting worse.* The young women had lived hellacious lives. The room was silent as the women exchanged glances. They had gotten part of the information they came for, but it wasn't helpful. They wanted some sort of closure.

Why does it matter so much to me? Beatrice wondered. She hadn't even known the young women. As she glanced around to the others gathered in the room, the thought struck her that it didn't matter that the young women were perfect strangers—tragedy could affect any one of them. In times of grief, it was bits and pieces of comforting gestures that kept you going.

They were still talking about something, but Beatrice did not care to follow along anymore. It was as if the Martelino sisters had never existed. They came here for a better life and got killed, probably by some gang. What was the world coming to?

Annie looked at Beatrice with a sadness in her dark eyes. She must have been thinking similar thoughts.

Beatrice took a bite of her pumpkin chocolate

chip muffin and let the flavor take her mind away from the young women with no family, save each other.

After the women had grilled him some more to no avail, Mr. Hathaway left, and DeeAnn was back to lying on the couch with her friends fussing over her. Beatrice asked if she was actually going to hire someone from the agency.

"I don't think so," DeeAnn said. "Lawd, if I could just have another pain pill. I have to wait until two to take the next one."

"Why?" Beatrice wondered.

"Jacob is withholding them. I guess he thought I was using too many of them," DeeAnn said.

"Well, how does he know?" Beatrice said. "Is he suddenly a doctor?"

"She was taking them willy-nilly," Annie said. "She's only supposed to take two a day. These pills are very addictive. Her husband is just concerned."

"Humph. Did the doctor mention anything about whiskey? That will take the edge off," Beatrice said.

"Her daddy always said it's good for what ails you," Annie said with a mocking tone that made them all laugh—including Beatrice.

"I'm willing to try anything," DeeAnn said.

"Where do you keep your booze?" Beatrice asked.

"In the kitchen cabinet below the sink," DeeAnn said.

"You better be careful mixing booze with those pills," Annie said. "You'll get all loopy."

"Loopier than usual?" DeeAnn said and laughed.

"What do you think of all this, Annie?" Beatrice heard DeeAnn say as she opened the kitchen cabinet door.

"I'm not sure what to think. It sounds to me like Transatlantic is a hair away from involvement in human trafficking. The man can say what he wants and call it what he wants, but I'm betting everything is not as rosy as it sounds."

"I thought he was real nice," DeeAnn said. "Seemed like he wanted to help people."

"He did seem nice," Annie said. "But then again, he's not the only person working in his company. And I'm not sure where that's going to lead us in terms of the murders."

Beatrice poured a glass of Jack Daniel's and carried the golden elixir into the living room. "I agree. After all, it was someone here who killed them. We need to avenge these young women." She handed the glass to DeeAnn.

DeeAnn drank from the glass. "Eww, that's nasty stuff." She turned to Annie. "What's this I hear about you going to another crop tonight?"

"Word travels fast around here," Annie said. "Yes, I'm going over to the Drummond house tonight for a crop with friends of Marina and Esmeralda."

Beatrice stopped in her tracks. "What did you say?"

"I'm going to—"

"The Drummond house?"

Annie nodded. "What's wrong?"

Beatrice told them about her own recent trip to the Drummond place.

"What an odd coinshidenshe," DeeAnn said with a bit of a slur to her words.

"Loopy," Bea said. "It doesn't take much."

Chapter 36

After everybody cleaned up, they all lingered a bit. DeeAnn took another sip of the whiskey. She was not fond of the drink, but she thought it might be taking the edge off her pain. "I'd love to go to that crop with you, Annie."

"Maybe another time," Annie replied. "After your back is better."

"Plan on going back?" DeeAnn asked.

"I don't know. I haven't been to the first one yet. I can't imagine scrapbooking two nights in a row. I'm pretty comfortable with our group the way it is. I'm wondering what these women might have to say about the Martelinos."

"Get the scoop," DeeAnn said. "You know, it's kind of odd that there's another crop going on across town . . . weekly, like ours. Almost like a parallel universe kind of thing."

"We are not the only scrapbookers in town," Annie said.

Cookie opened DeeAnn's front door, walked in, and sat down on the edge of the couch where

DeeAnn was propped up with pillows. They were all getting used to her wandering in and out of their houses.

"What are you going to do about that man?" Cookie asked. "I saw him leave."

DeeAnn shrugged.

"You're not going to hire someone from his agency, are you?"

"Hell, no," DeeAnn said. "I don't need any help right now and it seems like a whole lot of trouble."

"I agree that something is not quite right there," Beatrice said. "But he may not know that."

"What do you mean, Bea?" Annie asked.

"Well, he's the head of the company and seems to have romantic notions about it. His daddy starting it to help his momma's people and all that. But it's a huge company now. I'd wager he doesn't know half the employees."

"Good point," Cookie said. "But I don't know enough about the business to make an educated opinion."

DeeAnn studied Cookie for a moment. The person sitting on the couch next to her was actually acting like herself . . . for the first time in months. The murder cases seemed to spark something in her. DeeAnn's eyes momentarily caught Annie's, who also seemed to notice the spark in Cookie.

Cookie cleared her throat. She had noticed the exchanged look. "For some reason, these cases really touch me. Young women, basically, without a family, without a past, trying to make their way. The more I think about it, the more I remember feelings I must have had. Sometimes images come to me and I'm not sure if they are quite memories."

DeeAnn's heart sank. Poor Cookie. Would she ever remember? Or was she destined to never know where she came from? The dead sisters and their story must be setting off some triggers for her.

"Their stories are so sad," Beatrice said after a few minutes of quiet. She then slipped on her coat and left—which left Annie, DeeAnn, and Cookie still in the living room.

"You know, Cookie, I've often wondered how much you *want* to remember," DeeAnn said.

Cookie lifted her head in surprise and looked directly at DeeAnn. "Sometimes I want to—other times I'm afraid."

"What are you afraid of?"

"Afraid I'm not a very good person. Afraid of something I might have done . . . something not right," she said.

A hush fell over the room.

"Oh now, Cookie," DeeAnn said a few moments later. "You and I don't see eye to eye on a lot of things, but I know you're a good sort. We all do."

"That's true," Annie said. "You may have something mixed up because of the way you disappeared from jail. Someone took you, remember. You didn't escape. And you surely didn't hurt those girls who were killed, back then, if that's what you're thinking. They found the killer. He's in prison now."

"When I think I know myself, I know I couldn't hurt anything," Cookie said. "But other times . . ." She shrugged. "Sometimes I feel a darkness inside me. I don't know what else to call it."

"Oh goodness, honey," DeeAnn said. "We all have that. You're not alone. Who knows what any one of us is capable of? Good or bad."

"Or what life has in store for us," Annie said. "Look at Sheila and all of these changes she's dealing with."

"And DeeAnn," Cookie said quietly.

DeeAnn suddenly felt a flush creeping over her. It was as if someone had opened a window to see right inside of her.

"DeeAnn?" Annie said, looking confused.

"Oh" DeeAnn waved her off—"it's just me getting older. Thinking about retiring. Stuff like that."

"Big stuff, DeeAnn," Cookie said, reaching out for her hand. "I don't know. I mean, look at me. I don't remember much. I'm not an expert, but I think it's important to acknowledge changes in our lives while we are living them. That's the best way to move forward."

No, DeeAnn wanted to say, *it's best not to look at anything too deeply.*

Annie's cell phone beeped. She picked it up and hit the TALK button. "Yes?" Her eyes widened. "Really? I'll be right over. Oh. Then we'll see you tonight."

"Well, my word, you look like the cat that swallowed . . . something," DeeAnn said.

"That was Randy," Annie said. "Our friend Mr. Hathaway is at Pamela's right now, arguing with her and some young man. I told Randy I'd go over there, but he didn't think that was a good idea. I still might drop by. Randy's trying to figure out what they are saying."

"What do you mean by that?" DeeAnn asked.

"There's a lot of Spanish being flung around," Annie said, gathering her things.

"I thought Randy knew Spanish," DeeAnn said.

"No. He speaks French, not Spanish, but he can make out some words. We'll talk about it tonight. He's coming with me to the crop."

"Can I come, too?" Cookie asked.

"Of course," Annie said. "Do you speak Spanish?"

Cookie shrugged. "I have no idea."

Chapter 37

Annie was certain that the blue Cadillac parked outside Pamela's Pie Palace belonged to Christopher Hathaway. So he was still there. *Good.*

She pulled into the spot next to the Cadillac, sat in her car, and waited. After about fifteen minutes, the door to the Pie Palace opened. Pamela was with Mr. Hathaway and carrying a box of something—it looked like files.

As the two of them walked over to Hathaway's car, Annie opened her car door. "Hey."

"Hi Annie," Pamela said, smiling her perfect smile with perfect lips and perfect teeth.

"Do you need some help with that?" Annie asked, reaching out as Christopher Hathaway opened his trunk.

"I'm fine, Annie," Pamela said and dropped the box into his trunk. "Just a bunch of old files to go into storage at Hathaway."

"Why would you store your files there?" Annie said.

"Why don't you mind your own business?" Hathaway

snapped. "The way our company manages things is none of your concern."

"Well, I—"

"It's okay, Annie." Pamela smiled again. "Why don't you go inside and get some pie?"

"That's what I came for, but I've lost my appetite," she said and headed back to her own car. As she pulled away, she could have sworn she saw Pamela shove Christopher Hathaway.

Annie and Cookie picked up Randy from Elsie's B and B.

"You're right on time," Randy said with surprise, placing his scrapbooking bag in the backseat next to Cookie.

Annie ignored the good-natured jab. "So what happened today?" she asked as he slid into the passenger seat.

"Well," Randy said, shrugging, "I don't know what to make of it, but Pamela was very upset. I've never heard her raise her voice like that before."

Annie turned her signal on and then made a turn. "What exactly did you overhear?"

"I heard the word 'sponsor' and the word 'money.' And the name Jorge over and over again."

"Jorge?"

"Yes," Randy said. "He works at Pamela's. Doesn't speak much English, and he seems . . . I don't know, kind of quiet."

"What's he do there?" Cookie asked from the backseat.

"A little bit of everything," Randy said. "He's

harmless. Washes dishes. Helps with the supplies. Assists Pamela. Just whatever."

"He can't be that harmless if he was involved in the kerfuffle," Annie said.

Randy thought a moment. "That's true. That's one of the odd things about all this. I mean, usually he's so quiet and gets his work done. I wonder if it has to do something with Immigration."

"Could be. We should check him out," Annie said. "I'll run him through my databases."

"One more thing," Randy added. "They did mention the Martelino sisters several times."

Annie felt a chill creep up her spine.

"Of course he did," Cookie said. "We asked him about them. I'm sure he's unhappy with the attention. Even if he's on the up-and-up, nobody wants that kind of attention."

Annie pulled into the long driveway of the Drummond house.

"This is where we are scrapping?" Randy said, then let his jaw drop. "I thought this place was abandoned."

"So did I," Annie said.

"Beatrice did, too," Cookie said as she opened her car door. "Beatrice told me she used to know this family very well."

Randy stood for a minute as if he was remembering something. "Yes, I think I remember this place. Didn't they used to sell apples?"

"You're asking the wrong people," Annie said, opening her trunk and lifting her bag out of it. Cookie also reached in for her own tattered bag of supplies.

"I'll have to ask Mom about it," Randy remarked.

The three of them walked up the sidewalk together. Leaves were scattered across the lawn and crunched beneath their feet. The moon was peeking through the clouds. The steps creaked as they ascended the porch. Laughter came from within the house.

Annie wasn't sure if the place truly looked abandoned—but it did need a paint job. The paint on the clapboard had long ago faded away, giving the house a gray color that easily blended into the night.

She rang the doorbell and Irina answered. "Come in, Annie. You brought friends. Good!" She opened her arms wide and they all entered. "The crop is already happening. But there's space for you all."

They followed her into the dining room, which had been transformed since Annie had last been there. Six women were gathered around two long crop tables, four at one table and two at the other. Annie and her crew set up at the less crowded table.

"Everybody," Irina said. "This is Annie Chamovitz. She's a reporter. We met the other day. I told you all about her."

Annie looked up and smiled at the women. "And these are my friends, Randy and Cookie."

Cookie smiled and Randy nodded.

"Please help yourself to some food once you are settled in," Irina said.

Annie turned in the direction Irina had gestured and saw a table brimming with food. A heavy, spicy scent filled the air and made Annie's mouth water. Some of the croppers already had plates of food at their tables. Chips and salsa, paper bowls full of a stew that looked like chili, and flat bread with cheese and beans on it.

"The food looks and smells incredible," Annie said, wandering over to the table and then seeing the plates of tiny colorful cookies and cakes. So pretty.

"*Paciencia*," Randy said as he reached over and placed a round white cookie on his plate.

"You know it?" Irina asked.

He smiled and nodded. "Of course. We'd call them meringue cookies. I love them. Did you make them? They're beautiful."

"Yes, thank you. I enjoy making things look nice and pretty," Irina said.

After they filled their plates and sat down at the tables to scrapbook, Annie took a quick glance around the tables. Except for one, the women were mostly young, in their twenties. Irina was the oldest.

One of the younger women held up her page with a photo of a baby on it, framed in purple.

"Is she yours?" Annie asked.

The young woman nodded. "Yes, six months old. I'm Mary. This is my girl Sophia."

"Beautiful," Annie said, watching Mary beam. Mothers were the same everywhere. No matter where the cropping table was, when mothers got together and scrapped, they were always proud of their kids and loved to swap stories.

"Give me that!" a woman from the corner of the table said to another. "I want to use that paper."

Annie looked her way just as the woman who had cried out took a drink of beer.

The women all stopped and looked up as a young man entered the room.

"What are you doing here?" one of the women said.

"He always comes for some food. You'd think he never eats," Irina said and rolled her eyes. "Get some food and go. This is women's business." She spoke in Spanish, smiling.

"Yes, ma'am," he said, reaching for a plate, then turning to spot Randy. "Oh, Mr. Swanson," he said, noticeably nervous. "What are you doing here?"

"I'm cropping, Jorge," Randy said.

Jorge grinned. "Really?"

"Yes," Randy said with an edge in his voice.

Jorge looked away and went about filling his plate with food.

Annie looked around the room. The women's laughter and general demeanor had changed when Jorge entered the room.

When he finally left, Irina waved her hand. "He's my nephew. I told my sister I'd keep an eye on him. But he's a pain in the ass."

Annie grinned. It seemed the other women agreed, based on their laughter. Randy kept his eyes on his scrapbook, but she noted a slight stiffening in his jaw.

A few of the women were gathered around a die-cut machine. Annie found them fascinating but had never really gotten the hang of it, so she left her spot at the table and watched as the women placed a cartridge in the machine, then some cardstock. When the paper came out, it was perforated with beautiful flourishes and spirals.

"I love that," she said. "What design is that?"

"I did this myself," said the small woman standing next to her. "The designs are mine."

"Wow. Amazing," Annie said. "Do you work in the industry?"

The woman laughed. "No. I work as a maid. I'm thinking about going back to school. I've been talking to some people about it. I'm Rosa," she said, extending her hand.

"Annie. Nice to meet you. Tell me, Rosa, did you know the Martelino sisters?"

"Know them?" Rosa said. "I lived with them."

Annie's heart nearly lurched out of her chest. Could this be the break she'd been seeking?

Chapter 38

"Annie seems mighty excited about something," Jon said after Beatrice hung up the phone.

Beatrice nodded. "Last night, she found the Martelino sisters' roommate and she's going to visit her tomorrow over at the Riverside Apartments."

"You look worried," Jon said.

"Well, hells bells. All I've been hearing about is that there's gangs over there. I hope she takes someone with her."

"She should take Bryant," Jon said. "He's a good officer."

"I thought he was transferring to Charlottesville or somewhere. Wonder what happened," Beatrice said. "Anyway, he's unpleasant and Annie really doesn't like him. Maybe she'll take the sheriff over with her."

"You know, last night when I went to the grocery store, I saw Detective Bryant at the store. He had a bottle of wine and flowers. Romance is in the air," Jon said, moving his eyebrows around in a peculiar way.

"I can't imagine," Beatrice said, ignoring the eyebrow thing. "Poor woman."

"Everybody deserves a little romance in their lives." Jon grinned, then reached over and grabbed her hand. "Look at us, *mon amie.*"

Beatrice warmed. It was true that most people wondered what Jon saw in her. She was certain half the town thought she was a crazy old lady who liked to talk about the universe and tell people exactly what she thought. "Well, now, that's true. To the outside world we may not look well-suited . . ."

"But who cares about them?" Jon said, lifting his chin.

"Indeed. How about some lunch?"

"What do you have in mind?"

"Egg salad on rye bread, followed by some apple pie."

"*Oui.*"

Beatrice puttered around in the kitchen with Jon on her heels. They worked together to create lunch and then sat down to eat.

"The other thing that Annie found out is that a lot of these immigrants are living together to make ends meet. There were four women at the crop last night who share a two-bedroom apartment," Beatrice said.

Jon shrugged. "Not pleasant, I'm sure. But that's not too bad. I've heard of two or three entire families sharing an apartment."

"My understanding is that there are laws to prevent that," Beatrice said.

"I don't know. It may be up to the landlords."

"Who is the landlord over there, again?" Beatrice sorted through her creaky brain. "Oh yes, I wanted to look this up. It's the Kraft Corporation and I wondered if it's Pamela's Krafts."

She rose from the table and walked to her desktop computer. Within a few moments, she had ascertained that yes, it was indeed the same company. She remembered that they were the ones who'd bought the Drummonds' property. The Drummonds and the Krafts? Something about that made her very uncomfortable. She couldn't quite say why. On a lark, she typed in the names and *Cumberland Creek*. The search engine brought up a number of things. As she read over the list, it hit her with a stone-cold thud.

She remembered. But Lawd, she was a child then. Could it be the Krafts still had it in for the Drummonds and that's why they were so determined to get hold of all the Drummonds' property? It couldn't be; surely she was an old fool with an overactive imagination.

"Edward Drummond Convicted of Murdering 16-year-old Jenny Kraft." Jon read aloud, coming up behind her. "Oh my goodness."

Next on the list of articles was an academic paper entitled "The Drummonds and the Krafts: How a Young Woman's Death Led to One Family's Downfall."

"Ridiculous," Beatrice said. "That happened so long ago. Besides, the Krafts have more money than God. No family fell, like what that article claims." She looked up at Jon, whose eyes were lit with curiosity. "But, here, let me think. The patriarch of the Kraft family owns some land over there by the Drummonds. Maybe the Drummonds bought that land from them. Maybe the Krafts did have a hard time at one point. I just don't know."

"It's unlike you to not know everybody's business," Jon said with a knowing look.

"We were never that close with the Krafts," Beatrice went on. "Daddy never liked them—and my first husband didn't care for them one way or the other. Said they were bootleggers. Said their moonshine had sent more than one person over the edge."

"There you have it," Jon said. "History is poking at us again."

"Around here, it feels like I'm living history," Beatrice said.

Chapter 39

"So, was Rosa on the list of people who bought that paper from Sheila?" DeeAnn asked.

"No," Annie said, sitting down at the crop table.

They were all sitting in Sheila's basement, like they did most Saturday nights. Karen had driven DeeAnn over and made certain she was situated before she left.

"Are you certain you don't want to stay?" Randy had asked her.

"I have plans," said Karen.

"A hot date," DeeAnn said.

"Yes, so hot that I'm coming back at eleven to pick up my mommy," Karen said and smiled. Her blond hair was swept up off her long neck.

Gosh, DeeAnn loved her daughter's nice, long neck—inherited from her father, Jacob, who was as tall and skinny as DeeAnn was round.

"See you later," Karen said and then walked out.

"Who is she seeing tonight?" Vera asked.

"I have no idea," DeeAnn responded. "I don't know if I even have a right to ask, you know? I mean she'll soon be twenty-six. She lives on her own. It's none of my business. But I am dying to know."

"Do you hear that, Mom?" Randy put in.

Paige appeared to not be paying attention, but she grunted.

Once the group had settled in—photos and paper pulled out and placed on the table—DeeAnn cleared her throat. "I do wish Karen would tell me who it is. I mean, is she deliberately keeping it secret?"

"Probably not," Randy said. "She probably doesn't know where the relationship's going and doesn't think it's worth telling you about."

"That's probably it," Annie said. "Did you tell your mom every time you went out on a date?"

DeeAnn blushed. "I didn't date that much. But yes, I did tell her."

"Me, too," Vera said. "I couldn't keep a secret from my mom if I tried." She stood up and headed for the counter in the small kitchenette. Sheila kept it well-stocked with food and drinks. "Can I get you something, DeeAnn?"

"Not right now, thanks."

"So what was the crop like last night?" Sheila asked, looking at Annie over the glasses perched on her nose.

"Interesting," Annie said.

"I loved it," Randy replied. "They played cool music, had great food, and they were a fun bunch of women."

"I agree," Annie said. "And I had a breakthrough with Rosa. I'm going to visit her tomorrow. She roomed with the Martelinos and seemed very willing to talk with me."

"Did you find out anything else about them while you were there?"

"They loved to scrapbook," Randy chimed in.

"I'm hoping to see some more of their scrapbooks tomorrow," Annie said, opening the Halloween book she was working on.

"I can't believe Halloween is next week," Vera said. "I still don't have Lizzie's costume finished."

"Are you taking her to the fire hall community party?" DeeAnn asked.

Vera nodded. "We'll trick or treat a little around the neighborhood, then we'll go to the fire hall. It sounds like fun. Prizes. Games. And it's safe. We won't have to go through all the candy and so on."

"These books will be cool once we get some photos for them," Annie said.

"I'm thinking of doing a seasonal book," Paige said. "You know, instead of organizing books by specific holidays, doing it by seasons."

"I like that idea," Cookie said.

"You always loved Halloween," Annie said to her.

Cookie nodded. "I think you're right. I'm so excited about Halloween. I can't wait to see Lizzie and the boys dressed up."

"Oh, it was more than that," Vera said a bit wistfully. "We were all involved one year in this ritual at my place. Do you remember that?"

Cookie's head tilted, her brows knitted.

"You called it a Samhain ritual. It was quite lovely," Vera said. "Very moving."

The room quieted.

"I have an idea," Annie said. "Let's do it again."

"The ritual?" Cookie asked.

Annie nodded. "I think I can remember enough to do it again. And maybe it will jog some memories, Cookie."

Cookie was biting her lip, but she looked up at Annie with a glimmer of hope in her eyes. "Maybe."

"Being a witch was so important to you," Vera said. "We thought you were half batty when you first started talking about it, but you taught me so much. Well, all of us. Maybe . . . I mean, since it meant so much to you . . . maybe the memories will come back."

"You know," Paige said. "I think about that night sometimes. It seemed like time stood still briefly."

"And then all hell broke loose," added Sheila.

Chapter 40

You're not kidding. All hell really did break loose, Annie thought, then took an orange jeweled embellishment and placed it next to her empty frame. The cops had interrupted their Samhain ritual, Cookie was carted off to jail for a murder she didn't commit, and then she escaped—or was taken. The next thing Annie knew, Bryant told her that he knew where Cookie was, but he couldn't tell her. Then Cookie had just shown up at their crop a few months ago. She said she had been struck by lightning and had lost much of her memory.

Cookie certainly did not seem like herself in many ways. But then again, many of the croppers had changed over the years. Sheila was now tending her sick daughter, along with the rest of her family, still running her scrapbook supply company and working as a designer. She appeared as if all the energy had been zapped from her. Paige, on the other hand, seemed more happy and content than Annie had ever seen her. Was that all because Randy had come back to town?

Annie looked at Vera, who was turning a page on her Halloween scrapbook. She was definitely happier than Annie had ever known her to be now that she was living with Eric in his house in the mountains. But she refused to marry him and that made Annie smile.

And then there was DeeAnn. Poor DeeAnn and her back. Her brows were knit together and she grimaced.

"Are you okay?" Annie said, reaching for a chip.

"The pain medicine just isn't enough," DeeAnn responded. "They won't give me what I need. I think I might find another doctor."

"Well, I would," Paige said. "If you're in pain and they won't give you anything for it."

"Land sakes," DeeAnn said. "I'm a grown woman. I'm also a big woman. Stands to reason I need more medicine than the average woman."

"That pain medicine is very addictive," Sheila said, looking out over her laptop. "They're probably doing the right thing."

"But she's in pain," Paige said, getting up with her empty glass from the table. "Can I get anybody anything?"

"More wine, please," DeeAnn said and handed over her glass.

"I don't think it would hurt for you to talk to your doctor," Annie said. "But it also wouldn't hurt to get a second opinion."

"True," Sheila said. "God knows, it took us awhile to find the right doctor for Donna. And we think we finally found the right medicine. She's been stable for a while. Though she still has moments . . . when she just sort of . . . stares off into space."

"Because of the medication?" Annie asked.

"It could be that or it could be a part of the way her epilepsy is manifesting. In any case, she can't go to school like that," said Sheila. "She can't be away from home. I'm afraid she may have to give up that scholarship." Her voice cracked. "The world was at her feet."

"But she is still alive," Cookie offered.

Sheila reached out and grabbed Cookie's hand. "Yes," she said in a hoarse voice.

"So what's going on with the Martelino cases?" Paige said after several moments. "What do we know?"

"Speaking of sad," Annie said. "The women we met last night were so sad."

"Angry, too," Randy said.

"Did they have any idea who may have killed the women?" Paige asked.

"If they did, they didn't tell us," Randy said.

"But they did tell us some important things. They were a part of a community—a community I never knew even existed right here in Cumberland Creek. They were loved—which makes it all the worse," Annie said.

"It doesn't seem like they ever dated," Randy said.

"Well, apparently they did have men interested in them from time to time, but nothing serious. So far, the only connection is that they are sisters that like to scrapbook," Annie said, pausing a few beats. "You know, Pamela had mentioned to me that she has a problem with her foreign workers disappearing. Just not showing up. Not giving a notice or anything. Have there been any cases like that since you've been there?" She looked at Randy.

"Yes. One woman disappeared shortly after I started working there. I remember her vividly because she spoke perfect English and was very friendly, then didn't show up one day. Pamela was livid."

"Pamela has a temper, it seems," Paige said.

"Oh boy, does she ever. Sometimes she behaves like a spoiled kid," Randy said. "I like her most of the time, but I've seen that temper flare. And it's not pretty."

"So we have no boyfriends and no leads," DeeAnn said. "But there is Hathaway Transatlantic. I'm with your mom on that," she said to Vera. "Something strange going on there."

"Oh I agree," Vera said. "But what? It's a huge company with offices all over the world. Yet, when Mama was looking for info, they couldn't find records of the Martelino sisters."

"Why would the company want to kill those girls anyway? That doesn't make sense," Annie said. "Why would two women living and working in Cumberland Creek warrant that kind of attention?"

The room silenced momentarily.

"It was probably some crazy guy who lives here," Vera said, breaking the quiet. "Someone like Leo Shirley. Yeah, maybe it was him." She could convince herself of any number of suspects. Any time there was a murder, Leo's name came up on her list of suspects. He was the town drunk and had a troubled existence. So far, though, he hadn't killed anyone.

Annie waved her off. "How many times have we tried to pin something on him? He's not good, that's for sure, but I don't think he has it in him these days to get up off the couch, let alone kill someone."

The women giggled around the table and murmured agreement with Annie.

"So there is still a killer out there. There's some lunatic running around Cumberland Creek." Vera said.

"I'm betting it has something to do with the gangs," Paige said.

Just then the door flew open. It was Karen.

DeeAnn looked at her watch. "Oh, you're a bit early."

"Just a bit," Karen said. "I thought you might need help gathering your stuff up."

"What I need is another pill," said DeeAnn.

"You can have one when you get home," Karen told her, starting to help gather her mother's things.

"How was the date?" Annie couldn't resist asking.

"Fine," Karen said. "Until he got a call and had to leave. Happens every time."

"What kind of call?" DeeAnn said, shoving her papers into her bag.

"I'm not sure. He doesn't talk about cop business too much."

The women all stilled.

"You're dating a cop?" Randy said.

"Yeah. It's not a big secret, is it?" she said, shoving a scrapbook into another one of DeeAnn's bags.

Nobody moved a muscle.

"Actually you haven't said anything about him to me. I didn't know he was a cop," DeeAnn managed to say.

But Annie could see the wheels in her head turning. Who could it be?

"Yeah," Karen said. "I'm dating Adam Bryant. You know him, right?"

Annie's heart nearly stopped beating as some of the women gasped. DeeAnn's face turned bright red and her mouth dropped. Annie had never seen her speechless before.

Chapter 41

By nine the next morning, half of Cumberland Creek knew what the other half already had known—that Karen and Adam were an item. And that included Beatrice, who was sitting at the breakfast table with Vera, Eric, Jon, and Elizabeth.

Bea didn't know quite what to say. When she thought of Karen, she immediately thought of her as a towheaded, barefoot child running around the neighborhood. Then there were her difficult teenage years. She had started using birth control; DeeAnn had found the pills. It was early, too early. How old had Karen been? Fifteen, maybe. She was involved in a drinking episode or two, as well. DeeAnn and Jacob had had a time with her.

Now, she was a grown woman. Almost twenty-six. A nurse. A responsible adult. What on earth would she see in an almost forty-year-old man? Beatrice couldn't imagine.

"Mother? Did you hear me?" Vera asked loudly.

"I'm not deaf. Of course, I heard you," Bea said and took a bite of her egg.

"What do you think?"

"I'm not sure what to think. I wonder if there aren't any young men her age. Why would she be interested in Bryant? He's too old for her. But then again, she's an adult. Maybe it will come to nothing."

Eric nodded. "That's what I said. I'm sure she'll get bored with him and move on."

"In the meantime, DeeAnn is mortified," Vera said after setting her coffee cup back down on the table.

"Why?" Jon spoke up. "Maybe they are in love. Love has no age limits."

Beatrice almost choked on her biscuit. Of course, Jon would say that—he was such a romantic.

"He's too old for her," Beatrice said again with finality. Jon shrugged.

"I'd be more concerned about his being a detective than his age, frankly," Eric said.

"That, too," Vera said. "I mean he's definitely in a dangerous line of work and I never felt like he was looking to raise a family."

"Well, he loves Lizzie," Beatrice said.

"Everybody loves me." Elizabeth grinned.

Vera laughed and reached over to tousle her red hair.

Beatrice did not want to think about her granddaughter growing up and meeting a man. It did not settle well in her mind. No, indeed. She hoped and prayed that her granddaughter would be spared too much heartbreak, but a bit was inevitable. Beatrice sighed. She decided to think about something else. At that moment, she decided to go and visit Emma Drummond again.

She couldn't get Emma off her mind. Had she

really killed her husband? If anybody had deserved it, he did. But still, to kill your husband?

Bea mulled all that over during her walk to Emma's abode. She remembered more about her friendship with Emma and was so glad she'd found her again, even if Emma was scared to leave her room.

When Beatrice walked into the lobby area of Mountain View Assisted Living, she was surprised to see Sheriff Bixby pass by her. He smiled and nodded. Such a nice man. *He must have someone here,* she mused.

She told the woman behind the reception desk she was there to see Emma and was told to go right down to her room.

Beatrice rapped at the door.

"Go away! I told you to go away!"

"Emma? It's me, Beatrice."

"Oh!" Emma said and opened the door. "I thought you were that arrogant Sheriff Bixby. If I were twenty years younger, I'd kick his ass."

Beatrice was taken aback. Emma had never spoken like that. She had always been quite timid.

"I'm sorry, Beatrice. I lost my temper. Please come in."

"I just saw him leaving," Bea said. "Was he bothering you?"

"I'd say," Emma said, reaching up to tuck a strand of gray hair back into her long ponytail. "He married my niece, you see."

"I didn't know that."

"They want to buy my house."

"Oh?"

"I love my house. I know I don't live there anymore, but it comforts me to know that Michelle does. I don't want him getting his greedy hands on it."

"Well, nobody says you have to sell," Bea said, sitting on the couch. "Are they pressuring you?"

Emma sighed deeply and punctuated it with something that sounded like a cry or a sob. "Threatening me is more like it."

Chapter 42

DeeAnn took her latest pain pill, then a bite of egg salad sandwich.

"Are you still not talking to me?" Karen asked.

"Why aren't you talking to your daughter?" Jacob asked as he walked into the kitchen.

DeeAnn's heart jumped and she bit her lip. Her daughter was dating Detective Bryant. How old was he anyway? Forty?

"She doesn't like the guy I'm dating, Dad," Karen said. "It's not like we're talking about marriage or anything. I like him. He's a lot of fun."

"What else is new?" Jacob said, reaching in the refrigerator for a beer. "Your mom never liked the boys you dated."

"I don't remember you being too thrilled with them, either," DeeAnn pointed out.

Jacob took a seat at the table. "So who is it this time?"

"Adam Bryant," said Karen.

Jacob set his bottle down and laughed. "I thought you said Adam Bryant. That's not what you said, is it?"

Karen's smile vanished. "Yep, that's him."

He shot DeeAnn a glare, as if it were her fault.

She glared right back. "What?"

"What is the big deal? What do you all know about him that I don't?" Karen asked.

"First, he's too old for you," Jacob told her. "Second, he's a cop."

"And third," DeeAnn finally spoke up "He's a sarcastic SOB. And I've suspected . . . I don't know. I've suspected that he's a womanizer."

"Womanizer? What is this? 1965?" Karen exclaimed.

"You know what I mean," DeeAnn said.

"What's wrong with being a cop?" Karen asked after a moment.

Her father spoke up. "Not a damn thing, except it's dangerous work. Do you want to be a cop's wife? Really?"

"Look, Mom, Dad, I'm not interested in getting married. We're just spending time together. I mean whatever time we can. Between his schedule and mine, we haven't seen that much of one another. I know he's older than me, but he's in great shape."

"Hold on right there. I don't want to hear about what great shape he's in." DeeAnn had lusted over the man from afar herself. She took a deep breath. Her daughter was grinning and DeeAnn's face heated. "Look, I know you're a grown woman. But you can't expect your dad and I to not voice our opinions about the men you date. We're your parents. It goes with the territory."

Karen had grown into a beautiful woman. How had DeeAnn not seen that? It was hard to see your children clearly, even when they were grown. Of course, Adam Bryant would find her attractive. She was long and lean like her dad, with long, blond hair, her mom's blue eyes, and a smile that would melt any man's heart. She was a woman who glowed with happiness, as well. And she deserved to be happy after all her struggles as a teen. But Adam Bryant?

"I hear you, Mom. And I'll think over everything you both have said to me," Karen stood, then leaned over and kissed her parents' foreheads. "I better get to work."

It almost made DeeAnn cry. Damn, she wanted to be angry, shake her fists at Karen, but she couldn't. She would have to bite her tongue about Adam—for the most part.

After Karen left, DeeAnn and Jacob sat quietly. He finished his beer and then stood up with a defiance that suddenly scared her.

"Jacob," she said with a tremor in her voice. "Please sit down."

"I'm going to find Bryant," he said. Stern. Serious.

A shot of panic zipped through DeeAnn. Jacob was not an easily disturbed man. In fact, he was easygoing. But when he got angry, he was serious.

"Now hold on," she said, standing a bit too quickly and becoming dizzy. Those pills! She landed hard back in her chair.

"DeeAnn?" he said, grabbing onto her. "What the hell just happened?"

"Just a little dizzy," she said. "Maybe I need a different kind of pain pill. These make me so lightheaded."

"We'll talk to the doctor about that tomorrow," Jacob said, crouching down beside her.

DeeAnn nodded her head. "And what about you?

You're going to kick Bryant's ass? I don't think that's what would happen. He's a cop. In great shape. Has a gun. Please."

"Nah." Jacob grinned. "Not that I haven't thought about coldcocking him from time to time. Especially now. But I would like to talk to him."

DeeAnn reached out and held his hand. The hand of the man she loved. The man she shared her life with. "Please don't do that." She took a deep breath. "We have to trust Karen."

His eyes met hers and then he looked away. "Okay, DeeAnn. For now."

Chapter 43

"I don't like this place," Randy said as Annie pulled into the parking lot of the Riverside Apartments.

"I don't either. That's why I asked you to come along."

"Your new best gay friend?" Randy smiled.

"Well, you are a man."

"That I am," he said and puffed his chest out.

"Rosa seemed to really like you," Annie said, shutting off the engine. Noting a group of guys at the other side of the parking lot, she and Randy shared a look.

"Ignore them." She opened her car door. As they disembarked from the car, she noticed Rosa walking across the parking lot. She must have been waiting for them. *Odd.*

"Hey," Rosa said. "I didn't want you guys to get freaked out by the gang."

"Gang?" Randy said.

She laughed. "Not really. They're just a bunch of

middle-aged losers that hang out in the parking lot because they don't have anything better to do."

Rosa was short and built like a spark plug. She gave off a "don't mess with me" vibe that Annie quite liked.

The parking lot was a mishmash of vehicles. Most of them were well used. There were a couple of motorcycles and many trucks, including one new one that was kitted-out, big and shiny.

Why would anybody need a truck that big? marveled Annie.

Randy seemed to like it. "I love trucks. This is a beaut."

"Beaut?" Annie teased.

"I'm in Virginia now," he said and winked at her.

They followed Rosa up two flights of stairs to her apartment.

"Please come in," she said. "What would you like to drink? A soft drink? Juice? How about coffee?"

"Coffee sounds good," Annie said and Randy nodded.

After they were settled on the worn, yet comfortable, sofa, Rosa brought in the coffee and a plate of cookies.

"Thank you. So this is where the Martelino sisters lived," Annie said, looking around.

"Yes," Rosa said. "We all lived here together." The place was small, but neat and orderly. There was a jumble of décor, as one would expect to find with several adults living in the same quarters.

"I'll be interviewing a new roommate later today. She's passed the Mendez eye," Rosa said.

"About that Mendez guy . . ." Annie said. "He threatened me."

"I'm not surprised," Rosa said. "He feels very protective of us."

"What? Why?"

"He's more than a landlord for many of us. He's a sponsor. He keeps a close eye on us."

"Is he married?" Randy asked.

"Yes," replied Rosa. "Has three kids. His wife keeps to herself. He's very old-school Latino, if you know what I mean. We tried to get her involved in scrapbooking, but no dice. She came to our crop once and he had a fit. He told her it was a waste of time. Of course, we knew that he wants all of her attention. Wants her at home with him to cook and clean." She rolled her eyes.

"So he doesn't like scrapbooking?" Annie asked.

"No," Rosa responded. "None of our men like it. At least none of the ones here. They make fun of us. Think we should be out at the bars trying to get laid, I guess. Or trying to get a husband."

"That's interesting," Annie said, remembering the scrapbooking pages found on the bodies of the sisters, the craft knife sticking up from the neck of Marina, and the ribbon wrapped around Esmeralda. Someone definitely did not like them scrapbooking.

"Some people have strange feelings about scrapbooking. It's odd to me that someone would care that much about how someone else spends their time," Rosa said. "But even Marina's boss . . . What's her name? . . . Pamela. She doesn't like scrapbooking."

"Really?" Annie said. "I had no idea."

"Interesting," Randy said.

"Tell me about the sisters," Annie said after a moment. She glanced over at the statue of Mary in the corner, with dried flowers circled around it. Rosary beads with a cross hung over the statue.

"Aye," Rosa said with a sigh. "I miss them. And I am so frightened. I had the locks all changed. They were nice women. Clean. Polite. Funny."

"When you say frightened"—Annie leaned in closer to her—"are you afraid that whoever killed them will come after you?"

"Yes. I don't know why someone would want to kill them. But they lived here. You know? Maybe whoever killed Marina and Esmeralda will want to kill me, too." Rosa shrugged and bit her lip.

"Have you seen anybody strange hanging around?" Randy asked.

"No, just the same old crew. The middle-aged guys in the parking lot."

"I heard there were gangs over here," Annie said. "It's hard to believe."

Rosa swallowed her cookie. "Who told you that?" Her tone was serious.

"The police," Annie said.

"Well, yes, there was a gang," Rosa said. "But I don't think there's one anymore. I think those old guys out there have taken care of it."

"What do you mean?" Randy asked.

"They consider themselves the watchers. They are . . . how do you say? . . . vigilantes. They've scared away the gangs as far as I know."

"Interesting," Annie said and grinned. "Hell hath no fury like a bunch of middle-aged guys?"

"Yes," Rosa said. "I know I called them losers, but several of them have families and didn't like the way things were going. So they took matters into their own hands."

"Sounds dangerous," Randy said.

Rosa nodded.

"You know, we tried to reach out to the Martelino family," Annie said, trying to steer the conversation back to them. "The guy from Hathaway said they were orphans. So sad."

"What? They weren't orphans," said Rosa. "He must have them confused with one of his other clients. They have a mother and a father and a brother."

Annie's heart started to race. "Where are they?"

"Unfortunately, they are in prison."

"Prison? All of them?" Annie asked.

Rosa nodded. "I think it's in Kansas."

Randy started to cough. Was he choking on his coffee? He patted his chest.

"Are you okay?" Annie asked.

He nodded, calming down, but his face was still red.

Randy may not be the best guy to take on these interviews, thought Annie. She turned back to Rosa. "Kansas?"

"They all came to the United States together. The girls came here. Their parents and their brother went to Kansas. I don't know what happened, but they ended up in prison."

"Do the police know this?" Annie asked, fuming.

"Of course," Rosa said. "I told them everything I know."

"We've been trying to reach the family to send our condolences."

"I can give you their information," said Rosa. "Why don't you come into their room with me? I'll find the address for you."

Could it be that easy? After all this? thought Annie.

When Annie walked into the bedroom, she tried to hold back a shiver. It was a happy room, with walls painted a soft yellow and bright decorations. A bookcase stocked with books stood in one corner. Another one held scrapbooks. A vanity table had makeup and a red and purple floral scarf flung across the top of it.

Those young women were alive a few short weeks ago, thought Annie. *They hadn't expected to meet their end, to have their lives stolen at such a young age.*

"Annie?" Randy said.

"Oh, let me get you a tissue," Rosa said, noticing Annie's tears.

What's wrong with me, thought Annie. *I'm a reporter! How unprofessional to cry like this.* But there was no point trying to stop. Only part of her was a reporter. She was a woman, a mother, a wife, a friend, a human. As she stood in the room that once belonged to the two sisters, filled with remnants of their young lives, sadness overwhelmed her.

Chapter 44

"So the police confirmed everything," Beatrice said to Annie the following day.

Annie nodded. It was Monday and she had stopped by Beatrice's house to pick up some fabric for Ben's Halloween costume. Beatrice had an attic full of fabric and old costumes. "Sheriff Bixby apologized for not telling me what he'd found out about the Martelino family. He said he'd only just recently found out himself. Evidently, they're all in prison for running drugs." *Could it be true? It seems so cliché.*

"I wonder if they knew they were running drugs," Jon said. "I just read an article somewhere about how some of these families are set up."

"By who?" Beatrice said.

Jon shrugged. "Anybody who knows their vulnerabilities or someone who has some kind of power over them."

"I don't know what their lives were like in Kansas," Annie said, "but Hathaway definitely had power over them. And he out and out lied to us. I'm betting he has something to do with all of this."

Beatrice's jaw set. "I didn't like the man. I don't think he's about helping people. He exploits them."

"That would appear to be the case," Annie said. "This may be a bigger story than the murder of two sisters. I have some work to do."

"Thanks for giving us the addresses," Beatrice said. "We can at least send them cards in prison, if nothing else. I've been meaning to ask you—what was the crop like at the Drummond house?"

"It was lovely. The house is in great shape on the inside."

"Yes, I noticed that myself. I told Emma that."

"Emma?"

"She's the woman who actually owns the place."

"She doesn't live there?"

"No, she lives at Mountain View Assisted Living. She's agoraphobic, for one thing. Evidently her daughter who lives at the place has the same problem."

"She wasn't at the crop. Just the woman who works for her and her friends."

"Emma told me the most troubling thing," Beatrice said. "She told me the sheriff had visited her and wanted to buy her place."

"That's interesting, but not necessarily troubling," Annie said.

"Well, maybe she was mistaken, but I don't think so. She said he threatened her," Beatrice said.

"What? Surely not," Jon said.

Beatrice shrugged. "She's not quite right in the head, I'll give you that. She's had a bit of a rough life. But I think basically she's still got it together. I don't know why she'd think he was threatening her if he wasn't."

"Sheriff Bixby seems like a decent sort," Annie said. "He's much easier to deal with than Bryant."

"Ain't that the truth," Beatrice said.

"Still," Annie said with a tilt of her head. Her brows knit.

Beatrice had come to know and love that look. Annie was thinking and you could almost see her brain work.

"I've known a lot of people who seemed nice at first. Why would he threaten Emma Drummond?"

"You know, she didn't really go into specifics and I didn't push her. But that property is the only piece of land left to what was once a vast chunk of land— all owned by her family and the Drummonds. They probably want to build more apartments or something," Beatrice said.

"But why would Sheriff Bixby care about that?"

"He's married to Emma's niece. Maybe she wants the land. I don't know. It's very odd."

Annie sat back in her chair and smiled. "This community is amazing. I swear almost everybody here is related or almost related."

"Huh!" Beatrice said. "It used to be even more like that. But with all the new people moving in, I'm not so sure who is who anymore."

"New people like me?" Jon spoke up and grinned.

"Yes. Who are you anyway?" Beatrice said with a giggle.

Later on, Beatrice mulled over the conversation. Emma Drummond may not be all together, but she wasn't suffering from dementia or anything like that. Agoraphobia was different. It was more of a disorder than a mental illness—at least that was Beatrice's understanding of it. But she couldn't understand why Emma couldn't be treated with some kind of medicine and lead a normal life.

Maybe next time she visited, she'd find out.

Beatrice found herself looking forward to her next visit with Emma. It was comforting to have a woman around who was her age and still had it halfway together. At the same time, it brought up unresolved feelings she'd had years ago about Emma's husband Paul. In those days, not much was known about domestic abuse and most people turned a blind eye to it. In some parts, among some social classes, it was still expected that some men would occasionally beat their wives. Beatrice couldn't abide it, even then. And she had opened her big mouth, which sent Emma as far away from her as possible.

Yet, that might be the reason Emma was so welcoming with Beatrice these days. Had Emma really killed Paul? How would Bea ever know for sure?

Chapter 45

"So, you've been taking the pills twice a day?" Dr. Flathers asked DeeAnn.

Jacob was standing closely beside her.

"I think so, though I may have taken more when it didn't seem like the pain was going away," DeeAnn said. She hated being in the doctor's office.

"I think you did take more, or you'd still have them," Dr. Flathers told her. "I'm only going to authorize this prescription for another week. If I have to, I'll send someone to your house to give you only two a day."

"For God's sake," DeeAnn said. "What is the big deal? I thought the pills were supposed to take away my pain. Why shouldn't I take another when one isn't working?"

"These pills are very addictive," Dr. Flathers said.

"But I'm a big woman," she replied.

The doctor took his glasses off and looked her in the eye. "I've taken that into consideration and given you the proper dosage. And if you hadn't noticed, you've actually lost some weight since you hurt your back. Now, if you're unhappy, you are welcome to get another medical opinion."

DeeAnn *had* lost weight. All of her pants were baggy. She'd been in too much pain to shop for new ones.

"But you've been our doctor for twenty years," Jacob said.

"I can still be your doctor and you can still get a second opinion. If you wish. But I would not be a good doctor if I allowed DeeAnn to abuse these pills," said Dr. Flathers.

"Abuse!" DeeAnn cried. "I'm not abusing them. I'm in pain. Constantly."

"Constantly?" Dr. Flathers asked, raising an eyebrow. "If that's the case, let's get another series of X-rays. Maybe there's something we missed."

"Okay," Jacob said. "Let's do that. Is there another pain medication we can give her?"

"Jacob!" DeeAnn hissed. "I like those."

"I can see that," Jacob said after a pause.

"There are others we can try, but anything in this group of painkillers will have the same addictive quality. This is the most effective kind of painkiller on the market. After a few more weeks, I'd like to see you go down to one a day," Dr. Flathers said. "But first, let's get more X-rays."

"Really?" DeeAnn said. "Do you know how uncomfortable and painful that's going to be?"

"Is she always this big of a pain in the ass?" DeeAnn heard a voice say from the hallway. In walked her daughter Tracy, who was supposed to be in Texas . . . in school.

"What are you doing here?" DeeAnn asked. Her spikes of mother's intuition were raised.

"You're a sight for sore eyes," Jacob said as his daughter hugged him.

"What's going on here? Did they call you in for reinforcement?" DeeAnn sat with her arms crossed.

"Not exactly, Mom," Tracy said, leaning over and kissing her. "I finished a couple finals and wanted to see you. That's all."

"All the way from Texas? I wasn't born yesterday," DeeAnn said, wondering who had set this up.

"No, indeed," Dr. Flathers said. "Here's the prescription. Two a day. Now I'll have my nurse make an X-ray appointment for you. Are you free today?"

DeeAnn snorted.

Jacob shifted his weight. "I really should be going back to work."

"I'm here," Tracy said. "I'll take you to get X-rayed and get your prescription filled. We can have a nice visit."

DeeAnn loved Tracy with all of her heart—and then some—but she had the bedside manner of a drill sergeant. DeeAnn was not looking forward to her being around when she didn't have the mettle to defend herself.

"Sounds good to me," Jacob said and kissed first Tracy, then DeeAnn. "Be a good patient."

"Humph," DeeAnn said, reaching for her cane. She hated the thing. It made her look old. But it helped manage the pain—a bit. "Might as well get this over with."

After her X-rays, during which the technicians managed to get her in some of the most god-awful and uncomfortable positions, Tracy drove her to the pharmacy, then home.

"Was that Cookie walking along the street?" Tracy asked her.

"Yes, that's just about the only thing she does now. She walks and walks. Sometimes she shows up at the strangest times."

"So she's no better, huh?"

DeeAnn shook her head. "I have to wonder if she'll ever get better. Or if she even wants to. She seems to really not like the doctor she's working with now. He follows her around and she says he's a pain. I don't think she wants to remember."

"Why wouldn't she?"

"I don't know, honey. I think there's something awful in her past she doesn't want to face." DeeAnn sighed.

"What could be more awful than being accused of murder, being arrested, then kidnapped and struck by lightning?" Tracy wondered.

"There's plenty that could be worse than that," DeeAnn said, thinking about the Martelino sisters. "Plenty."

Chapter 46

Sometimes Internet research wasn't enough. But today, there was hope.

A few years back, Hathaway Transatlantic had been investigated for human trafficking. Newspaper articles and research papers had been published on the net. Annie read and read, gobsmacked by the fact that Hathaway was still in business, skirting around the law with high-paid lawyers, no doubt. She read an article from a newspaper in Texas.

> As federal investigators raided the brick building in Houston, similar raids were happening at businesses in at least ten other cities in Texas and Louisiana.
>
> "Finger after finger was pointing to Hathaway *Transatlantic*," said US Attorney Chris Carpenter.
>
> Hathaway Transatlantic is an international employment referral business operating out of Wichita. Prosecutors say they filed charges after years of extensive investigation.

"There were court-ordered wiretaps, undercover projects, and long term physical surveillance," Carpenter said.

Authorities were able to arrest 23 of the 32 people accused of recruiting, transporting, and housing undocumented Spanish speaking immigrants who were already in the United States illegally and giving them low paying jobs at restaurants.

"In essence, they ran a takeout and delivery service," said Agent Smithers. "Not for food but rather for people. People they called 'amigos' who were in this country illegally."

Federal agents say the recruiters made millions off those "amigos" by collecting finders fees from greedy restaurant owners and managers looking for cheap labor. And while the workers broke laws to get into the United States, "it is also fair to say that they were exploited by the defendants," Smithers said.

Hathaway spokesperson Gary Laskowski says that with such a huge, multifaceted operation, it's difficult to police all of their operations, but in the future the company will endeavor to do more policing. Laskowski claims, however, that the management of the company did not know about these middleman operations.

Hmm. Of course not, Annie thought with a smirk. Almost all of the clippings she read were the same kind of story. The middlemen were the ones on the take. The company needed to police more. They paid fines and moved on. But one thing that never

came up was sex trafficking. Annie was at least
pleased about that.

Every incident mentioned involved restaurants,
which led her squarely back to Pamela. *Pamela, what
have you gotten yourself into?*

Annie pulled up the public records from the
county where the Pie Palace was located. Owners of
the property were listed as Pamela and Evan Kraft.
No real surprise there. And it didn't appear anything was unusual with the permits or plans.

Annie keyed PAMELA KRAFT into Google. The first
page was nothing more than PR pieces about
the restaurant, her Web site updates, and so on. The
second page listed some genealogy sites. *What the
heck?* Annie clicked one. Turns out Pamela was really
into genealogy. Well, that wasn't unusual. Especially
for someone who appeared to be enamored with
the past as Pamela was. Annie didn't get the whole
"rockabilly lifestyle" thing, but to each his or her own.

Annie scrolled through the Kraft family tree. *Interesting.* There was a Bixby connection. Looked like
Pamela's second cousin was Sheriff Bixby, who in
turn was married to a Drummond. That much she
already knew from Beatrice. Pings of her reporter's
intuition zoomed through her. *What is going on here?
Is this all just a coincidence that all of these folks are related? And are all involved somehow with the Martelinos?
Or not?*

Beatrice had said that Sheriff Bixby threatened
Emma Drummond. Surely that was a misunder-
standing. The woman was elderly and agoraphobic.
Perhaps he frightened her without meaning to.

But perhaps not.

Perhaps he wasn't as pleasant as he seemed.

Had Annie been taken in by a smiling sheriff? In some ways, Bryant was actually easier to deal with—at least he was honest, even if he was a sarcastic grump. But Sheriff Bixby? Always smiling, polite, and friendly. She should have suspected him from the beginning—not necessarily of committing murders, but of knowing more than what he'd been telling. Yes, she was certain of it, the more she mulled things over.

Annie planned her next steps—talk to Pamela again, talk to the sheriff, then talk with Bryant.

In the meantime, she had several of the Martelino sisters' scrapbooks to look through. Vera and Sheila were coming over tomorrow to help her sort through them. Maybe, just maybe, something in those books would point them to who killed the young women.

Annie didn't have the heart to sort through the scrapbooks alone. Not this time.

Chapter 47

It turned out that Mountain View Assisted Living actually did have a mountain view. Emma's room had one of the prettiest views Beatrice had ever seen from a window. Of course, the fact that it was fall helped. Fall in Cumberland Creek was a colorful, amazing experience. As Emma poured tea, Beatrice looked out the window at the crimsons, golds, reds, and bright, fiery oranges dotting the mountains.

As far as she could tell, her old friend still had her wits about her.

"Why haven't they given you medicine to deal with the fear of leaving your room?" Beatrice asked.

"I'm allergic," Emma said. "They've yet to find a medicine I don't react to."

Beatrice frowned. "That's too bad. I'd love to have you over to dinner sometime."

"Not possible," Emma said with finality. "You don't mind coming to see me, do you? This place isn't so bad." She gestured with her arm at her surroundings.

"Your place is lovely. Do you get many visitors?"

"I do. I have some family around. And several of the residents here come and visit with me."

"I wanted to ask you about Sheriff Bixby," Beatrice said and then took a sip of tea. *Why not get on with it*, she told herself. She didn't want to upset Emma, but she needed to know.

Emma placed her teacup back in her saucer. It was beautiful, delicate china, the kind that Bea hadn't seen in years. Pink roses had always brought Emma to mind. Nobody drank tea with beautiful china anymore.

"What about him?" asked Emma.

"Was he really threatening you, dear?"

"Oh, he wants to buy my house and I told him I'm not interested in selling."

"But, to threaten you? That takes balls."

"The thing is, the property is worth more than the house. I know that. He'd level the house and build something new. Well, he wouldn't build it himself. He'd sell it to that damned Kraft family and they'd build more apartments or a Walmart or something. My granddaddy built that house with his own two hands. And I'll be damned if I give it up."

"How did he threaten you?" Beatrice persisted.

"He said if I didn't sell willingly, he'd force me and that he's not beyond blackmail or coercion. That scared me because my Michelle is still living in the house and I don't want anything to happen to her. I'm not afraid of him. What can he do to me while I'm in here?" Emma looked out the window, the sunlight reflecting in her blue eyes.

"But he's an officer of the law," Beatrice said. "Surely he'd not do anything illegal?"

"Humph. I never liked those Bixbys. Sometimes

you give a redneck an education and all you have is an educated redneck. Bone deep, I'd say. I didn't like it when Chelsea married him. I still don't like it. But she's my niece, not my daughter, so what could I say?"

"Not much you can say, even if she was your daughter. Vera married Bill and I never really liked him. Well, that's not true. A few months in, when he lived with me I kind of liked him. But then, it just didn't work out between them," Beatrice said.

All in all, it was a good visit. Beatrice came to find out more about Sheriff Bixby and decided then and there that she'd pay the man a visit and tell him to back off her friend.

Back home, she told Jon what she'd learned and what she planned to do.

"Listen, Beatrice, he's a police officer. I don't think it's a good idea for you to go storming into his office," Jon said.

"He's still a person. How dare he threaten Emma? And, by the way, I wouldn't storm. I would sashay, of course."

Jon rolled his eyes. "I know you better than that. And I don't want to have to bail you out of jail."

"Okay. I promise I won't go storming into his office. But if I see him—"

Jon held up his hand in his dramatic French way as if to stop her from finishing the thought. "I do not want to know."

Bea shrugged. She could live with that. What the man didn't know wouldn't kill him.

Chapter 48

DeeAnn's kitchen table was covered in the Martelino sisters' scrapbooks. Some were haphazardly stacked, some wide open, and some were closed. But the Cumberland Creek scrapbookers were all enthralled. It was a reminder of one of the unspoken reasons they themselves scrapbooked—so that they left behind a neat and tidy pictorial record of their lives. Or at least the lives that they wanted others to know about.

They searched through the books for something—anything—that might be a clue. Not just to understand the cases, but to understand the young women and what brought them to the US. Each one of the sisters had a book focused on her childhood. A few pictures, some drawings, and journaling. All written in scribbled Spanish, which even Annie couldn't read.

But the last books they had been working on had more photos. Photos of friends, of one another, of the town, Christmas celebrations, picnics, and so on.

"They seem to go on a lot of picnics," Paige re-marked.

DeeAnn set a plate of still-warm brownies in the center of the table. Each woman reached for one. There was nothing like a warm brownie.

"They liked being outside, that much is clear," Sheila said with her mouth half full.

"Oh my GAWD, these brownies are good!" said Annie. "But back to the sisters—think about it. It must be so different here from where they grew up. They were probably in awe of the mountains and the seasons."

"I imagine," agreed DeeAnn, turning the page on the scrapbook she was looking over. Esmeralda had a good eye for color and placement of her photos.

"I just don't see anything here," Sheila said, shutting the book she had been looking over and reaching for another brownie.

DeeAnn turned the page again. It wasn't falling back into place and was a bit wavy. Something was off in the book. "Wait. This is strange."

"What?" Annie said, leaning over toward her.

DeeAnn flipped the page again. "I think a page is missing here."

"Let me see. You're right. Look." Sheila ran her finger along the inside of the book where the pages came together. "Someone ripped the page out."

"Maybe it's the page that the police found on her?" Annie wondered.

"Even if it is, what does that tell us?" Paige asked.

The women sat in silence for a few minutes in DeeAnn's kitchen, decorated in bright red straw-berry patterns—the curtains, the tablecloth, pot holders, and dish towels. Even her tea kettle had strawberries on it.

"I wonder if we can find where the missing page is in Marina's book," Sheila said.

"I think we have one more of her books over here," Paige said, reaching for the book in question and sliding it into the center of the table.

Jacob walked into the kitchen. "Hello, ladies."

Halfhearted hellos came from the circle of women around the table. They were engrossed in searching for clues.

Jacob went over to DeeAnn and kissed her. "I'm going to the store. You need anything?"

"No thanks," DeeAnn said, only half paying attention to him. They were on to something. She could feel it. Jacob's presence was disturbing the energy in the room and she wanted him to leave.

He left and it was as if the room sighed in relief.

"Here," Paige said. "Here's where the missing page is."

"Aha," Annie said, lifting the other books from the table and setting them on the floor. She set both books open to where the pages were missing. Pages before and after were about a hike or picnic, which was exactly what was on the pages found on their bodies.

"There must be something about this day," Annie said.

"We need to find out more about it. When was it? Who was there? What significance did it have in their lives?" said Vera.

"But why?" Sheila said. "How will that help?"

"Think about it, Sheila," Paige said.

"Oh don't make me think!" Sheila tittered. "That's the last thing I want to do!"

"Do you think a killer would leave clues so blatantly like that?" DeeAnn questioned.

"It wasn't really blatant," Annie said. "I mean, the police looked for fingerprints and stuff on the actual pages, but they didn't look in their scrapbooks. Why would they?"

"Besides, some killers like to leave clues. Deep down, they really want to get caught. It's a cry for help," Vera said.

All of the women looked at her. It was an odd thing to hear coming out of her mouth.

She frowned. "What? Don't you watch *CSI?*"

"What's that?" Paige asked.

"It's a TV show," Vera said.

"Oh, well you know how I feel about TV," Paige said.

"So all we need to do is figure out what happened on this day. Reconstruct it and it might lead us to the killer before he kills again," Vera said.

"Exactly," Annie replied. "First order of business is to get copies of the pages from the police. Then I'll talk to Rosa. Maybe she was there that day."

"I have a better idea," DeeAnn said. "Why don't you take the copies with you on Friday night. You're going to their crop, right?"

"Yes, but I'm not sure I want to wait until then. I feel a sense of urgency about this." Annie said. "Two women have been killed. We're not sure how many others there could be, given that employees have been disappearing from the Pie Palace for years, evidently. We don't know if they were all linked, but we know at least two were."

"Should we take the books to Bryant and tell him our theory?" Paige asked.

The mention of Bryant's name made DeeAnn's face redden. She still could not believe that Karen was dating him.

Annie didn't notice DeeAnn's embarrassment as she was deep in thought. "I think we should keep this all to ourselves for now, until we find something more substantial. Really, at this point, it's all conjecture."

The slight quiver in her voice led DeeAnn to believe it was more than that. She felt it in her bones that reconstructing the scrapbooked day was going to lead them straight to the killer.

Chapter 49

Armed with the scrapbooks that had pages torn out of them, Annie headed over to Rosa's apartment. She had called ahead and Rosa had said to please come.

Annie pulled into the parking lot. The same group of men were standing around a motorcycle. When they looked over at her, she remembered what Rosa had said about them being "middle-aged losers that hang out in the parking lot because they don't have anything better to do." She smiled at them and kind of waved. Most of them nodded their heads and smiled back. Annie almost laughed when she thought of how frightened she was the first time she had seen them standing there.

"Hey, Annie," Rosa said when she opened her door. "Please come in."

After they sat down and were situated at the kitchen table, Annie opened the scrapbooks. "We think this is where the pages were torn out."

"It certainly looks that way," Rosa agreed.

"Can you tell me anything about this day? It appears to be outside, some kind of gathering?"

"Humph," Rosa said, looking over the pictures. "I think this is the Pie Palace's annual employee picnic."

"Interesting. I didn't know they had one, but it seems like a nice thing to do."

"They say Pamela is great to work for."

Annie sifted through her thoughts. *Great to work for, but has a temper.* "Is it only employees that go to this picnic?"

"And their families," Rosa replied. "It's a big thing."

"It seems so simple."

"What does?"

"Our killer left scrapbook pages on the sisters. Both about the same day, the same event. He or she must have been there, don't you think? Any ideas?"

Rosa shook her head. "No, but I wish I did." But she seemed shaken.

"Are you sure?" Annie questioned.

Rosa bit her lip. "I'm sure it's nothing. . . ."

"If I had a dime for every time I've said that . . ." Annie smiled.

"It's just that Jorge creeps me out. I know he's Irina's nephew. But I don't know. The way he's always hanging around. There's something about him."

"Would he have been there that day?" Annie said.

Rosa nodded. "Maybe. He works at the Pie Palace. And he likes to take pictures. Maybe he even took the pictures on those pages."

A shiver traveled the length of Annie's spine. Was Jorge capable of murder? If he was, what was it about the sisters or their scrapbooks, that had set him off? She shook off her thoughts. "Irina said he was harmless."

"Who knows? He just creeps me out. I know that Marina did not like him. We talked about it. He asked her out once."

"He asked her out?" Annie's heart nearly leaped out of her chest.

"He sure did. He really liked her. She told him no. He tried for a while, but not very long. A few weeks maybe. Then Pamela stepped in and told him employees weren't allowed to date each other."

Pamela! Annie had thought all along that she knew more than she was telling. It was time for another visit.

"Thanks, Rosa. You've been very helpful," Annie said, glancing at her watch. It was getting late; the boys would be home soon. She needed to get home.

After saying good-bye, Annie almost ran into Bryant on the stairs. He was heading up as she was going down.

"Annie, what are you doing here?"

"Working on a story," she told him, clutching the scrapbooks to her chest.

"What have you got there?" he said, a crooked smirk forming.

"Scrapbooks, Adam," she said with an edge.

"What's going on?"

"I could ask you the same thing. What are you doing here?"

"Business."

"Police business?"

"Of course. Now let me see those scrapbooks."

Annie shrugged and handed him the books.

He stood on the stairs and flipped through the books. "What am I missing here?"

Annie's stomach flip-flopped. She'd never withheld information from the police before. She wasn't that kind of reporter; she was always cooperative. And they reciprocated. But this was Adam Bryant. Sarcastic. Usually not helpful. The man she had almost had an affair with. And he was dating twenty five-year-old Karen Fields.

"Annie?" Bryant said. "Earth to Annie."

"There's missing pages in those books," she blurted out. "We think the pages you and Bixby have came from these books."

"You just found that out?"

She nodded.

"And you were coming to find me, right? To tell me everything, right? Because you wouldn't keep this to yourself," he said in a patronizing tone.

"No," she said and took a deep breath. "I was on my way home. My boys will be home soon. I was still thinking things over."

"What things? What have you found out?"

"The pictures on those pages you have were taken at the Pie Palace's employee picnic."

"And?"

"Seems like your killer might have been there."

"You think it's that simple?" He handed the books back to her.

"Here's what I think. There's nothing like a disturbed man who has been recently spurned," Annie said.

Their eyes met, and then Bryant guffawed. "Women," he said and continued walking up the steps, leaving Annie and her scrapbooks behind.

Chapter 50

Vera had been stopping by to see Bea every morning after she dropped Elizabeth off at pre-school. Beatrice liked sitting with her grown, happy daughter, sharing coffee and muffins or something. Anything. It seemed as if they had reached a new level in their relationship. Vera was more mature and happier than Bea had ever seen her.

Vera had brought some of her homemade chocolate to sample. When Bea took a bite and let the chocolate wallow around on her tongue a bit, she was transported. *Lawd, I'm in heaven.*

Vera frowned. "What's wrong, Mama?"

"That's the best chocolate I've ever had in my life," Bea said in a hushed tone.

Vera waved her off, then tilted her head. "Well, the ingredients I used are some of the finest. It's single original dark chocolate from Ecuador. And the spices are all fresh and organic."

"It's extraordinary," Bea said. "I think you should take DeeAnn up on her offer. Have a side business selling chocolate."

Vera sat up straighter in her chair. "But I'm a dancer, Mama. I'm not a chocolatier."

"There's no reason you can't be both," Bea said. So much of her daughter's identity was wrapped up in dancing. Had Bea ever felt that way about the quantum physics that was her careeer? Oh yes, she had. How about that? She shared something in common with Vera. Bea's obsession with physics was the same as Vera's preoccupation with dancing—and maybe chocolate, as well.

"I suppose you're right. And maybe I could make a little more money with the chocolate. The studio is still struggling," Vera said.

"Why are you worried 'bout money? You're living with a man who has plenty."

"That's him, Mama. That's his money. To tell you the truth, it makes me feel odd sometimes, living in that gorgeous house, surrounded by luxury when I'm not sure if I can pay the rent on my studio."

Beatrice mulled that over. "I guess that would be strange."

"Well," Vera said, standing up. "I better get going. I've got some little dancers coming in this morning. What are you going to do today?"

"I'm not sure," Beatrice said.

Vera would not like the idea of her mother going to visit Sheriff Bixby on her own. She tended to be a little overprotective, as well as overly concerned with what other people thought. Beatrice, on the other hand, didn't give a rat's ass.

As soon as Vera left, Bea drove over to see Sheriff Bixby. She sifted through what she thought he could offer her as to why he threatened Emma. None of it would hold water as far as she was concerned. Who did he think he was?

The sheriff's building was well-kept, clean, and official looking. When Bea walked in, she noticed a lovely bouquet of flowers on the receptionist's desk. The woman behind the desk looked up and greeted her. It was all very nice and very different from the Cumberland Creek police station.

"Please have a seat, Ms. Matthews," the receptionist said pleasantly.

Beatrice sat down and halfheartedly browsed through a magazine until the receptionist said, "Ms. Matthews, the sheriff will see you now."

"Thank you," Bea said and followed the young, well-dressed woman through the door and down a hallway.

Sheriff Bixby was seated behind his desk when they entered the room. He stood and offered his hand to Beatrice. She shook it and they smiled at one another very pleasantly.

"Please have a seat," he told her. "Can I get you anything? Water? Coffee?"

"No thank you," Beatrice said. "I won't be here long."

"Well, what can I help you with?"

"I saw you coming out of Mountain View the other day."

He nodded.

"You were there to see my good friend, Emma Drummond," she continued.

"Yes, she's my wife's aunt. They were very close."

"Were?"

"Yes, you know how these things go. Family issues."

"I don't mean to pry, but Emma seems to think you threatened her."

Sheriff Bixby's eyebrows went up and the pleasant look on his face disappeared. "I don't know if you noticed," he said slowly, "but Emma is ill."

"I know about the agoraphobia. But the rest of her is as sharp as she used to be. I've known her my whole life."

He cackled. "Ms. Matthews, she ain't never been right. You gotta know that."

Beatrice tilted her head and leaned in. "What I know is, her husband used to beat her to a pulp. I saw it."

Sheriff Bixby bit his lip, looked out his window, and then back at Beatrice.

"And," Beatrice went on, "that does tend to mess with a woman's mind. But are you saying she made it up? That you didn't threaten her?"

"Look, I'm not sure this is any of your business, but I will tell you she may have taken what I said as a threat. I don't need to threaten poor old Emma Drummond. Why would I do that?"

"That's what I want to know."

"Take my word." He smiled.

Lawd the man is full of smiles and charm. If he'd been wearing a bow tie, she'd have left a long time ago. Bea's daddy used to say never trust a man wearing a bow tie, especially a charming and smiling one.

"I'm eighty-five years old," Beatrice said. "Your good looks, fancy mustache, and charm mean nothing to me. I've seen a million good old boys like you."

"Now, Ms. Math—"

She stood. "What do you want with Emma Drummond?"

Sheriff Bixby remained seated and just stared back at her, silently. He wasn't going to tell her a thing.

Chapter 51

Annie followed the steps to Pamela's office. Pamela was at her desk, on the phone. She made eye contact with Annie and then held her finger up.

"Hmm-hmm," Pamela said into the phone. "Okay. Thanks so much." She hung up the phone and smiled at Annie. "Hey, Annie, what can I do for you?"

"I need to talk to you about your employee picnic," Annie said, getting right to the point.

"Please sit down," Pamela said. "I'm not sure what the picnic has to do with anything. I've already given Bryant a list of everybody who was there."

"Bryant?" Annie said as a pang of anger shot through her. When they'd talked, he had treated that bit of information as inconsequential. *Bastard*.

Pamela nodded. "He just left here. I explained to him that the people who were there were employees, spouses, children, and a few close friends. But I do keep a list because they were only allowed to bring one guest each." She paused. "I also have a holiday party each year. I used to have a Halloween party, but it just got to be too much. I like doing these parties. They're great for morale."

"Would you happen to have a copy of your list that you can give me?" Annie asked. She was still seething but maintaining her composure.

"Certainly," Pamela said. "I just need to print it off." She turned around, pulled up her computer screen, and clicked around a bit. "Bryant wouldn't tell me what he wanted with the list. Can you?"

Annie smirked. "Certainly. Both of the scrapbook pages found on the victims were pages about the same day—the employee picnic. So we were thinking the pages might have some relevance, like—"

"The killer was at my picnic?" Pamela lowered her voice as if she didn't want anybody to hear her.

"Who knows?" Annie said. "But it's a lead."

Pamela sat back in her large, red leather chair and looked as though she was wilting.

"Are you okay?" Annie said. "Can I get you something?"

"Oh, I'm fine. It's just a lot to digest. An employee dead in my freezer. Murdered. And now, there's a good chance it was someone who works for me that killed her and maybe her sister."

"It is a lot. I think we reporters and cops forget sometimes that not everybody is as used to murder as we are." Annie smiled sympathetically.

"I'm thinking about my current staff and wondering which of them were at the picnic. In the restaurant business, the turnover is so awful. Fortunately, I do have some employees that have stayed with me for years."

"But not the kitchen staff?"

"Right. Well, now, the chefs do stay awhile. I try to keep them on. But the dishwashers, busboys—"

"All of whom are foreign?"

Pamela nodded. "It seems as if we get them on their way to somewhere else. They get their working permits, green cards, then they leave. Some of them stick around until they get an education. Like Jorge. He is taking online classes in business. I imagine he won't be here by this time next year."

Annie remembered Irina's reaction to Jorge at the crop. "Do you do background checks?"

"On Americans, I do," said Pamela, handing Annie the sheet with the list of picnic attendees. "Hathaway checks into background of the immigrants they send me."

"Tell me, is Mr. Hathaway always difficult?" Annie asked.

"Humph. I don't know. I rarely deal with the man. My husband Evan is the one who got us involved with them. I will say Hathaway appealed to my husband's pocketbook and my sense of altruism." Pamela tapped her long, red nails on the desk. It was nearly spotless.

"Your husband?" Annie asked. "I thought this place was *your* baby."

"What made you think that? Kraft Corporation owns it, just like it does half of Cumberland Creek."

"What?"

"My husband bought me out when we married. It's been great, for the most part. I don't have to worry about the money, just running the place and the creative aspects. His people take care of the rest."

Annie's respect for Pamela took a nosedive.

Up until then, she had thought of her as a smart, independent woman. "What else does your husband own?"

"Well, it's not just my husband. I own half of the Kraft company, of course, but he runs it. Let me think of some places we own that you might know. The Riverside Apartments? Vera's dance studio? Several empty buildings on Main Street."

Annie had no idea. Her stomach tightened as she thought about those new apartments and how close they were to the park where Esmeralda's body was found. Also how close they were to the Drummond place. How had the Drummonds managed to keep it from the Krafts? And what, if anything, did it all have to do with two murdered sisters?

Chapter 52

"Well, hello, Cookie," Beatrice said when she opened the door. "Come in, dear. We're stuffing our faces with apple pie and ice cream. Join us." She led Cookie into the kitchen.

"Thanks," Cookie said and sat at the table with Jon, who smiled and nodded in between bites of pie.

Beatrice set an extra plate of pie on the table. Cookie reached for a fork and dug in.

"What's on your mind, dear?" Beatrice asked.

Cookie had put on some weight. These days she ate anything set in front of her. It was a good weight gain in Beatrice's mind—the woman had been entirely too thin.

Cookie shrugged. "I've been thinking about the Martelino sisters. How sad it is. I went for a walk over by where they lived." She had been walking a lot lately. It was part of her healing process. At least, that's what her doctor said. "Have you noticed how close the apartments are to the Drummond place? I mean from a certain angle? It's not something you'd notice right away."

"Yes," Jon said. "We were walking over there the other day and noticed the same thing."

"There's a Mexican woman living in the Drummond place," Beatrice offered. "I was a little surprised by that. In fact, I was surprised that people are still living there at all. It doesn't look like it from the outside. But Emma says that's on purpose, to put off robbers. What do you think? Why does this remind you of the sisters?"

"I'm certain I saw one of them—I think it was Marina—about a week before she died, sitting on the steps of the house with a man," Cookie said. "I just remembered it when I was over there."

"A man?" Beatrice didn't want to get too excited, but maybe this was the break they had all been waiting for.

"I was just walking down there and I suddenly remembered. You know how my memory is," Cookie said, meeting Bea's eyes and then looking away in embarrassment.

"What's wrong?"

"I just feel . . . so helpless most of the time. I feel like I should be able to remember things by now."

"Honey, you were struck by lightning. You're lucky to be alive," Beatrice said.

"I just feel like I'm missing . . . something. I have this longing, this aching. I don't know what it is," Cookie said.

"You're missing yourself," Beatrice said after a beat. "I don't believe I'd ever known a young woman like you before. You were so solid in your skin. I didn't always agree with everything you said. I never liked your veganism," Beatrice joked, "but you were so solid. So you. I'm certain that sense of self is what you're missing." She sat back in her chair. "I think about our conversation at the jail sometimes."

The three of them sat, eating their pie and ice cream.

"Should we call the police?" Jon finally asked.

"For what?" Beatrice said.

"About what Cookie remembered. A man?"

"Yes, Jon's right. I should call Bryant," Cookie said.

"Don't forget to tell Annie, too," Bea said. "Why don't I call Annie and you call Bryant. We'll get 'em both over here."

But once they made the calls, Bryant wanted Cookie to go to the station to give a description of the man she'd seen with Marina and Annie was helping Ben with his math homework.

"I don't know Bea, I just don't understand this math," Annie had said over the phone.

"I'll be over, dear," Beatrice said. "I can help. In the meantime, you think about who that man could have been with Marina. What were they doing on the front porch of the Drummond house?"

"I will. Thanks Bea. You're a life saver."

Well, Beatrice wasn't so sure about that. But she did know math. She loved math. For her, it was the poetry of the universe. But then again, so was pie.

Chapter 53

Karen and Tracy were on to DeeAnn. They had enough medical background to know that she had way too many pills.

"What have you done, Mom?" Tracy said. "How did you get so many pills?"

DeeAnn stood and crossed her arms. "I don't need to answer to you. For God's sake, you're my daughter."

"Mom. You went to another doctor, didn't you?" Karen picked up the bottles and looked them over. "Yep. That's what you did."

The room went silent as DeeAnn's daughters took her in.

DeeAnn didn't back down. "Look. I'm in a lot of pain. Doctor Flathers doesn't seem to get it. I'm a big woman. Those little ole painkillers he gives me are just not helping."

"What did he say about surgery?" Tracy said.

"He said he'd like to wait awhile and see if the disk slips back into place. In the meantime, he gave me a shot. Didn't do any damn good. I have a life, you know? I've got to get back to the shop. There's your dad, the house, my friends. I can't function when I'm in pain."

"Mama, pain is a funny thing," Tracy said. "You know they've done all kinds of studies about it. Sometimes people get, I don't know, used to their pain, but still take pills to numb it, instead of trying to develop a tolerance. Are you okay?"

"What the hell do you mean?" DeeAnn said. "I'm not okay. I'm in pain! I keep telling you that."

"That's not what she means, Mom. She means is everything okay . . . in your life?" Karen said.

DeeAnn was floored. Of course everything was okay in her life. Why did her daughters think it wasn't? She turned and walked out of the kitchen to plop herself on the couch. She didn't want to talk with her daughters about her life. What was there to talk about? It was the same as it ever was.

"Mom?" Karen followed her in the room. She was trailed by her sister. "I know you think of us as little girls. But look at us. We're grown women. We're educated. And we love you. We think you might have a problem."

"What kind of problem?" DeeAnn said.

"With the pills, Ma. The doctor said there's no reason you should be in such horrible pain," Tracy said.

"What the hell does he know? I'm going to get another opinion," DeeAnn snapped.

"Okay," Karen said. "You do that. And I'll go with you." She sat down on the couch next to her.

DeeAnn was confused—did her daughters think she was addicted to painkillers? Or addicted to pain? Or both? Was it all in her mind? Was she in pain? She sighed—of course she was in pain; it wasn't in her mind. She knew that much. Why didn't they? They didn't know how it pinched at her and sent jags of pain through her lower half.

"I'd have thought that two nurses would be a bit more sympathetic," DeeAnn said. "I'm a little surprised."

"I *am* sympathetic," Karen said, pushing her hair back behind her ears. "I also know how easily people get addicted to these things. You haven't been yourself."

DeeAnn felt something blooming in her chest. Was it fear? Was she addicted? "I'm not sure I know what you mean. I'm not addicted to anything. I'm as much myself as I ever was. I'm just getting older. I was even thinking about retiring before this happened."

"Retiring? You? I can't see that," Tracy said.

"Well, baking is hard work. Physical. And my back has been bothering me for quite some time," DeeAnn said.

"What would you do with yourself?" Karen asked.

"What does anybody do with themselves when they retire?" DeeAnn sighed. "I thought, I don't know, I'd hang around with my daughters and maybe someday be a grandma."

"Don't look at me," Karen said. "I'm not interested in kids right now."

"But you and Adam?" Tracy asked.

Karen groaned. "Look. I keep telling you people, I like him. But I'm not looking for marriage. If I were, I think he'd be a great husband and father."

DeeAnn sat forward.

"But I'm not. We're just having fun right now. So don't go making wedding plans, Mom."

"Oh, I know things are different now," DeeAnn said. "Women have a lot more options. And I think it's great. I raised you both to be strong, independent women." Her voice cracked. "And that's exactly what I've got."

Chapter 54

"The police took Jorge this morning," Randy whispered into the phone. "Came here and got him early, like at five-thirty."

"What? Why?" Annie said.

"I'm not sure, but I think someone saw him with one of the sisters before—"

"Maybe that's who Cookie saw. She was at the station last night giving them a description," Annie said.

"Cookie? I wouldn't trust her memory."

"Memory is an odd thing. She suddenly remembered seeing Marina sitting with a man on the front porch of the Drummond house," Annie said.

"Just because they were sitting there doesn't mean he killed her. He's odd, but I don't think he'd hurt a fly."

Where had Annie heard that before? People who killed were often everyday sorts that momentarily lost it. Was Jorge a killer? She took a deep breath and calmed herself. Randy was right. Just because Marina had been seen with Jorge before her death didn't mean he'd killed her. The police must just be questioning him.

"I guess I should go down to the station. Who picked him up, Bryant or Sheriff Bixby?" asked Annie.

"Bryant."

"Shoot, I was afraid you were going to say that."

Randy laughed. "I've got to get back to work."

Annie finished loading the dishwasher and then drove to the station, shifting through the cases in her mind yet again. What did the police know? Two sisters were dead. Both of them had scrapbooking pages on their bodies, documenting the same day.

The sisters weren't involved in any of the assorted gang activities in Cumberland Creek, but their deaths were not accidental or coincidental. Someone was making a statement. A cry for help?

That profile might fit Jorge, despite what Randy thought. Jorge didn't seem quite together—maybe he was disturbed.

And then there was Hathaway *Transatlantic*. Could they have embroiled the sisters in something that got them killed? But what? That didn't make much sense, even though Annie saw them for what they were—a shade away from human trafficking. But she couldn't imagine what would involve them in the murder of women in small-town Cumberland Creek. What had the sisters known? What had they had that was worth killing them for?

As she pulled into the police station parking lot, Pamela's cherry red 1957 Chevy roared in front of her. And what about Pamela? Did Pamela have it in her to kill?

Annie grimaced at the thought. Women did kill, she reminded herself. But Pamela seemed genuinely distraught over the murder of Marina. Of course, it could be an act, but what would Pamela's motive be? Why would she kill her own employees? That didn't make sense.

What did make sense was that Pamela was at the police station. Likely there to help Jorge, who was probably frightened beyond belief. He seemed very little-boy-like.

Annie opened the door to a crowded waiting area. There sat Pamela with Irina, Jorge's aunt. They looked up at Annie. Pamela looked worried, but Irina looked haunted, stricken.

"Any ideas you have about writing a story about Jorge, you can just forget it," said Pamela.

"I'm just here to see what's happening," Annie said. "It's part of the story I'm already working on. If he's innocent, there's no reason I need to write about this."

Pamela seemed awfully protective of Jorge. Was she hiding something?

"Of course, he's innocent," Irina said. "Of course he is." She was adamant. Her eyes flared with anger.

Annie left to find the bathroom, then slipped down the hall to have a look around. The doors were all closed. A uniformed officer passed by her and she turned to go back to the waiting area.

At the corner she heard voices so she stopped and listened. She peeked around the corner and saw Bryant standing in the waiting area, shaking

Pamela's hand, then Irina's. Then he started walking down the hallway toward her.

Damn.

"What are you doing here?" he said when he approached her.

"I was in the ladies' room. You know what goes on in there, right?"

Bryant placed his hands on his hips. "That's not what I meant, Annie. Come to my office please."

"Yeah, I don't know. I'm in kind of a hurry. Maybe for a few minutes." She followed him down the snaking gray hallway.

After they were situated, he looked at her and said, "Spill."

"I was just here checking on Jorge. Someone said you brought him in." Why did she feel like she was lying, when she was telling the truth?

"We just brought him in to see if he knew anything about the murders or the sisters. He's not a suspect," Bryant said. "You could have just asked me. It's really not a big deal."

"How close are you to solving this case?"

"Very."

"Can you give me any details?"

"Of course not."

"But you can say that Jorge is not a suspect."

"Not at this point."

"Interesting that his aunt and employer both came in so quickly," Annie said, gauging Bryant's reaction carefully.

He lifted one eyebrow. "I guess they care about him or something."

"Was he dating Marina?" Annie hated to ask, but she had to.

He guffawed. "No. He wanted to, but nothing came of it."

"I'm assuming he's the man Cookie saw with her at the Drummond place?" Annie asked.

Bryant nodded.

"What were they doing together, then?"

"I think there was a scrapbooking crop there that night and they had stepped outside for some air. It was a Friday night."

"What was Cookie doing there?" Annie wondered out loud.

Adam tensed and moved around in his seat. "Ask her. She's your friend, isn't she?"

"I will," Annie said.

"Have you been back to the apartments?" Bryant asked.

"Not since the day I saw you there. I haven't seen any evidence of gangs, Adam."

"What do you think a gang looks like?" he asked in a patronizing tone.

"Not like the group of middle-aged guys standing around in the parking lot," Annie answered quickly.

"You need to adjust your vision. Don't trust just anybody."

"I don't. But the only time I've felt threatened over there is by the manager of the place. And I haven't seen him since that day at the grocery store."

Bryant looked at her with his head tilted and eyebrows hitched. "Be careful, Annie. Gang members come in all shapes, ages, sizes . . . and genders."

"Were the sisters involved with a gang?" she asked again. She was certain she'd asked that question a million times or more.

"Not that I know of."

"Their deaths seem linked and personal and, well, I have to say it's just not making any sense to me. I can't figure out what the motive would be for killing two young women who mostly kept to themselves, worked hard, liked to get together with friends and scrapbook. I just don't know!" She flung her arms out.

"Most murders are linked to drugs these days," Bryant said. "Once you rule that out, it gets murkier."

His office door opened. A uniformed officer entered the room and handed him a file.

"Thanks," Bryant said, accepting the file.

"So are you saying their deaths had nothing to do with drugs?" Annie asked as the officer left the room.

"I think we can safely rule that out," Bryant replied.

"The other motive for murder is passion," Annie said almost to herself. "Money. Secrets they may have stumbled on."

Adam looked up from his files quickly, blinked, then looked away.

Something caught in Annie's chest. The young women had stumbled upon someone's secret. Bryant must be on the trail of that secret. And it was a big one. The momentary look in his eyes, the lifting of his chin at that precise moment told her that.

"Annie, leave the sleuthing up to us, and I promise we'll let you know once we find out something."

If only she could believe that. If she left it up to him, she'd never get the story.

Chapter 55

"Can I come in?" Sheriff Bixby asked Beatrice.

When she had opened the door, Bea was so shocked to see him that she had forgotten her manners. "Oh, I'm sorry, Sheriff. Please come in." She led him into the living room and gestured for him to sit on the couch.

As he sat, he let out a huge sigh. "Now, Ms. Matthews, I'm a little concerned about Emma."

"What? Why?" she said, sitting down next to him.

"I'm going to be straight with you," Sheriff Bixby said. "I hate to get you involved in family business, but it concerned me that she thought I was threatening her."

Beatrice sat back against the cushion. "It concerned me, too."

"I was talking with her about her will, you see. Now, it's not what you're thinking. I can assure you."

"Humph."

"My wife and I have never been in her will, and we are fine with that. We do okay, Ms. Matthews.

We're not too concerned about that old house and property of hers. Besides which, it's kind of a delicate matter. I hated to bring it up to her."

"I imagine."

"For years, the place was to be left to Michelle."

"As it should be," Beatrice chimed in.

"Indeed," the sheriff said. "I agree."

"So what's the problem?"

"Recently Emma's will was changed."

"You mean Michelle isn't going to get the place?" Beatrice said. "I find that hard to believe."

"No, no. Not that exactly. But another person has been added. You know Michelle is alone. No man in her life. No kids. So, someone was added in case something happened to Michelle, right?"

"Oh I see. Well, that makes sense. Emma doesn't want the Kraft Corporation to get their hands on the place." Beatrice thought about asking who the new beneficiary was, but she didn't want to pry.

"Neither do I," he said firmly.

That surprised Beatrice. She found herself liking the man as he continued to talk.

"The minute they purchased the other parcel, they had a construction crew over there. It was some of the prettiest land. All those apple trees, gone."

"I hear you. It was pretty. Old, too. One of the first orchards in the state," Beatrice told him. "It's hard to see that happen. I was walking around over there and barely recognized the landscape. I used to know it so well." She sighed. "Time marches on. Can I get you anything to drink?"

"Thanks, Ms. Matthews, but I'm fine. I just want to

be clear with you. I never intended to upset Emma. That bothered me, you see."

"Well, now, I'm glad you came over to straighten it out. I can see where Emma might have misunderstood the conversation."

"The family sent me over to talk to her. I told them it wasn't a good idea. I think she's intimidated by me."

"Why would she be intimidated by you?"

"Not just me, Ms. Matthews, but most men." He looked away.

"You know then," Bea said softly. "You know how she was beaten."

He nodded. "We all do, now."

"I knew it back then," Bea said, her voice suddenly quivering. "And there wasn't a damn thing I could do about it."

"In those days, there weren't any social services, no Oprah Winfreys, either. I can't imagine what she went through."

"I should have done something." It was a confession Bea felt deep in her bones and in the center of her chest.

"You did, didn't you? At least that's how the story goes. You stood up for her."

Bea nodded. "I did. But then I didn't see her again for forty years." Suddenly Beatrice's old heart felt like it was splitting wide open. She clutched her chest and tried not to cry. *Old fool,* she told herself. *I am an old fool.*

"Are you okay?" Sheriff Bixby asked.

She waved her hand. "Oh, I'm fine. Just thinking about all the time that's gone by. How I missed her.

Regrets. I've got plenty of them. But not reaching out to her sooner is at the top of my list."

"Thank your lucky stars you didn't, Ms. Matthews," Sheriff Bixby said in a somber tone. "I'm sure Paul would have killed you if you had."

"What?"

"That's why Emma never contacted you. She didn't want him to hurt you."

"How do you know that?" Beatrice said incredulously.

"My wife. She's got plenty of stories about the family. But that's something everybody agrees to. Paul threatened to kill you on more than one occasion. Ms. Emma had no choice but to turn her back on your friendship. That's what we figure."

Beatrice didn't know what to think. It felt a mite too personal for her taste. How could he know such things? *Family.* She knew enough about family tales to know that sometimes there was a glimmer of truth to them.

She remembered that Emma had said she killed Paul. Bea was just now starting to believe it.

Chapter 56

DeeAnn always looked forward to Halloween. She loved baking Halloween goodies—maybe even more than Christmas goodies.

Some years, she planned themes for Halloween. Last year's Harry Potter was probably the best, and it was so successful that they were offering it again this year—butter beer cookies, wizard hat cupcakes, mini-treacle tarts, Hedwig cookies, peppermint humbugs, and so on. According to Jill, who called her with an update every day, things were going smoothly at the bakery.

DeeAnn was grateful that she was up and about, even if it was just for short periods of time. She still couldn't drive and she still couldn't work. It was difficult to be patient with herself.

She flipped off the TV and sighed. It was the day before Halloween and she was bored. Karen was at work and Tracy was still asleep upstairs.

DeeAnn was certain that Tracy had come home to make sure she didn't become a painkiller addict. The thought of that made DeeAnn giggle. Her, an addict!

Women like her did not become drug addicts. Her daughters were being overprotective.

Her doorbell rang and it startled her. She wasn't expecting anybody.

She opened the door and there stood Christopher Hathaway from Hathaway Transatlantic.

"Can I come in?" he asked.

Her first thought was to say no, but she shrugged off her instinct. "Of course. I'm just a little surprised to see you, but please do come in."

"I'm sorry to barge in like this," he said, following her to the living room. "It's very rare that I'm in the area so I thought I'd take the chance to talk with you a bit."

DeeAnn sat down, not waiting until he sat, as her back was feeling prickly.

Finally he also sat down. "I was just over at your bakery. It's lovely. And you have a bustling business." His voice had a patronizing tone.

She smiled. "It's because it's Halloween."

"I think I can help you out. Help you earn more money."

"Really? How?"

"By helping you hire some very hard working Mexicans."

DeeAnn took a deep breath. She was going to have to lay it on the line with him. It was no good trying to be polite with some people—they just didn't get it. "I don't think I'm interested in your services. I'm very happy with the people I have working for me now."

"All of them?"

"Absolutely, even the vegan baker. She's done a great job."

"You're overpaying them. You should be keeping more of your profit."

"I do okay. I don't see any reason to not pay them well."

He leaned in closer to her, which made her very uncomfortable. "I'm trying to get you to see the big picture."

"Mr. Hathaway, how do you know that I *don't* see the big picture? I've had this business for years and have always paid my employees well. It's about respect. If it doesn't work out, then I let them go. It's that simple. But I have good folks working for me and I treat them well. Sounds like a sound business principle to me."

Mr. Hathaway rolled his eyes.

"Did you just roll your eyes at me?" DeeAnn said, trying not to raise her voice. "Please leave my home."

"Mom?" Tracy came down the stairs. "Everything okay?"

"I'm sorry. I was just trying to help," Mr. Hathaway said, looking deflated.

"It's fine," DeeAnn said to Tracy. "I was just showing Mr. Hathaway to the door."

But he remained seated. "I'm not a very good salesperson, am I?"

"How do I know?" DeeAnn said. "I'm simply not interested in your services. You can't get blood from a turnip."

He smiled. "True enough. Well, I think I need to start thinking about a new job. My daddy is going to fire me over this."

"Over this?" DeeAnn said, surprised.

"You're not the only person to reject me. I haven't

gotten any new clients in years and well"—he shrugged—"I think Hathaway Transatlantic might be on its last legs." Suddenly all of his swagger was gone. He looked bereft.

"Can I get you a cup of coffee? Water?" DeeAnn asked, feeling sorry for him.

He nodded. "I'd love a cup of coffee."

"I'll get it, Mom. Stay where you are," Tracy ordered.

While Tracy was in the kitchen Mr. Hathaway continued. "It's kind of sad. My dad started the business with the best of intentions. But things have changed so much and gotten out of hand in some cases."

"What do you mean?" DeeAnn asked, finally showing some interest.

"Well, it's getting harder and harder to police all of our business. The people on the ground, the sponsors and so on. So many of them . . . well, we caught one running drugs. Another had a prostitution ring. That's not what my daddy had in mind."

"Maybe you need to pull back," DeeAnn offered.

Tracy came into the room with two steaming cups of coffee. "Cream or sugar?" she asked as she set the cups down on the table.

"Nothing for me," Mr. Hathaway said to Tracy. Then to DeeAnn he asked, "What do you mean, pull back?"

"Get back to the company's original mission. Close some of your offices. Gather your forces, your good guys, get rid of everybody else. Clean house."

His eyes widened. "DeeAnn Fields, you are brilliant."

"Well, now. Thanks for that."

"I guess I knew it already. I just needed to hear someone else say it."

DeeAnn sipped from her coffee. "What do you know about the Martelino sisters? Do you think their deaths had anything to do with the company?"

Mr. Hathaway shook his head. "At first, I thought they might, given the trouble we've been having. But, no, the operations here are clean. Those girls were good people. Their friends and employers all check out."

"Except their parents are in prison," DeeAnn said.

"I maintain they were set up," he said. "It happens. We're trying to help. We've hired a very good lawyer. Maybe they'll be out soon."

"Humph. So if none of Hathaway's folks had anything to do with the Martelino murders, who did?"

Mr. Hathaway was silent for a moment before speaking. "What we've found in terms of crime and our immigrant workers is that most of the time—not all of the time—it's their intermediaries or sponsors that are taking advantage of them and getting them involved in illegal activities."

"Who would that be in the Martelino case? I know they weren't involved in anything shady—or at least not as far as we've been able to find. Who was their sponsor?"

"Pamela Kraft and the Kraft Corporation."

Chapter 57

"I know," Annie said to DeeAnn over the phone. "It does seem suspicious. I mean, the Krafts own half of Cumberland Creek from what I can tell."

"I don't dislike Pamela. I find it hard to believe she'd be involved in any kind of shenanigans, let alone murder," DeeAnn said.

"And I have to say, she seemed as if she genuinely liked Marina. She was grieving. But her husband might be another matter." Annie made a mental note to check him out further. On the face of things, he appeared legit—but she hadn't scratched past the surface yet.

"I wouldn't know him if I tripped over him. He keeps a low profile for a wealthy guy, I have to say. Have you checked out Hathaway?"

"Yes, and everything he told you is right on the money. They've been sinking for quite some time. They need to do a lot of policing to clean up their reputation. Well, I have to run. I'm going to Irina's crop again tonight."

"Are you going to keep going to both crops?" DeeAnn asked.

"Maybe for a while, until I figure some things out. I'll see you tomorrow."

Mike had taken the boys out for the evening, for pizza and some last minute costume purchases, so Annie was on her own.

She sometimes didn't know what to do with herself when by herself—which was odd since she spent most of every day alone. It was different, she supposed when she was alone during the day because she was working. When she had free time, she felt a bit like a caged animal let loose, having to decide what to do first.

But tonight she had an agenda.

As she pulled into the driveway of the Drummond house, she noticed that something was different. There were more and brighter lights coming from the windows and all of the drapes were pulled back.

She walked up the crumbling sidewalk and rapped on the door.

Irina answered, welcoming her warmly. "Hi, Annie, please come in."

Annie rolled her scrapbook case in behind her and felt as if she had entered a jewelry box glowing with rich colors—fuchsia, crimson, purple, emerald green, ocean blue. Festive lights were strung across the room, and tables overflowed with colorful items. Papier-mâché sugar skulls were hanging from the center light fixture in the hallway.

"What's this?" Annie said, approaching one of the tables. In the center was a huge framed photograph of Esmeralda and Marina and surrounding them were lit candles and sugar skulls in a variety of forms—cookies, candy, cupcakes. They were so lovely, Annie could hardly believe that the detailed designs were on replicas of human skulls.

"Today is the Day of the Dead," Irina said. "We remember our departed loved ones on this day."

"Oh yes!" Annie said. How could she have forgotten? She used to have a friend in college who celebrated. "It's just gorgeous!"

"Well, you know how I love to make things nice and pretty," Irina said.

A number of the women were already scrapbooking, so Annie claimed her spot next to Rosa. She smiled at her. "How are you?"

"Great," she said. "I'm working on this book for my boss' daughter. It's kind of hard making a scrapbook for someone else. She just turned sixteen and they had this huge party. This is my gift to her."

"Ah," Annie said. "I love the way you cut that photo into a star shape. Did you do that by hand?"

Rosa laughed. "No. I used this." She held up a template.

"Exactly what I would do. I'm going to get some food and then I'll be right back." Annie didn't know anybody that could cut a photo into a perfect star like that, except maybe Sheila. Templates helped a lot.

As she turned toward the food table, she ran smack into Jorge.

"I'm sorry!" he said awkwardly.

"Jorge!" his aunt Irina said with a harsh edge to her voice that frightened even Annie. "What the hell are you doing with the pretty white lady?" She said it in Spanish. Evidently she didn't know that Annie also knew Spanish.

"It's okay," Annie managed to say. "I ran into him."

"So sorry, Annie," he said, and with his head bent low he left the room.

"He's a pain in the ass," Irina said.

"I think he's nice," Annie said loud enough that she hoped Jorge heard. "He seems sweet." It also seemed as if he was being picked on by his dear old auntie with the good gig in the big house. Had her concern for him at the station been completely fake?

Irina changed the subject. "Help yourself, Annie. We've got plenty of goodies here tonight." She walked away and went to her spot at the table.

"She can be so hard on him," Rosa whispered to Annie when she got back to the table with a plate of sugar cookies shaped like skulls and decorated lavishly with flowers and swirls and flourishes. "I feel sorry for him sometimes."

"Rosa?" said Irina.

Rosa turned around. "Yes?"

"I've got your order of new paper right here," said Irina.

"Do you sell scrapbooking materials?" Annie asked.

Irina nodded. "Yes, but only part time. I'm so busy taking care of Ms. Drummond."

"Speaking of Ms. Drummond," Annie said. "Where is she?"

"What do you mean?" Irina asked.

"I mean, where is she? This is her house, right? Why doesn't she come to the crops?"

Irina laughed. "Ms. Drummond is in her rooms upstairs. She allows me to have the crops, but she doesn't like to socialize. It's part of her illness."

Annie tasted a cookie. It wasn't bad, but like most cookies with decorative icing, she found it a bit too sweet. "Sorry to hear that. Is it something like agoraphobia?"

"Yes, exactly. It runs in the family, I'm afraid."

"There's no medication?"

Irina tilted her head. "It doesn't seem to help her. Like her mother, she is allergic to most of it."

"Her moth—"Annie was interrupted by laughter at the end of the table, but things were clicking and zinging through her brain.

People who worked in others' homes knew all the family secrets, didn't they? It was an unspoken code that they never told—and yet Irina had just blurted out some personal information about Emma and Michelle as if it were nothing. Maybe it was. Maybe Annie was making too much of it. But that, coupled with the way she had just treated her nephew, left Annie with a sudden dislike of the woman.

She looked carefully at the woman next to her. Rosa seemed to like Irina, and she certainly knew her better than Annie did.

Then again, after all these years, Annie was learning to trust her intuition, no matter the cold, hard facts.

Chapter 58

Beatrice loved waking up with Elizabeth between her and Jon in their big king size bed. She knew it wasn't in vogue to still share a bed with almost-five-year-olds, but when Elizabeth stayed with her, Beatrice left it up to her. She looked like a clichéd sleeping angel, curled between her and Jon.

Bea struggled to loosen herself from the blankets without waking anybody up. She planned on pumpkin pancakes this morning, one of her favorite breakfasts for the fall. It had become a tradition for Halloween morning.

She was so pleased that she would be taking Elizabeth trick or treating this year, then on to the fire hall for the community party. Vera and the others were all going to try to stop by the party, including Annie with her boys, so there would be no scrapbooking party tonight, but they were getting together later to do another Halloween ritual. Beatrice had thought about going—in truth she still thought about going. She might just leave Elizabeth with Jon and attend after all.

After breakfast, Annie called her.

"Are you ready for tonight?" Beatrice said. "Are the boys excited?"

"Yes and yes," Annie said. "It's going to be a busy one. But listen, I have a question for you."

"Yes?" Beatrice asked.

"What do you know about Michelle Drummond's housekeeper Irina and her nephew Jorge?"

"Nothing, really," Beatrice said. "Why?"

"I don't know. I just had the weirdest feeling about them last night."

"Last night?"

"Yes, I went to their crop, which was pretty cool. It had this Day of the Dead theme."

"What kind of weird feeling did you have?"

"It's hard to explain, really," Annie said, but she tried to articulate her feelings while Beatrice listened.

"You probably just stepped into the middle of a family thing. Kind of like I did with Emma."

"What happened?" Annie asked.

Beatrice relayed the story of seeing Sheriff Bixby at Mountain View and then visiting with him later. On Annie's end of the phone, she heard a scuffling in the background, followed by a crash.

"I've got to go," Annie said.

Beatrice laughed. "It sure sounds like it." Those boys of Annie's were a handful.

Jon and Lizzie were outside raking leaves, and then they planned to carve a jack-o-lantern. Of all the joys Elizabeth had brought Beatrice, seeing her with Jon was a huge one.

Bea finished loading the dishwasher, wiped off the counters, and finally went upstairs to change. She'd been in her nightclothes all morning.

When she came back downstairs she was surprised to see Detective Bryant, Jon, and Lizzie in her living room. Lizzie loved Bryant and was sitting on his lap, chatting away about Halloween.

"You need to promise me that you will check out each piece of candy you get or let a grownup do it, before you eat it," Bryant was saying to her.

"Okay, I promise," she said solemnly.

"Well, look what the cat dragged in," Beatrice said.

"Beatrice," Bryant said, looking up at her, then back at Lizzie. "I've got to talk to your grandmother alone, okay?"

Lizzie wrapped her arms around him and kissed him on the cheek before she and Jon went into the kitchen.

"What can I help you with?" Beatrice said as she sat down in her favorite armchair.

"I hear that you've been buddying up to the local sheriff," Bryant said.

Bea didn't like his tone. Why did he have to be so sarcastic? "Well, that's not exactlty true. And I hear you've been buddying up to a woman who's half your age," she retorted.

He reddened. "That's my personal life. Not your concern. Or any of your cronies'."

"Cronies?" Bea's voice raised. She took a deep breath. "What do you want? Honestly, just get on with it."

"I've been working pretty hard on the cases of the murdered sisters and trying to combine efforts with the sheriff."

"And?"

"I wondered if you might have any leads for me."

Beatrice sat back against her chair cushion. "Do you think I killed those women?"

"No no no! I just keep tabs on Bixby. I don't trust the man. The feeling is mutual."

"He's a lawman, Bryant," Beatrice said. "I'm surprised at you."

"He's a sheriff. He works at the will of the people. A lot of politics goes into his job. A lot of winks and slaps on the back."

Beatrice thought about that a moment. "Well, that's true. But that doesn't mean he's a bad guy."

"No, I know that. He's just a different animal from me. So have you found anything about the cases from him?"

"No, we had a personal conversation. His wife's aunt, Emma Drummond, is my old friend and I ran into him the other day at Mountain View. We've just been discussing her and, um, well, family matters, if you must know."

Bryant raised an eyebrow and nodded his head as if that somehow meant a lot to him. "That it?"

"I think so. Small talk, you know. Nothing else," Bea said. "Sorry I can't help you. I wish I could. You know, we were able to send cards to the Martelino family and I thought I'd feel better after that. But I sure would feel a whole lot better if you'd find their killer."

"We all would, Beatrice," Bryant said. "Believe me, we all would feel much better if these cases were solved."

Chapter 59

After handing out candy in the early evening to a parade of little ghosts, goblins, and fairy princesses, DeeAnn, Jacob, and Tracy headed over to the fire hall where the community gathering was being held. DeeAnn's new pills seemed to be doing the trick and since Tracy and Karen hadn't taken away the second prescription of pills she'd gotten, she was able to take as many as she wanted.

Usually DeeAnn would walk to the fire hall, but she didn't want to overexert herself, for fear of stopping whatever healing had already taken place so they'd driven. Her friends had saved a space for her at a table. Jacob gravitated toward the men in the corner, all looking a bit out of place. Tracy sat next to her.

Long card tables were set end to end, making rows of tables extending from one end of the room to the next. Orange and black paper covered the tables. A centerpiece stood in the middle of each— pumpkins with fall flowers, orange, yellow, gold, and crimson. Black and orange streamers were strewn across the room, with orange and black balloons in each of the four corners. It was Halloween, all right, and the Cumberland Creek fire hall was decorated to the hilt.

Spider-Man sauntered up next to DeeAnn.

"Well, hello there, Sam," she said.

"How did you know it was me?" asked Annie's son, who evidently at the last minute had decided he wasn't too cool or too old to celebrate Halloween.

"It was a good guess," DeeAnn said, looking over at the little boy next to him who was dressed as an old man. "Who are you supposed to be?"

"Mozart, of course," Ben said.

"Mozart?" Who ever heard of a Mozart costume? "Well, I guess you know what you're doing," she said. "I wouldn't know him if I tripped over him."

"But he's already dead," Ben said, deadpan.

"I know that," DeeAnn laughed. "I meant, if he were alive, I still wouldn't know who he was. Or what he'd look like. Are you certain he looked like you, with the fancy hair, and such?"

Annie grinned. "Oh yes. He researched it."

"Very nice," Tracy said. "Maybe you'll win the contest tonight."

A large man dressed as a clown walked by the table and Sheila gasped. "I just find them so creepy!"

Annie did a double take and a questioning look came over her face, but then she appeared to shrug it off.

"Clowns?" DeeAnn asked.

"Yes, and that one is so big! A grown man dressed as a clown!" said Sheila.

"A lot of people here are dressed up," Paige said. "I wish Randy were here to see it. I bet him that there would be some adults in costumes. But he had to work tonight. He's trying out some new recipes."

"Yeah, so did Karen," DeeAnn said. "Halloween can be a nightmare in the ER."

Beatrice chortled. "Sound likes a title for one of those campy horror movies."

Jon was sitting next to Bea with Elizabeth on his lap. She was dressed as a giraffe—a costume her grandmother had made for her.

"It's time for the contest, young lady," Jon said, guiding her out of his lap.

The children began to line up for the costume competition and then so did the teenagers, and then finally the adults—the few of them that were participating. The clown was nowhere in sight, much to Sheila's contentment.

Elizabeth ended up winning the competition in her age group for most original costume.

"Beatrice, you are such a talented seamstress," DeeAnn said after Elizabeth came back to the table with her trophy.

"Well, now don't make a big deal of it. I've been making costumes for many years. When I was growing up we all learned to sew. I'm not sure what the kids are learning these days."

"I'm sure you don't want to know, Mama," Vera said. "I don't think I do, either."

Detective Bryant paraded by the table. He was dressed in jeans and a sweatshirt, off duty. DeeAnn wanted to grab him, shake him, and tell him to back off her daughter. Instead, she smiled and nodded politely . . . but it was killing her.

"Don't look now," Paige said. "He's heading toward your husband."

DeeAnn's heart lurched in her chest. "Ohmigoodness!" She covered her face with her hands. "I can't look," she said as the others around her laughed. "What's happening?"

"He shook Jacob's hand and is smiling at him," Paige said in a low voice. "Jacob is not smiling back."

"Oh Lordy, what should I do?" DeeAnn's eyes were still closed, her face hot, pulse racing.

"Oh c'mon," Bea said. "They're polite adults. It's going to be fine."

"They are going outside," Paige whispered in a horrified tone.

"Okay. I take that *polite adults* thing back," Bea said.

"Let me go and check out the situation," Jon said, rising from his chair.

"What? No, it's none of your business," Bea said. "I don't want you getting hurt."

"I'm a man. This is man's business," he said and left.

DeeAnn opened her eyes and noted that other men around the room were also moving toward the door. *Poor Bryant,* she thought.

"This is the biggest bunch of crap I've ever seen," Tracy said and got up from the table. "I'm going to put a stop to this. Karen is a grown woman. It's nobody's business what she's doing with Adam. I don't like it, either; he's so old. But it's none of our business. Dad just needs to back off."

DeeAnn sat back in her chair. She felt frozen and couldn't move even if she wanted to.

"You stay put," Vera said to DeeAnn. "You don't need to hurt yourself over this. I'm sure it will be fine."

But DeeAnn was not so sure. Tracy was right. On the one hand, it was nobody's business. But on the other hand, what Tracy didn't understand was that both she and her sister would always be their parents' business. And in a small community like Cumberland Creek, dating a man like Adam Bryant—no matter what age you were—was going to set tongues wagging. That's just the way it was.

Oh yes, many folks in Cumberland Creek had come a long way. The murmurs about a Jewish family living in town had faded—or at least gone behind closed doors, and one of their own had come back to live here as an openly gay man. That never would have happened ten years ago.

But DeeAnn knew that if you scratched beneath the surface, all of the prejudices were lurking beyond the picket fences and the neatly trimmed lawns. Paige and Earl had yet to be welcomed back into their church community. Annie and her family were always running up against bumps and ignorance. Her own twenty-five-year-old daughter dating a local detective who was almost twice her age? Well, people were talking. The more DeeAnn thought about it, the more it pissed her off. The more she wanted to tell people to back off. But she couldn't, because she didn't like it, either. So she sucked in her breath. Karen was old enough to know actions led to consequences. It was her life, not DeeAnn's.

The door flung open and one of the men high-tailed it into the fire hall kitchen and quickly came back out with some ice. If DeeAnn's intuition was correct, a man was down.

Jon slinked back into the room and came to their table in a midst of a crowd of middle schoolers roaming around. "Well, that's that."

DeeAnn couldn't speak. Had Bryant hurt her husband?

"What happened?" Bea asked.

"Bryant is bleeding a bit. I think he's going to have a black eye," Jon said.

"What?"

All of the women at the table turned to look at him.

"It's all over now. I think he went home. It was only one punch, but Jacob made it a good one." Jon grinned.

Chapter 60

After all the fuss at the Halloween party, the scrapbookers plus Beatrice got together in Vera's basement. They moved a bunch of furniture around and created a circular space in which to hold the Halloween ritual.

The women gathered around. Cookie stood next to a decorated table. She was dressed in the same blue dress she had worn the first time they held the ritual. It was made of a deep blue velvet with large, flowing sleeves and hemline. Annie's stomach tightened as she remembered the night that Cookie first wore it—the night she was arrested for murder based on some flimsy evidence that had never added up and a botched investigation that never made sense.

Paige was in charge. She and Cookie had come up with the ritual based on what Paige remembered and by looking over some books on Wicca. Each one of them had brought pictures of people they had lost. The photos of deceased people adorned the table, along with a huge seashell, a statue of Mary, candles, a wooden bowl of water, flowers, and silk scarves.

Once again, Annie was struck that although each item on the table was not usually pretty by itself, gathered together they had a simple beauty. "This reminds me of the Day of the Dead celebration over at the Drummond place last night."

Cookie smiled. "So many cultures have similar celebrations and rituals."

Annie reached for Cookie's hand. "I remember the first time we did this like it was yesterday. You said something about women have been meeting like this for generations, gathering around the fire or the altar. Some of the things here represent some deep connections we have and always will."

Paige grabbed Cookie's other hand. "We are safe here."

"Can we get on with it?" Beatrice said, but she held onto Vera and DeeAnn's hands. They were all in a circle, holding hands.

"Okay, first I'll call quarters," Paige said, letting go of Cookie and DeeAnn's hands and placing herself in the center of the circle. "Hail to the North," she said with her arms out, palms up, facing Sheila's fireplace. "Place of patience, endurance, stability, and earth." She dipped her hand into a bowl of dirt and let it fall back into the bowl. "Hail to the East." She picked up a feather and placed it in the bowl. "Place of wisdom, intellect, perception, and inspiration. Air," she added with a flourish of the feather.

She struck a match and lit the black candles on the table. "Hail to the South, place of passion, strength, energy, and willpower. Place of fire."

As Paige welcomed each element, or called quarters

as she put it, Annie watched Cookie as much as she could without making her uncomfortable. Cookie's spirituality had been so important to her before the accident. They were all hoping that going through this ritual struck a chord in her.

After Paige was done reciting, they all sat and ate a vegan feast prepared by her and Cookie.

"So do you remember anything?" Beatrice asked.

Cookie looked up at the women, who were all focused on her. "I can't say that I remember specific details. But it felt familiar and comforting."

"Well, that's something," Vera said. "That sounds like a good start."

Everybody mumbled in agreement.

"I have to say, the first time we did the ritual, it felt that way to me as well," Annie said. "I was surprised. I mean, I'm Jewish. Yet this felt comforting to me. From the first."

"Well, it should be," Beatrice said. "All of these rituals are based on ancient ways. These things, like the seashell, have symbolized the sacred feminine for generations. You sort of pick up on these things by osmosis."

Cookie reached for the huge seashell on the table and held it in her hands.

Is she trying to remember again? Annie wondered.

"Oh Mama, you're such a smarty-pants," Vera said.

"Pshaw," Beatrice said.

"False humility never got you anywhere, Bea," Sheila pointed out.

"I still haven't been able to figure out what happened to the Martelino sisters," Beatrice said. It felt fitting to talk about them tonight, on this feast of the dead.

"Sad," Vera said.

"We're not very close to solving the cases," Annie said.

DeeAnn cleared her throat. "That man from Hathaway cleared up a few things for me. I don't think they had anything to do with it."

"Humph," Beatrice said. "What makes you say that?"

"He told me about the problems they were having and how they might go out of business. He said the company has gotten too big to police and some of the employers and sponsors are taking advantage," DeeAnn said.

"That makes sense," Annie said. "The articles I've been reading about arrests and things all back that up. It was the intermediaries who were lax."

"In this case, that would be . . . ?" Vera questioned.

"Pamela or the Kraft Corporation," DeeAnn finished.

The room sat in silence.

"They seem on the up and up," Annie finally said. "I've looked into them. They seem squeaky clean on the face of things."

"Heck. It's a huge company. It could be someone that worksh for them that Pamela doeshn't even know." DeeAnn was sweating profusely and slurring her words a bit.

"Are you okay?" Annie asked.

"Yeah, why?"

"You're sweating and slurring your words."

"That's just the medicine," DeeAnn said, waving her off. "I feel fine. I'm in no pain."

Paige frowned. "DeeAnn—"

"Really?" DeeAnn said. "You're going to ashk me

about my *medishine again*? Haven't I had enough drama for tonight, what with my idiot hushband punching Bryant in the nose?"

Paige held up her hand as if to say *You'll get nothing more from me*.

"Well, on that note, I need to get going," Annie said, standing up from the table.

"Early night?" Beatrice said.

"Not really," Annie said. "I just have a little work to do."

After everybody said their good-byes, she took off down the dark, empty street alone, her bag flung over her shoulder and her cell phone in her hand. She liked to keep her phone close when she traveled in the dark. Not all of the streets were well lit.

As she rounded the first corner, she felt as if someone were watching her. *Strange*. The Halloween festivities were over. Not many folks would be out or looking out their windows. A thump of a footfall sounded from somewhere behind her.

As Annie turned, things became a blur of color. The clown from the fire hall reached for her and pulled his face close to hers, opening his mouth. She twisted and kneed him in the crotch; he bent over, groaning, and she kneed him again in the head, ignoring the pain rippling through her knee. He went down.

"Help!" she yelled and saw Mrs. Green coming out of her house wielding a shotgun.

"Wait! Don't shoot! Please, just call 9-1-1," Annie said, feeling her chest nearly explode with the pounding of her heart and her knee reeling with pain.

"I done that already, missy," Mrs. Green said. "Figured you needed backup until the police get here." She was in her robe, with curlers in her hair.

"Well, thank you," Annie said, trying to catch her breath.

The police were there momentarily and Annie found the strength to face her attacker, who the medics were trying to awaken. Vera and the others had come running down the street as soon as the sirens sounded. Cookie's arm went around Annie as a police officer took off the clown mask.

"Jorge," Annie said with a pang of disappointment traveling through her. "Oh Jorge, what have you done?"

Chapter 61

Twenty-six-year-old Jorge Mendez is currently being held on assault charges by the Cumberland Creek Police. Mendez, an assistant manager at Pamela's Pie Palace, had recently been questioned about the murders of Marina and Esmeralda Martelino.

Mendez, an immigrant from Mexico, assaulted a Cumberland Creek woman on Halloween night while he was dressed in a clown costume.

"Freaky," Beatrice said as she lowered the Sunday newspaper. "What was a grown man doing dressed up in a clown costume, anyway?"

Jon shrugged. "I don't think it's that big of a deal. It was Halloween. But going after Annie . . . that I don't understand. What did he want?"

"He wanted to hurt her, maybe kill her, Jon. Just like he probably did to those other women," Beatrice said.

"No, I meant, why Annie? I know he wanted to

hurt her. But why *her*? Do you really think he's the killer?"

"He's got some problems," Beatrice said. "Don't you think?"

Jon shrugged. "It does seem that way. Some men . . . I don't know . . . are quite macho. But it doesn't mean they are killers. Look at Jacob."

"Well, someone has needed to punch Bryant in the nose for years. I'm glad he was off duty so that he can't bust Jacob for assaulting a police officer or something."

"In France, it's typical for an older man to be with a younger woman and vice versa. I don't understand Americans' view on this subject. I mean, look at us. I'm a lot younger than you. What is the big deal?"

Beatrice thought a moment. "I know what you're saying is true. We have a fairly puritanical culture and it's kind of ridiculous, given the fact that sex is everywhere these days. But I think Jacob was acting as a protective dad. I'm not sure it's the age thing, the cop thing, or the ass thing . . ."

"Ass thing?"

"The fact that Bryant can be a real ass. As a dad, Jacob has every right to express his dislike. But I don't agree with his methods. We can't go around beating up people we don't like." Beatrice grinned. "Would that I could, I'd have beaten up well . . . just about everybody I know."

"I know you better than that," Jon said, leaning in to her.

"Yeah, you kinda do. How about some pie?"

"Oh, I think I can have a slice or two."

"It's the last of the pumpkin pie," Bea said, handing him a slice.

"We can always make more," Jon said with a hopeful note in his voice, taking a forkful.

Beatrice sat down with her own slice of pie and dug in. "Annie said that she thought Jorge was nice. She said she picked up on some tension between him and Irina but that he seemed nice. It worries Annie, I think, when she's wrong."

Jon chortled. "Like someone else I know."

"I'm wrong all the time," Beatrice said with a grin.

The day stretched out before them and it left Bea wondering what it would hold. Who would have thought a man dressed as a clown would have attacked Annie on Halloween night? *Poor thing.*

Bea smacked her lips after her last bit of pie and wondered what would come next. Did they have a killer in Jorge Mendez? It had to be. If not, who else had killed those young women? None of it made sense—murder rarely did. But if Jorge had the kind of temper and personality to attack Annie on Halloween, he definitely might have an inclination toward murder.

Bea worried about Annie, who had said the murders would be her last story. Bea couldn't imagine it, Annie without a story. It seemed unfathomable. In any case, it was the second time within a year that her life had been threatened. It pained Beatrice to admit, but maybe Mike was right. Maybe she should give up reporting.

Beatrice had always thought women could do anything. But when it came to her friend Annie risking her life . . . she didn't like it. No story was worth that. It had taken Annie awhile to get over the last incident; it was what had led her to her initial thoughts of retiring. And then the murders happened. And the assault.

But Annie had handled herself. She took him down. Beatrice grinned.

"What are you smiling about?" Jon said.

"I'm thinking about Annie taking that big clown to the ground."

"Yep. She's a hell of a woman."

Indeed.

Beatrice was still mulling over Annie, imagining her tackling Jorge, when the phone rang. It was Cookie.

"Oh, Beatrice. I'm suddenly remembering so much. The dead sisters, the ritual, all of it is shaking something loose in me. One thing I remembered tonight is how much I love you."

Beatrice's heart fluttered. She quickly got a grip on her emotions. "Now, Cookie, Let's not get carried away."

"You know what?"

Beatrice heard the joy in Cookie's voice.

"That's exactly what I expected you to say."

Chapter 62

DeeAnn was excited. It was the first crop she had gone to outside her own house in weeks. The doctor thought it would be okay and on Monday, she'd finally start going back to work half days.

When she walked into Sheila's basement scrapbooking headquarters, it felt like a second home. She was unprepared for the emotions that came bubbling forward.

"DeeAnn?" Sheila said. "Are you okay?"

All of the others were already at the table—Paige, Randy, Vera, Annie, and Cookie, who was looking livelier than she had felt in quite some time. They all looked up at DeeAnn.

She nodded. "I'm fine. Just happy to be here."

DeeAnn took her place next to Paige, who was already at work on a heritage album. She and Randy were working on it together. They had been doing family research and decided to record it in albums, scrapbooking a family history. It made sense.

DeeAnn loved seeing them together—and loved seeing all three of them together. Earl had come a long way. Hell, they all had. If she had known five or ten years ago that she'd be at the scrapbooking table with a Jewish woman, a witch, and a gay man, she probably would never have believed it. Time did some awful things to people—but it also held some wonderful surprises.

"DeeAnn, you should eat some of Vera's chocolates tonight," Randy said. "They are divine. I told her if you didn't sell them, we would. I'll get her into the Pie Palace."

Annie stiffened at the mention of the Pie Palace.

"Look, it's where I work. Okay?" Randy rolled his eyes.

DeeAnn ignored him. "I told Vera that we would carry her chocolate when she was ready," She bit into one. "Ohmigoodness. Very good!"

"Thanks," Vera said. "I'm having a lot of fun with it. We can talk about selling it later, okay DeeAnn?"

DeeAnn nodded. Of all of the women at the table, Vera had probably changed the most. She'd been through hell and had come out stronger and happier—more centered than any of them, perhaps.

"Well, what's going on with the whole Jorge thing?" DeeAnn said as she spread her pages out on the table.

"They're still holding him for the assault," Annie said.

"Really?" DeeAnn said. "It's been a week. That's odd."

"They must have their reasons," Paige said.

"I think he's guilty as sin," Vera said, looking up from her scrapbook. "I'm sure he killed the sisters and God knows who else."

Sheila laughed. "You know what, Vera? If I had a

dime for every time you've said that and have been wrong . . ."

"Well, now. I know that's true," Vera said, her blue eyes sparkling. She was a beautiful woman. Always had been, but these days, she positively glowed. "But this time? He attacked Annie. That's all I need to know about the man."

The room quieted.

"How are you, Annie?" Randy asked, reaching for her hand.

"I'm good. Really. That was nothing compared to being tied up in the B and B. I feel strong. I took care of myself. I've done it before. When I was a young investigative reporter, I used to get into some tight spots. But that was before I married Mike. And certainly before I had kids. Of course, my greatest fear is that my boys will grow up without me."

It was unlike Annie to offer up so much personal information so they all listened intently as she continued talking.

"I worry that I'll miss out on watching them grow up by doing something stupid. By chasing after a story for an editor who doesn't really pay me enough and certainly doesn't even really respect me. It's just a job. So not worth the risk."

After a few beats of silence, Cookie lifted her glass. "Hear, hear, Annie! Here's to a new life. Renewal. Health. Happiness. All of it!"

They all cheered and toasted Annie then settled into their scrapbooking, eating, and chatting.

"Damn, the chocolate is gone," Paige said. "What did you bring, DeeAnn?"

"Nothing to eat. Just brought my gorgeous self over here. I figured that was enough." DeeAnn smiled.

"Next time, bring food, you old bat." Paige laughed.

"It's the price of admission," Sheila said, grinning.

"Well, we'll see what we can do." DeeAnn felt proud as she realized her friends were missing her baked goods. Maybe, once she got on her feet completely, she'd continue working awhile longer. Maybe she'd retire next year. Or the year after. One thing having the back problem had taught her was that there was more to life than her bakery. She still ached to bake. Maybe the thing to do was to pull back, just a bit. Like Annie, DeeAnn was ready to make some changes.

"What fancy-schmancy scrapbooking thing are you working on?" DeeAnn said to Sheila.

"I'm writing my letter of resignation," Sheila said.

"What?" It was a collective question.

She looked up at the table of croppers around her. They had all been so busy with events in their lives that maybe they hadn't seen the circles beneath her eyes, the weight she'd lost, jagged nerves fraying.

"I can't do it anymore," Sheila said. "My Donna is not getting any better. It's taking awhile to find the right medicine. I'm tired of trying to balance it all. It's been a little crazy."

"But this is your dream," Vera said weakly.

"It used to be my dream," Sheila said. "Now my dream is to have a healthy daughter."

Chapter 63

Change was in the air at the Cumberland Creek scrapbooking crop. DeeAnn was going back to work on Monday. Sheila was quitting her dream job. Paige, Randy, and Earl were one big happy family. And Vera was thinking of starting a side business selling her chocolate.

Besides all that, Annie was giving up the only job she'd ever really wanted. She was ready, but she didn't know what came next. "I'm going to call it a night, friends."

"So early?" Sheila said.

Annie nodded. She was tired. And worried. The murder cases still hadn't been solved even though most of the community was already acting as if it were. Jorge had attacked her and that branded him as a violent man. A violent, *foreign* man. So it was easy for people to assume that he'd killed the Martelino sisters.

Annie wasn't so sure.

"I'll walk with you," Cookie said. "I'm tired, too."

They said their good-byes, grabbed their bags and headed out.

As they walked down the street, Annie sensed Cookie had something to say. Pockets of light came from the streetlights, followed by stretches of dark.

"I feel like we're not alone." Cookie stopped walking to look around.

"I don't see anybody," Annie said. "Are you okay?"

"I wish you'd stop asking me that. I'm fine. My memories are coming back so fast now that sometimes it gives me a headache." Cookie grinned. "It turns out my doctor isn't really a doctor. At least not in the way we thought."

"What?"

"I can't tell everybody this. Just you, Annie. You're my best friend. And you know how to keep a secret. I know you can be trusted."

"What is it?" Annie asked.

"The man you know as my doctor is a doctor, but he's also my colleague. It turns out that I'm a kind of operative." Cookie smiled like the Cheshire cat. "Imagine that."

Annie was floored at first, but as she sifted through some memories, it started to make sense. "What kind of operative?"

"I can't tell you that. What I can tell you is that it's not CIA or FBI. It's a special force, of a sort."

"Does this mean you'll leave us?" Annie said.

"Once I'm designated as completely healthy, I have no idea where they'll send me. But there will be ways we can keep in touch. I promise."

That settled Annie's stomach. A bit. "What were you doing here? Who were you investigating?"

"I can't go into specifics, but we were here because

of the New Mountain Order and the way they were abusing the crystals on the mountain." Cookie smiled again. "The mission was a success," she added.

"Well, that's good to know," Annie said, stopping at the corner of Cookie's street, which is where she usually turned off when they walked together. "I'll miss you, Cookie." She hugged her.

"I'm not going anywhere just yet," Cookie said. "I've got a long way to go. I'm still in my little house, thanks to the folks from my agency who have been paying for the place. I'll be there for some time." She paused. "Good night, Annie."

"Good night." Annie watched Cookie walk away for a few seconds before turning up the street to head home. *Cookie, an operative?* She must be an important one if her agency was paying the bills and working with her on her memories. But, as Cookie had said, the Martelino sisters and the ritual had shaken something up in her memories. For the first time in months, Annie felt a glimmer of hope for Cookie.

It was a chilly autumn night, and Annie thought she smelled rain. The wind was kicking up, scattering leaves across the sidewalk. She pulled her scarf in tighter. The weather forecasters were calling for the first snow of the year tomorrow. She believed it.

Suddenly, a person was standing in front of her on the sidewalk. A woman. Annie couldn't see her face, but for a moment it looked like Vera.

Startled, Annie stepped back, outside of the light and into the shadows. "Vera?" she said quietly.

The woman's hand went up and Annie realized that a gun was pointed toward her. A shot sounded and she hit the sidewalk hard as pain ripped through her body. Was she shot? Had she been shot?

"Cumberland Creek Police. Stand down," Annie heard a voice yell. "Drop the gun."

"Drop the gun. Stand down," the voice said again before Annie drifted away.

Annie came to in the ambulance. "Have I been shot?" she asked the paramedic hovering over her.

"No, ma'am. You've had a bit of a shock and you have quite a bump on your head."

"Hurts," Annie said and fell back into a cloud of fitful sleep.

"What's going on? Where's my wife?" Annie heard Mike's voice as she drifted awake again. She opened her eyes. She was in a room. She turned her head. No, a hallway . . . and there was her man.

"Annie. God," Mike said, tears in his eyes. "What happened?"

"Sir, we need you to step away for a moment," Annie heard through the haze. "She's going to be fine. She's just had a nasty fall and has a bump on her head. Probably a concussion."

"Mike?" Annie reached for his hand.

His arm extended around the doctor and his hand, strong, secure, held hers. As always.

When she next opened her eyes, Mike was sitting on the edge of her bed as if guarding her. "She's had a bad time of it. I don't think she can talk," he said defensively to Bryant and Bixby.

"We're not here to ask her questions," Sheriff Bixby said. "We're here to give her answers."

"Answers?" Annie muttered.

Mike stood. "You're awake." He leaned in and kissed her gently.

"You've helped us catch a murderer," Bryant said. "It's the least we can do."

"Nice shiner," Annie managed to say to him and smiled.

"Yours is prettier," Bryant replied.

"Answers?" Mike said impatiently.

"We let Jorge go this morning. After talking with him, we knew he was covering for somebody," Bryant said. "He was scared. We were keeping him for his own safety."

Annie's head ached. Things were not making much sense to her. *Kept him for his own safety?*

"It was his aunt," Sheriff Bixby said. "Irina. She killed both Martelinos and was going to kill you. Jorge suspected her. He suspects that she also killed others over the years, but we have no proof of that yet."

"Irina?" Annie managed to say. She pictured the older woman's face, her calm composure, the way she tended to Michelle Drummond. And then Annie also remembered how she'd called her nephew names and snapped at him. But still, kill someone?

"Why?" Mike asked. "Why? I don't understand."

"Turns out Emma Drummond had changed her will recently to include Irina. Emma's fortune was to be split between Michelle and Irina. But Irina had already started making plans to get rid of Michelle. She didn't get far. Esmeralda found out and told Marina. They confronted her," Bryant said.

"So she got rid of them before killing Michelle. It was the only way she could get away with it," Sheriff Bixby said.

Annie's stomach twisted. The young women had been killed for the sake of money.

"Why the crafting tools and scrapbook pages?" Annie asked. "I don't get it."

Bryant shrugged. "Irina is a deeply disturbed woman. I'm surprised she's held it together this long. We've asked her about it and she just said she likes to make things nice and pretty."

Annie shivered. She remembered the woman saying those exact same words to her.

"You must have known she'd come after Annie. You were already on the street," Mike said. His voice registered at least two octaves higher than normal.

"We thought she might come after Annie because she was afraid Annie was on to her. We didn't know for sure. It was just a theory," Sheriff Bixby said. "But we kept an eye on her and wouldn't have let anything happen to Annie."

"You set her up. Something did happen to her," Mike said. "She has a concussion. It could have been so much worse. What the hell is wrong with you?"

"Look Mike, we were very careful about this. She's going to be fine. I'd never jeopardize Annie's life," Bryant said a little too emphatically.

Mike's eye's narrowed. "I should have beat the shit out of you years ago."

"What? Whoa—" Sheriff Bixby moved quickly to stand between them.

"Mike—"

"I'm glad Jacob hit you, you son of a bitch," Mike raged. "How dare you use my wife like that! I catch you around Annie again . . ."

Bryant started to leave the room then turned and looked at Annie, momentarily revealing far too much emotion with his eyes.

Annie looked away.

"Later, Bryant," Sheriff Bixby said forcefully.

"I'm so glad you won't have to work with him again," Mike said. "I'm so glad this is your last story."

Annie's chest felt a burn of emotion. Tears stung her eyes and a wave of nausea overcame her. "I feel sick," she said, and reached for a nearby container.

Chapter 64

"Well, how about that?" Emma said when Beatrice explained the Irina situation to her. "You mean she was eventually planning to kill Michelle so that she could have everything when I go?"

Beatrice nodded. "I'm sorry to be the bearer of bad news."

They were in Emma's small room looking out of her window at the view of the mountains. Most of the leaves were gone and the black trees stood out against the bright sky.

"I trusted her," Emma said, looking crestfallen. The light played across her papery, wrinkled skin.

"It's awful what money can do to people," Beatrice said. "But somehow Marina and Esmeralda found out about her plot to kill Michelle."

"How?"

"Jorge told us they found her filling pill capsules with some kind of poison. She tried to shrug it off, but Marina knew about the change in your will because Irina told her about it," Bea said.

"So she killed Marina because she knew too much," Emma said, her face fallen, head nodding back and forth slowly.

"And Esmeralda, too, just in case Marina had told her," Beatrice said.

The two of them sat a few minutes and listened to some old bluegrass music playing over the radio. Sounds of the banjo filled the room as they looked out the window and then fussed over their tea.

"What about that poor man? I saw his name in the paper for assaulting that reporter," Emma eventually asked.

"Jorge is out of jail," Beatrice said. "He wasn't really planning to attack Annie that night. He was trying to warn her."

"He knew, then?"

"He strongly suspected. But he was afraid of Irina," Beatrice said. "Still, he was keeping an eye on her, evidently, and trying to warn Annie. But she let him have it before he could explain. She's tough."

Beatrice was thrilled that Annie seemed to have gotten her spark back. After the incident at Elsie's B and B, Beatrice hadn't been sure she ever would. Bea did feel sorry for Jorge—just a bit. After all, what did he think he was doing approaching a woman late on Halloween night while dressed in a clown costume?

"How on earth did the woman get Marina's body into the freezer at the Pie Palace?" Emma asked. "And why?"

"Jorge says that Irina knew Marina was working alone one night and took advantage of it, attacked and killed her, then panicked and shoved her tiny body into the freezer—with a scrapbooking page. It's so warped."

"Warped is right," Emma said.

"Well, at least Michelle is okay. Irina never did get to poison her," Beatrice said. "I was over there yesterday and the new caretaker seems nice. She also said that they'll be trying some new medicine on Michelle. She seemed hopeful that Michelle could tolerate it. Maybe you would, too."

"Oh, I don't know. I'm comfortable here. I'm not sure my body can take another shock." Emma paused. "Funny, when I was young, I burned to see the world. Now, I just want peace. And I think I've found it here in my little apartment."

A feeling of peace fell over Beatrice, as well. Emma was happy. After all these years. All it took was a dead husband and a pretty little apartment.

"Emma, what did you mean when you said you killed Paul?" Beatrice asked. "Did you intentionally let him die when he had the heart attack? Surely not."

Emma's eyes filled with tears. "I did, Bea. It was my only way out."

As Beatrice had dinner with her own husband, she relayed the conversation to him.

Jon drank from his wineglass before speaking. "After her horrible life with her husband it sounds like she's finally content, I know the feeling." He reached out and grasped Bea's hand for a moment.

"Me, too," said Beatrice, as she spread more butter onto her bread. Butter made everything better.

"It's so good to know that the police have found their killer," Jon said. "It surprises me when I hear about female killers."

"I don't know why. Women are every bit as capable of murder as men," Beatrice said, thinking of Emma. "You ought to know that by now."

Jon nodded. "Yes. But I like to think of them as the gentler sex."

Beatrice grunted. "Whatever." She resisted rolling her eyes.

Jon snoozed on the couch while Beatrice looked over the news on the computer. It was true. Jorge had been released. *Good*. She read how Irina had worked for the Drummond family for six years. *Six years!* The article went on to say that she had a record in Mexico, which Hathaway Transatlantic had overlooked when placing her. *Humph*.

> "Sometimes, it's just an oversight," said Detective Adam Bryant of the Cumberland Creek Police. "Other times, families and friends help get criminals out of the country by paying agencies more money. Hathaway is currently under investigation. Not for the first time, I might add."

"Hathaway!" Beatrice muttered with vehemence.

"What?" Jon said, sitting up, looking dazed. And cute. Cute as could be.

Beatrice made her way over to the couch and snuggled next to him. "Nothing, Jon. Relax. Go back to sleep."

He slid his arm around her and she relaxed into the warmth of his touch.

Chapter 65

It was another Saturday night crop, just like any other. Except it really wasn't.

Annie looked like hell—pale and thinner than usual. Cookie sat quietly and stared off into space. Vera was busily working on her Halloween scrapbook. Paige and Randy were chattering about some family reunion and suddenly everything stopped when Sheila made the announcement that she had quit her dream job. Just like that.

"Are you certain?" Vera asked.

"Absolutely," Sheila said. "I'll be freelancing from home to finish up some projects I've been working on. Then I'm done. It was too much for me."

"That's too bad," Annie said. "I know how much it meant to you."

"Well, what about you?" Sheila said.

"What do you mean?" Annie said.

"You're doing the same thing," Sheila said. "Giving up a job you love for your family."

"I hadn't thought of it like that," Vera said.

"I've been a reporter for twenty-five years," Annie

said as she sorted through some photos. "It's not the same thing at all. Um . . . or maybe it is. I don't know. . . ." Her voice trailed off.

"We all do what we have to do," Paige said. "Look at me. I'm still teaching and I wanted to retire years ago." She shrugged.

"Besides," Sheila said. "I'm not really giving it up. I'll be freelancing a good long while. I just can't continue going like I have been. Once I get Donna on the right track with her health, it should be fine. It's just bad timing."

"I think it sucks," DeeAnn said. "Why doesn't Steve help you out more with Donna? She's his kid, too."

A hush fell over the room.

"Now, DeeAnn, you know Steve helps where he can. His job is important. He still makes more money than I do and it takes him away from home a lot," Sheila said. "And to tell you the truth, I want to be the one taking care of her. Call me old-fashioned or whatever you want."

"I totally get that," Vera said.

Murmurs of agreement came from the others around the table.

"Just don't forget to take care of yourself," Cookie said.

"I'm trying," Sheila said. "Quitting my job is the first step."

"But didn't you say how it nourished you?" DeeAnn asked.

Annie looked up from what she was doing.

"Yes," Sheila said after a moment. "And I'll always have the confidence the job gave me. But it's not the job, but the actual work that nourished me. The art.

I'll have to think of a better way. Right now, I've been given the go-ahead from my boss to come up with a line of paper dolls, at a much slower pace than what I've been doing. Donna and I are going to do it together."

"How fantastic," DeeAnn said.

Murmurs of agreement swirled around the table again.

DeeAnn bit into a lemon cupcake. She wasn't a big fan of lemon, but the cupcake was good and refreshing.

"No sugar," Cookie said. "Can you believe it? I found the recipe in a book at the library. I really like them. What do you think?"

"I think it'sh good," DeeAnn said. "I can't believe there'sh no sugar in it. But maybe that'sh why I like it so much. I don't usually like lemon."

"You're slurring your words again," Paige said.

"Well, I'm off my medicine, so it must be the booze," DeeAnn said. "Maybe I shouldn't have had that third glass of wine." She giggled. "Damn smart, independent daughters made me stop taking those pain pills. And I gotta tell you, they were right. I might have been on my way to addiction." She looked around the table at her friends.

Sheila had gone back to the paper she was meticulously cutting out with tiny scissors. Annie and Vera were comparing their Halloween books. They appeared to be zipping right through those scrapbooks. Maybe doing a premade scrapbook was a good idea. DeeAnn had never tried it. In fact, she thought it was kind of cheating. But she was slowly changing her mind—about a lot of things. She'd never imagined liking a vegan anything, nor a sugarless cupcake.

Now that she was down two sizes, she might embrace a healthier lifestyle. It was all good, no matter what her overprotective daughters thought.

"I've been thinking about Jorge," Cookie said. "I hope he's okay. I'm guessing Irina was abusive to him."

"You're right," Annie said. "She was. He was scared of her. And it turns out that she was abusing Michelle Drummond, too."

"What?" DeeAnn said. "How awful! To take advantage of a sick woman like that!"

"They are trying to get her medicine squared away," Annie said. "It appears she has a bunch. They're not sure how many doctors have given her which medicine and so on. It's a mess. She doesn't have to be on that many meds. Once they get her off of everything, she might turn out to be the healthiest person in Cumberland Creek."

"I doubt that," Vera said. "It would be nice, of course. But Sheila and I went to school with her and she's always had problems."

"But nowadays medicine is so much better," Sheila said. "Let's hope she can leave her house soon."

"They've come a long way with medicine," DeeAnn agreed. "I mean two weeks ago, I was still flat on my back. And now here I am."

Chapter 66

Annie's head hurt. She reached in her bag for another ibuprofen. She sighed. It could have been worse. Irina could have shot her. She could be dead. Years ago that same thought had occurred to her one too many times, which is one of the reasons she and Mike had moved to Cumberland Creek.

Annie pasted the final photo of her boys onto the page. She had already put it in a pumpkin-shaped frame and trimmed the corners off. She thought about the fear she saw in her boys' eyes when she lay in the hospital room and she knew she had made the right choice to quit her job.

"How are you feeling, Annie?" Randy asked after he closed his own scrapbook.

"Better. I filed my story and I am officially done."

Randy grinned at her. "Good for you."

"Did they ever figure out who slashed your tire?" Sheila asked.

"It was Jorge," Annie said. "He was coerced into it by Irina. It had nothing to do with the Mendez guy.

He's just a bit overprotective, very macho, but probably harmless."

"Humph. That's what they all say," Randy said, making the women laugh.

"What are you going to do now?" Vera asked when the laughter died down.

Annie shrugged. "I don't know." In some strange way that felt good. It felt good to not have her life planned to the nth degree. She was looking forward to spending more time with the boys and her husband, reading, watching some old movies, spending time with her friends—and writing. Writing fed her—not just stringing words and facts together as a journalist.

The doorbell rang, interrupting Annie from her reverie. Sheila rose from the table. "We're all here. I don't know who this could be," she muttered.

Annie heard the sliding glass door open.

"Well, look what the cat dragged in," Sheila said.

Annie turned to see Pamela and Jorge standing there with pies in their arms. Pamela held a bottle of something under an arm.

"I've heard so much about this crop," Pamela said with a flourish that only she could manage. "Just look at you all."

Jorge stood sheepishly beside her and looked Annie's way. "This is for you, Annie. I made it myself." He spoke quietly with a slight accent. He handed her a pie box with a card on top of it. "Thank you for everything and I just wanted to say . . . sorry about Irina."

Annie's heart nearly leaped out of her chest. "Jorge, you don't need to apologize for her." She took the pie and card from him. She knew what kind of pie it was without even looking inside the box. Everybody knew how she adored that chocolate-cherry pie. "Thanks so much for the pie."

"What do you have there?" DeeAnn said to Pamela.

"Chocolate and banana cream." Pamela walked over to the counter where all the food was set out and slid her box next to some chocolate chip cookies. "Who wants a slice?"

As Pamela doled out the slices of pie, the crop took on even more of a party atmosphere. Annie looked around at her friends, both old and new. Pamela was her usual vision of perfection in her fitted red dress and rockabilly style. Jorge was quiet, yet appeared more centered than the other times she had seen him, as he spoke with Randy off to the side of the room. Pamela handed out glasses of champagne, which Annie happily helped her with.

"I want to make a toast to you all," Pamela said and then cleared her throat. "I've enjoyed getting to know each one of you over the years. I thank you for your patronage and your friendship.

"Jorge and I want to thank Annie, in particular, for her dogged determination." Pamela took a deep breath. "And for putting her life on the line. We are so glad you're okay. In fact"—she looked directly at Annie with a tear in the corner of her eye—"if it wasn't for you, Annie, I'm not certain either one of us would still be alive. Irina was on a path of destruction. We could have been next. You stopped her. Thank you." She lifted her glass.

Annie felt her face flush.

"Hear, hear," DeeAnn said and lifted her glass.

"To Annie!" Randy said, as he and Jorge joined the group and they all lifted their glasses to her.

Tears pricked at Annie's eyes. She was speechless. She had never been thanked like that before. "I'm, ah, not sure what to say." She smiled, willing the tears away.

Cookie put her hand on Annie's shoulder and she suddenly felt a bit more at ease.

"You don't have to say anything. Just soak it in." The light in Cookie's green eyes was back.

Annie took in the rest of the people in the room and felt a surge of warmth. For years, she had searched for good friends and now she had them. DeeAnn, skinnier, and on the path to wellness; Sheila, the artist-scrapbooker, still finding her way, but keeping her family at the center of her life; Paige, whole and happy now that her son was home; Randy, who had become so dear to Annie and Vera, the dancer and maybe-chocolatier, living with the most ineligible bachelor in Cumberland Creek. It was quite a group.

They were all scrapbookers, gathering weekly to share photos, techniques, and stories about their lives and families. It created a bond as they laughed, shared, and ate together. Who knew when she'd accepted Vera's invite five years ago, that she would still be there, pressing memories into albums? As she looked around the table at the women surrounding her, toasting her, she looked deep into her own heart and knew their stories and connections weren't just about scrapbooking. The hobby had brought them together, but it was the friendship that kept them going strong.

Annie didn't know what came next in her life.

She'd shared some of her best moments with her scrapbooking friends. She had also gone through hell with them. They'd seen each other through cheating husbands and divorce, hard financial times, health problems, and murder investigations. But they were all still there. Thanks to their friendship, Annie wasn't too concerned about the next phase of her life. Lifted, strengthened, and loved, she was ready to move forward.

Glossary of Basic Scrapbooking Terms

Acid-Free: Acid is a chemical found in paper that will disintegrate the paper over time. It will ruin photos. It's very important that all papers, pens, and other supplies say "acid-free," or eventually the acid may ruin cherished photos and layouts.

Adhesive: Any kind of glue or tape can be considered an adhesive. In scrapbooking, there are several kinds of adhesives. Tape runners, glue sticks, and glue dots are a few.

Brad: This is similar to a typical split pin, but it is found in many different sizes, shapes, and colors. It is commonly used for embellishments.

Challenge: Within the scrapbooking community, "challenges" are issued in groups as a way to instill motivation.

Crop: Technically, "to crop" means "to cut down a photo." However, "a crop" is when scrapbookers get together and scrapbook. A crop can be anything from a group of friends getting together to a more official gathering where scrapbook materials are for sale, games are played, and challenges are issued. Online crops are a good alternative for people who don't have a local scrapbook community.

Die cut: This is a shape or letter cut from paper or cardstock, usually by machine or by using a template.

Embellishment: An embellishment is an item, other than words or photos, that enhances a scrapbook page. Typical embellishments are ribbons, fabric, and stickers.

Eyelet: These small metal circles, similar to the metal rings found on shoes for threading laces, are used in the scrapbook context as a decoration and can hold elements on a page.

Journaling: This is the term for writing on scrapbook pages. It includes everything from titles to full pages of thoughts, feelings, and memories about the photos displayed.

Mat: Photos in scrapbooks are framed with a mat. Scrapbookers mat with coordinating papers on layouts, often using colors found in the photos.

Page Protector: These are clear, acid-free covers that are used to protect finished pages.

Permanent: Adhesives that will stay are deemed permanent.

Photo Corner: A photo is held to a page by slipping the corners of the photo into photo corners. They usually stick on one side.

Post-Bound Album: This term refers to an album that uses metal posts to hold the binding together. These albums can be extended with more posts to make them thicker. Usually page protectors are already included on the album pages.

Punch: This is a tool used to "punch" decorative shapes in paper or cardstock.

Punchie: The paper shapes that result from using a paper punch tool are known as punchies. These can be used on a page for a decorative effect.

Repositionable Adhesive: Magically, this adhesive does not create a permanent bond until dry, so you can move an element dabbed with the adhesive around on the page until you find just the perfect spot.

Scraplift: When a scrapbooker copies someone's page layout or design, she has scraplifted.

Scrapper's Block: This is a creativity block.

Strap-Hinge Album: An album can utilize straps to allow the pages to lie completely flat when the album is open. To add pages to this album, the straps are unhinged.

Template: A template is a guide for cutting shapes, drawing, or writing on a page. Templates are usually made of plastic or cardboard.

Trimmer: A trimmer is a tool used for straight-cutting photos.

Vellum: Vellum is a thicker, semitransparent paper with a smooth finish.

Basic Card Making Tips

1. Your handmade card begins with a blank card to decorate. You can either buy blank cards that are pre-scored so they fold easily, or make your own from cardstock. Pre-scored blank cards typically measure 5" x 6½", which is a perfect size for mailing.
2. Add paper. Patterned paper makes a great background on cards. You can either cover the card front entirely with paper or cut the paper slightly smaller than the card and glue it on the center. Papers patterned with small, all-over prints are easy to use— but don't dismiss papers with larger designs. You can use papers made for card making, or cut up a 12" x 12" sheet of scrapbook paper . . . one sheet will cover 4 cards!
3. Accent with embellishments. Your card might feature a single stamped message or image, a cluster of silk flowers, stickers, rubber stamps, or metal and paper embellishments—just about anything! Lay out your card embellishments, then experiment with the placement until

you're happy. If attaching elements with brads, you might secure the brad to the paper before attaching the paper to the card front in order to conceal the brad prongs.

4. Don't forget the envelope. You can decorate the outside of your envelope to match your card—stamp it, or add stickers, for example. If you're planning to mail the card, you'll want to make sure the accents won't get caught in the postal machines, but if you're handing the card over, then you can embellish to your heart's content!

Scrapbook Essentials for the Beginner

Getting Started with Scrapbooking

When you first start to scrapbook, the amount of products and choices available can be overwhelming. It's best to keep it simple until you develop your own style and see exactly what you need. Basically, this hobby can be as complicated or as simple as you want. Here is all you really need:

1. Photos
2. Archival scrapbooks and acid-free paper
3. Adhesive
4. Scissors
5. Sheet protectors

Advice on Cropping

Basically, two kinds of crops exist. An "official" crop is when a scrapbook seller is involved. At an official crop, participants sample and purchase products, along with participating in contests and giveaways. The second kind of crop is an informal gathering of friends on at least a semi-regular basis

to share, scrapbook, eat, and gossip, just like the
Cumberland Creek croppers.

1. In both cases, food and drinks are usually
   served. Finger food is most appropriate.
   The usual drinks are nonalcoholic, but
   sometimes wine is served. There should be
   plenty of space for snacking around the
   scrapbooking area. If something spills, you
   don't want your cherished photos to get
   ruined.
2. If you have an official crop, it's imperative
   that your scrapbook seller doesn't come on
   too strong. Scrapbook materials sell themselves. Scrapbookers know what they want
   and need.
3. Be prepared to share. If you have a die-cut
   machine, for example, bring it along, show
   others how to use it, and so on. Crops are
   about generosity of the spirit. This generosity can entail something as small as
   paper that you purchased and decided not
   to use. Someone will find a use for it.
4. Make sure the scrapbooking area has a lot
   of surface space, such as long tables, where
   scrapbookers can spread out. (Some even
   use the floor.)
5. Be open to giving scrapbooking advice and
   receiving it. You can always ignore advice if
   it's bad.
6. Get organized before you crop. You don't
   need fancy boxes and organizing systems.
   Place the photos you want to crop within
   an envelope, and you are ready to go.

7. Go with realistic expectations. You probably won't get a whole scrapbook done during the crop. Focus on several pages.

8. Always ask what you can bring, such as food, drinks, cups, plates, and so on.

9. If you're the host, have plenty of garbage bags around the scrapbooking area. Ideally, have one small bag for each person. That way scrapbookers can throw away unusable scraps as they go along, which makes cleanup much easier.

10. If you're the host, make certain the scrapbooking area has plenty of good lighting, as well as an adequate number of electricity outlets.

Frugal Scrapbooking Tips

Spend your money where it counts. The scrapbook itself is the carrier of all your memories and creativity. Splurge there.

1. You can find perfectly fine scrapbooking paper in discount stores, along with stickers, pens, and sometimes glue. If it's labeled "archival," it's safe.

2. You can cut your own paper and make matting, borders, journal boxes, and so on. You don't need fancy templates, though they make it easier.

3. Check on some online auction sites, like eBay, for scrapbooking materials and tools.

4. Reuse and recycle as much as you can. Keep a box of paper scraps, for example, that you might be able to use for a border,

mat, or journal box. Commit to not buying anything else until what you've already purchased has been used.

5. Wait for special coupons. Some national crafts stores run excellent coupons—sometimes 40 percent off. Wait for the coupons, and then go and buy something on your wish list that you could not otherwise afford.

6. If you have Internet access, you have a wealth of information available to you for free. You can find free clip art, ideas for titles for your pages, or even poems, fonts, and so on.

Digital and Hybrid Scrapbooking

Digital scrapbooking involves using your computer and a photo-editing program to create part or all of your scrapbook page. Hybrid scrapbooking is a combination of digital scrapbooking and traditional paper scrapbooking. For example, you might print off some online scrapbooking elements, cut them out, and then use them on your traditional paper scrapbook page.

Digital scrapbooking allows you to do the following:

1. Print an element out on photo paper to put in a scrapbook album. Remember a scrapbook page can be 8½ x 11 inches or smaller, so you can print from your home printer.

2. Send files to a print shop for printing—a good option for bigger pages.

3. Upload an image of a page to an online photo gallery for sharing with others. (I highly recommend Smilebox for this purpose and as a way of getting used to the idea of digital scrapbooking.)
4. E-mail a copy of a page to family and friends.
5. Burn a copy of a page to a DVD for safe-keeping or use a USB flash drive for this purpose.

Great Ways to Learn Digital Scrapbooking

A really good way to transition from conventional paper scrapbooking to digital scrapbooking is to explore these Web sites:

1. Smilebox (www.smilebox.com) is a very user-friendly Web site that allows you to choose a scrapbook design and personalize it with your own photos, embellishments, and journaling, and then share your scrapbook via e-mail, social networks, burned DVDs, and print.
2. Digital Scrapbooking HQ (www.digital scrapbookinghq.com) offers a blog with great tips on digital scrapbooking, as well as tutorials and sometimes freebies.
3. Sweet Shoppe Designs (www.sweetshoppe designs.com) is not only an online shop that sells digital scrapbooking supplies, but it is also a repository of good information and a source of plenty of freebies. My advice it to rely on freebies as much as

you can until you see if you like digital scrapbooking. There are many digital scrapbooking freebies on the Web.

Digital Scrapbooking Apps

You can approach digital scrapbooking by using apps for your devices and/or apps for your computer.

For your devices (apps I've used on my iPad):

1. Coolibah. This app is free and easy to follow, and I highly recommend it. But here's the rub: you can use only the kits they have in their gallery. They have plenty to choose from, but if you want more or a different kind of design, you must look elsewhere.
2. Martha Stewart CraftStudio. This app is designed so well. For instance, it has little digital drawers to hold all the materials, including paper, and you open them with just a touch. It offers glitter, stamps, pens, and glue. It's great fun to play with. This app is best for greeting cards and mini scrapbooks.

For the computer:

1. Photoshop Elements (PE). PE is a less complex version of Photoshop, and while I can see that it is user-friendly, it's just a bit too complicated for me to learn with the hectic life I lead. But I'd like to learn more.

2. MyMemories Suite. This is what I like using the most. You can jump right in and scrapbook with simplicity. MyMemories Suite allows you to do more complex techniques, like layering and shadowing, which I have yet to get into. They offer paper, elements, types, and more, but you can also import your own.

If you enjoyed *Scrapbook of the Dead*
be sure not to miss Mollie Cox Bryan's

A CRAFTY CHRISTMAS

Christmas is just around the corner, and the ladies
of the Cumberland Creek Scrapbook Crop are
thrilled when Sheila wins the first place prize
in a scrapbooking design contest: a ten-day
scrapbook-themed cruise in the Caribbean.
Vera and Paige decide to tag along, which should
pose the perfect opportunity to learn some new
techniques, mingle with fellow croppers, and get
in some rest and relaxation before the chaos of
Christmas. But when Sheila finds a famous crafter
dead, and investigators determine she was
poisoned, the luxury cruise veers toward disaster as
Sheila becomes the number one suspect—or was
she really the intended victim? Just as the croppers
begin unwrapping the truth, a storm strands them
at sea, and they'll find it's harder than ever to
survive the holidays with a killer on deck . . .

Keep reading for a special excerpt.

A Kensington mass-market paperback and e-book
on sale now!

Chapter 1

Was that a person lying half in the shadows of the ship's deck?

When Sheila had tripped, her eyeglasses flew off her face. She'd stumbled and landed on her knees, groping around for them. On this, her second day of running on the deck of the cruise ship, images of disaster ticked at her brain. What if she couldn't find her glasses? What if they were broken? She didn't have a spare. Finally, she found them and slipped them on.

Now, what was it she tripped over? What was she touching as she groped around?

She tried to get a better view as she struggled to her feet. But the sun hadn't cracked the Caribbean sky yet this morning, and the ship's lights were dim. The glasses weren't helping, either. It looked like there was a sack shaped like a body lying on the deck, with an arm strewn over the path. *That can't be right.* She pulled the glasses off her face. *These are not my glasses.*

A huge floodlight flicked on, and Sheila now saw

the object she was looking at was indeed a person,
lying there in a most uncomfortable position.
Drunk, of course. She thought she saw her own glasses
just beyond the person's arm, and as she reached
for them, a member of the ship's crew came walking over.

"Is everything okay here?"

"My glasses. I tripped," she said, stumbling back-
ward over the person's arm again.

"What's this?"

"It looks like someone had quite a night," Sheila
said, smiling. She was no prude and enjoyed a drink
or two, but she'd never seen so much drinking in
her life as what she had witnessed on this cruise.

The crew member's expression grew pained as he
leaned in closer, shaking the person gently.

"Dead," the man said.

"What?" Sheila said with a sharp tone, dropping
her glasses. Was he joking with her? What a sick joke.

"Stay right there," he said, and pulled out his cell
phone. "I'll call security."

"I'm in the middle of my run," she said, dazed.

"Ma'am," he said. All business. Very stern. "I need
you to stay here."

"Well, all right," she said, picking up her glasses
and slipping them on. Her heart was thumping
against her rib cage.

As she stood next to the crumpled body on the
deck, she crouched over to take a better look. She
blinked. The side of the face was clear: mouth open
and skin sickly blue. Sheila stood fast. Yes, that was
a dead person on the deck. And she had been
groping around the body. Touching the body as
she searched for her glasses. As soon as it sank in,

she proceeded to do what any normal, red-blooded woman would do. She watched everything melt around her . . . and she swooned.

When she came to, she heard a familiar voice. "She runs every day," the voice said. "Nothing unusual about that."

Sheila blinked her eyes. Where was she? She looked around. There was a CPR poster, a table with medical supplies, and she was lying on a cot, underneath a soft blanket. She figured she was in the infirmary—and, man, her head throbbed. She reached her hand to her forehead and felt the swollen area. It hurt to touch it. When she'd passed out, she must have fallen forward. Of course. She was such a klutz. Why couldn't she have swooned with grace, like they did in the movies?

As she lay on the cot, her mind patching together what had happened, she began to feel sick. She'd tripped over a dead person, and what was more, she'd been pawing around the body to find her glasses. Where were they, anyway?

She started to sit up, but dizziness overtook her. She wanted to cry.

Here she was on a scrapbooking cruise, as the guest of honor—a once-in-a-lifetime opportunity—and she couldn't even sit up.

"Mrs. Rogers? Please don't sit up yet," said a male voice coming from the side of the room. She couldn't see without twisting her aching head. "You took quite a fall and have a nasty head injury. We don't think it's a concussion, but we need to keep an eye on you."

"Sheila!" a familiar voice said, and Vera's face came into view. "How do you feel?"

"Like hell," she managed to say. "What happened?"

Vera's presence calmed her. She was Sheila's best friend. They'd known each other their whole lives. It was hard to imagine life without Vera.

Vera's mouth twisted. "I was hoping you could tell us. We were paged. They said you had an accident. We came rushing down here. And this security guy starts questioning me like I'm a common criminal. Then he starts questioning us about you."

"Vera, you're babbling," Paige said as she came up behind Vera.

Paige was here, too. That was good. Another friend whom she'd known for a long time. And for some reason, Sheila felt like she needed as many as she could get.

"I tripped and fell during my run," Sheila said, nearing tears.

"That's not like you," Vera said. "You've been running your whole life. I don't think I've ever known you to fall."

"She said she tripped," Paige said. "Anybody can trip."

"Yes, I fell over a . . . body," Sheila said. "I've got this horrible headache. Anybody know where my glasses are?"

"Here." Paige handed them to her.

"No, these aren't mine."

"You fell over a body?" Vera asked, ignoring the part about the eyeglasses.

Sheila nodded.

"These are the only glasses I see here," Paige told her, and then turned. "Any idea where her glasses are?"

"Those aren't hers?" the male voice said.

Sheila sighed in frustration. "No, they are not mine. I'm sure I had them when I passed out. I think. Maybe they fell off again. These glasses must belong to the . . . the deceased."

"Which means that the dead woman has your glasses on," Vera said, smirking, then giggling.

"What's so funny?" Paige asked.

Vera shrugged and laughed. "It just seems funny. I don't think she has any need for eyeglasses if she's dead, is all."

These two had been sniping at one another since they'd gotten on board. Paige was mad because Vera had brought Eric along on what was supposed to be a girls-only trip. Vera became upset when she realized Paige was mad, yet Paige's son had joined them on board to surprise his mother. Yet another man.

"Hi, Sheila." The male voice suddenly merged with a face as he gently moved the two women away. "I'm Doctor Sweeney. How do you feel? Head hurt?"

She nodded. A nurse brought her an ice pack.

"Let's keep the ice on that bump for a while. I'll get you some pain medicine. Are you allergic to anything?"

"Nothing," she said. "I'd really like my glasses. Everything is a blur."

"We have someone working on that," he said. The nurse brought water and some pills. "This should help with the pain. I hope your vision is a blur because you don't have your glasses. You really smacked your head."

"Well, here they are," said another man, who walked into the room. He was tall, well built, and wearing a linen suit. His long, black dreadlocks were pulled back into a ponytail.

He handed Sheila her glasses, and she slid them on her face. The world around her took on a familiar clarity.

"Mrs. Rogers, I'm Matthew Kirtley, from Ahoy Security. I have a few questions for you," he said. His voice was softer than what his body and his professional attitude would have led one to believe.

"Can it wait?" the doctor said. "We're not sure how she's doing."

"Certainly," Matthew said, and smiled. "Whenever you're up to it. My vic is not going anywhere. Well, nobody is. That's one of the interesting things about security on a ship. Nobody's going anywhere. Not even the murderer."

"Murder?" Sheila said. Her hand went to her chest. Paige and Vera rushed to her side; both paled at the word that stuck in the air and hovered around them.

Finally, Matthew Kirtley cleared his throat in the quiet room, which made Sheila's heart nearly leap out of her chest. They were on a cruise ship with a dead body and a murderer.

Nobody's going anywhere. Not even the murderer.

Grab These Cozy Mysteries
from
Kensington Books